Pip Harry has worked as a magazine journalist, university lecturer, camp counsellor, pool lifeguard and check-out chick. She has contested six Head of the River regattas as a rower and coach but never took home the title. This novel is a suitable consolation prize. Pip lives on the Northern Beaches in Sydney with her family. When not at a keyboard, she can be found searching for the perfect flat white or swimming in the ocean.

UQP published Pip's debut novel, *I'll Tell You Mine*, which won the 2013 Australian Family Therapists' Awards for Children's Literature.

www.pipharry.com
@piphaz

Also by Pip Harry

I'll Tell You Mine

HEAD OF THE RIVER

PIP HARRY

UQP

First published 2014 by University of Queensland Press
PO Box 6042, St Lucia, Queensland 4067 Australia

www.uqp.com.au
uqp@uqp.uq.edu.au

Cover design by Jo Hunt
Cover photographs by Fuse/Thinkstock; nikkytok/iStock
Typeset in 11/15 pt Bembo by Post Pre-press Group, Brisbane
Printed in Australia by McPherson's Printing Group

This project has been assisted by the Commonwealth
Government through the Australian Council, its arts
funding and advisory body.

Cataloguing-in-Publication Data
National Library of Australia

Cataloguing-in-Publication entry is available
from the National Library of Australia
http://catalogue.nla.gov.au

Harry, Pip, author.
Head of the river / Pip Harry.
Twins – Juvenile fiction.
Rowing – Juvenile fiction.
Doping in sports – Juvenile fiction.

ISBN 978 0 7022 5326 3 (pbk)
ISBN 978 0 7022 5311 9 (pdf)
ISBN 978 0 7022 5312 6 (epub)
ISBN 978 0 7022 5313 3 (kindle)

A823.4

University of Queensland Press uses papers that are natural, renewable
and recyclable products made from wood grown in sustainable
forests. The logging and manufacturing processes conform to
the environmental regulations of the country of origin.

For John

'Believe me, my young friend, there is nothing –
absolutely nothing – half so much worth doing as
simply messing about in boats.'

Kenneth Grahame, *The Wind in the Willows*

Author's note

The Victorian Head of the River is the oldest continuous schoolboy rowing event in the world, dating back to 1868, when it was a two-boat race between Melbourne Grammar and Scotch College staged on the Yarra River in Melbourne. Today it is held between the eleven Associated Public Schools on Victoria's Lake Nagambie.

Although girls from co-ed schools have been rowing in the Head of the River since 1972, a dedicated event, The Head of the Schoolgirls' Regatta was first held in 1985 on Lake Wendouree, Ballarat. Today it is held on the Barwon River in Geelong. Both events draw huge crowds and public interest.

The winner of the first eight in the boys' and girls' division is crowned 'Head of the River'. A prestigious and highly sought after award for the brave young rowers that compete each year.

Heads of the River are also run annually in South Australia, New South Wales, Queensland, Tasmania and Western Australia. The name 'Head of the River' is taken from similar international regattas, including the famous event staged on the River Thames in London since 1926.

The author acknowledges some changes to the running and location of the Head of the River in this novel, due to creative licence.

Glossary

Blade – Flat end of an oar.

Bow – Back of the boat.

Bowside – Left side of boat (if you are a rower sitting in the boat).

Catch a crab – When the oar becomes trapped under the water.

Check – To stop the boat with turned blades.

Coxen (cox) – Person who steers the boat and offers in-boat strategy.

Easy oar – Call to stop rowing.

Eight – Boat containing eight rowers and a cox.

Ergometer (Erg, Ergo) – Stationary indoor rowing machine on which rowers are tested and train.

Rigger – Triangle-shaped outrigger on which oars are attached.

Scull – Single boat with one rower.

Slide – The runners on which the wheels of the seat run.

Stern – Front of the boat.

Stroke – The rower who sits in the front seat and sets the pace for the crew.

Strokeside – Right side of boat.

Zoot suit (Zootie) – All-in-one rowing suit.

Repechage: A rowing heat in which the best competitors who have lost in a previous round compete for the remaining places in the next round.

Positions in the boat: (From the front of a coxed eight) Cox, stroke seat, seven seat, six seat, five seat, four seat, three seat, two seat and bow seat.

Monday, 4 April

Two days after Head of the River

Cristian

Assembly is like a funeral. There are no overconfident victory speeches from the Captains of Boats or pats on the back for a 'job well done boys and girls'. Nobody holds aloft the precious Head of the River cup. Instead of a cheesy victory song like 'Holy Grail' or 'We Are the Champions' playing, there's a hushed silence.

Eight hundred students sit perfectly still and upright. A quiet sea of green blazers and white shirts. Usually, this would be the time our principal Mr Kentwell would ask us to settle down. 'Monday morning, people, let's get it done'. Today, there's no need. Gripping the lectern emblazoned with our school crest, 'Harley Grammar – Success Smiles on Effort', he has our full attention.

'As I'm sure you are aware the APS Head of the River was held on Saturday at the Barwon River in Geelong,' Mr Kentwell says. 'It's customary to hold a celebratory assembly and to announce the results of our hardworking rowing team as the culmination of a very successful season, however, this year we felt that wasn't an appropriate course of action. One of our students is seriously ill,' he says.

A girl in front of me starts to sob loudly and I want to lean over and say, 'Stop being such a drama queen. You weren't even friends. This has nothing to do with you.' I wish it had nothing to do with me.

Gossip swirls and Mr Kentwell momentarily loses control of the room.

Around the hall are guys I've rowed with for the past four years. I can pick them out by the slope of their shoulders, crookedness of haircuts or the way their ears stick out. Up close I know what they smell like when they're scared to death.

Nick, our stroke, is two rows in front of me. His head is dipped slightly to the right side as it is in the boat. Leaning into our riggers helps us find the balance. It's hard to shake the habit on dry land. Charley, Mal, Julian ... they're all here. It's tradition for Head of the River crews to sit together during this assembly. Last year I was even on stage. Here at Harley, winners are elevated.

But this year the rowing team is blown like dandelion fluff all over the room.

'We wish a speedy recovery to this very well-liked member of our school community,' says Mr Kentwell. 'Some housekeeping – it's been requested that no flowers are sent to the hospital and no visitors are permitted at this critical stage. However, counselling is available for any students who witnessed this incident, particularly the rowers. Please see your home room teacher to make an appointment.'

That's it. The briefest of reports and onto the day-to-day running of the school – a visiting author, music exams, the upcoming school fete and the Year Ten trip to Papua New Guinea to walk the Kokoda trail.

There's so much more to say than Mr Kentwell's five-minute wrap up. I want to take the microphone and speak up, before everyone clatters out of the room to PE, chem or history classes. Could I put up my hand? Ask for a minute of everyone's precious time?

I could tell the students what colour skin turns when all the oxygen runs out of it. What a body looks like when the heart stops beating. How you can completely forget every single thing you learnt in Outdoor Ed about how to do CPR, how many breaths and what angle to tilt the chin. And all you can do is stand there like a statue while paramedics pound away, hoping for life to return.

I could tell them what it sounds like when a chest compression breaks a rib. Like cracking a stick, if you want to know.

Leni

I try to leave the house without detection, but Mum pounces on me as I'm heading for the front door with my schoolbag.

'Not so fast, Leni. I've made you an appointment with Dr Chang,' she says.

Dr Chang has been my GP since kindy. He's a kind Asian man who's liberal with jellybeans, but I don't want to see him today. I want to be at school with my crew, trying to make sense of what happened at the Head of the River.

'But I don't want to miss assembly,' I complain as she bundles me into the car.

'You need a check-up, sweetie,' Mum says firmly.

I knew I couldn't get away with letting her know I wasn't feeling well after the regatta. Mum's been a pediatric nurse at the Royal Children's for twelve years. No cough or sniffle has ever gone unnoticed by her.

'How do you feel?' she asks as she squeezes into a parking spot outside the clinic, which is already heaving with people and germs.

'Fine.'

'And how do you really feel?' she presses.

'Tired,' I admit, although actually I'm beyond exhausted. So knackered and sore I could barely get out of bed. 'My throat hurts.' Probably from shouting all day at the regatta.

'Saturday was quite a shock,' she says.

'I'm so worried.'

I hardly slept last night thinking of the accident. Of one of my best friends being stuck in hospital.

'I know,' says Mum, patting my knee. 'We all are. Any news?'

'Nothing,' I say, shaking my phone, as if the lost news might fall out.

We sit next to the healthiest looking person in the clinic. Across the room a man wearing a chicken beanie coughs up phlegm into a dirty hanky. I breathe under my hand. I don't want to get sick before nationals. They're only a fortnight away. And then there's the AIS trials. State crew selections. This is the worst possible time to be at a doctor's surgery.

Mum talks shop with Dr Chang, who's holding a plastic container of my urine. It's bright yellow. He puts it into a plastic bag and labels it.

Funny, I thought today would be the best day of my life. I thought I'd be swimming in relief, accepting accolades and sitting up on stage with my crew. Instead, I'm wrestling in a tangle of anxiety. Waiting for a test result that might ruin all my plans.

'How are things at the Royal, Jodie?' Dr Chang asks.

'Busy,' says Mum tightly.

Mum leans into me. I can smell the garlic she had last night for dinner – sour and close in my ear. 'It'll be okay, Leni,' she says. 'Whatever the result.'

I look down at my hands, which are clenched shut.

'Roll up your sleeve, Leni, and let's take some bloods,' says Dr Chang. 'Which is your writing hand?'

What he should be asking is, which is your turning hand on the oar? I hold out my right arm.

My head is heavy with pain and I have an urge to lie down in Mum's lap and let her stroke my forehead with her cool palm. But I'm seventeen, so that might look weird. I sit up tall as Dr Chang prepares the needles. Staring at a tatty food pyramid poster on the wall. Dr Chang's face is expressionless as he plunges the needle into my skin. He would make an excellent poker player.

'Just a couple more, you're being very brave,' he says, as if I'm a toddler. These are the longest seconds of my life.

Longer than the quiet, panicky silence before the starter's gun. Longer than being six and busting to get out of bed and look at Santa's presents, longer than waiting for a winter tram in the freezing rain without an umbrella. Longer than hearing paramedics say, 'I've got no pulse', when someone you love is lying on the ground, not a single part of their body moving on its own. Longer than any seconds of my life so far.

The wrong result here and everything might fall apart, even more than they have already. They might disintegrate.

October

Six months to Head of the River

Leni

The Yarra Classic is the craziest event on the rowing calendar. Hundreds of eights row in staggered starts down the 8.6-kilometre length of the Yarra River. The course is full of odd bends and kinks and the aim is to get the fastest time and avoid hitting bridges, islands, the rocky banks or each other.

We're coming down the tail end of the race in the blazing heat. We've had a clean run but I'm rushing the slide and everyone's desperate to get to the end. Our hands and bums hurt and I'm not the only one thinking of the sausage sandwich and can of cold soft drink that waits for us on the bank.

'Come on girls, let's finish off!' screams Aiko, our cox. She's cute, peppy and everyone likes her. She gets away with bossing us around in the boat. 'You can still get St Ann's!'

We've managed to hold off the other schoolgirl first eights, but our arch rivals, St Ann's, slipped ahead in the melee.

We won't know for sure until we get handicap times, but as we cross the line and collapse, I have a sinking feeling we are second best today. I don't like being second best.

On the bank our coach, Laura, is weaving through other bikes and spectators, trying to make her voice heard.

'Don't just sit there, Harley, row off the start!' she yells. 'Come on, Leni! Get them going!'

I sit forward and take a jelly stroke. We wobble, completely spent, out of the way. Dozens of eights are clawing for the finish line, blades reaching out like insect legs.

'I'm. So. Freaking. Knackered,' whines Rachel in the seven seat, directly behind me. I can feel her heavy breath on the back of my neck. As usual, she's behind on pre-season training, leaving it to the rest of us to pull her along. The sound of her voice makes me tense. She complains constantly and only seems to do rowing to keep an eye on her boyfriend down at the river. I've actually seen her take her hand off her oar to fix her hair – mid stroke.

'Everyone's stuffed. Let's just get the boat in,' I say.

'Yes, sir,' Rachel says.

I roll my eyes and keep rowing. Rachel will follow me. It's hard not to in rowing.

Laura gathers us in a grassy spot out of the way of the crowds. She has the results of the race, on times.

'Firstly, I'm thrilled with how you raced today. It was strong, consistent rowing,' she says.

'St Ann's beat us,' I prompt, glumly.

'St Ann's won the Schoolgirls Division One in 33.04. You guys were second in 33.24.'

'They were twenty seconds ahead?' says Rachel. She sighs through her nose. 'They always beat us.'

'Let's not be too disappointed. Second is a very solid result.'

Solid. Something about the word makes me unhappy. I'm the stroke of our crew and when we don't win, I take it personally. I'm desperate to be elected Captain of Boats in a few weeks' time, so every race counts.

'This is a pre-season, fun race. So we have a little competition on our hands. Gives us something to train for,' Laura says. 'Get a feed and hit the drinks station. Meet back at the boat to row home in an hour and a half.'

Penny Mission grabs me as I head for the school tent on shaky legs. She's in Year Ten – the year below me – and seems keen to be mates. She's sweet, but I'm so busy training I don't have much time for new friends.

'Don't worry about St Ann's,' she says. 'You rowed really well today. We all did.'

Penny was a ballerina before she ditched pliés for oars and she still stands with slightly ducked feet – toes pointing outward. Her long limbs and graceful touch mean she's risen quickly to the top crew. I should get to know her. She's quieter and more thoughtful than the other girls. Sometimes I hardly even notice she's in the boat. That can be a good quality in an eight.

She gives me a hug, which I find awkward and wriggle out of. I don't like touching, especially in public.

9

'We beat thirteen other first crews today,' she reminds me.

'But not the crew that counts,' I add.

Penny droops and looks deflated. I can never see the glass half full. My brother, Cristian, says it's not a good character trait.

'Come on,' I say, forcing a smile. 'Let's eat. I'm so hungry I could eat half a cow.'

Instead of standing with the other parents drinking from plastic champagne glasses and eating dainty chicken sandwiches, my parents are tinkering with boats. They've been tinkering with boats my whole life. Dad's adjusting the height of a rigger. Mum's oiling a squeaky seat wheel. Dad's the Harley Grammar boat caretaker, so he fixes, tunes and cleans all sixty boats in our fleet.

Mum has a smudge of grease on her cheek and she's dressed in cargo shorts and an old T-shirt. I feel an itch of embarrassment. The other rowing mothers have white teeth and done-up hair, Broome pearls and designer jeans. The dads wear polo shirts and aviator sunnies. They carry long lens SLR cameras and the *Saturday Age*.

'Leni!' calls Mum. 'Great race.'

Dad puts his screwdriver in his tool belt and sweeps me into an oily, sweaty hug. The kind you can't wriggle out of. He should be racing with his own masters crew today, but work on the boats comes first.

'Dad, what did I say about PDAs?'

'No PDAs ever?' he says, smiling. 'I saw the end of your race. Very well done, Elena.'

'But we came second,' I say. 'St Ann's beat us again.'

'What's wrong with second?' says Dad. It's a loaded question.

My parents' rowing medals are framed and adorn every spare wall in our house. There are Olympic medals, too. Dad's is silver. Mum's is gold.

'Lovely wind up at the end, good pacing,' says Mum. She shakes my hand, her grip still so strong.

Mum puts an arm around Dad and he kisses her nose.

The story goes, my parents first made eyes at each other across the dance floor at the athletes bar at the Olympic Village in Seoul – post racing. It was 1988. Mum had a perm and Dad had a sixpack. Dad was rowing in the Romanian eight and Mum was stroke of the Australian pair.

Dad says he had to carry Mum back to her room after she literally became legless on four champagnes. She's 6 feet, so he must've been keen. Mum says he was the perfect gentleman, sleeping on the floor next to her bed while the rest of the village danced until the sun came up.

'Wait a minute, Dad slept on the floor? Then why do they need thousands of condoms in the Olympic Village?' said Cristian when Mum told the story for the millionth time. 'You two must have been complete dorks.'

'Ewwww,' I said. 'If you ever mention our parents and condoms in the same sentence again I will puke.'

They kept in contact by writing letters and talking by phone for hours. After the fall of communism in Romania in 1989 Dad was finally free to come to Australia, marry

Mum and row for the Aussie team. You can see why Cristian and I pretty much came out of the womb with tiny oars in our hands.

Dad looks at his watch. 'Ooh. Cristian races now. Jodie, finish for me?'

Dad sprints towards the car park to grab a lift back to the start. He hates to miss our races.

Mum throws me a screwdriver. 'Come on, Leni, we have work to do.'

After I've helped Mum with the boats, I grab a sushi roll and a steak sandwich from the parents' lavish picnic and head down to the bank with Penny. We sit on the grassy hill as the Harley boys second eight crew cruise over the line looking powerful.

'Where are the firsts?' I ask. Cristian's crew should be in by now.

The seconds are pumped as they pull their boat off the water. They've been training well. Buzz surrounds them.

'Maybe the firsts got beaten by the seconds?' says Penny. 'People are talking about Sam Cam being the next big thing.' On cue, Sam Camero carries his blades up the bank, his zootie pulled down past his hips.

Penny follows my eyes to Sam's lean torso.

'Pretty gorgeous, isn't he?' she says.

'I dunno, I guess.'

I pick at a blade of grass and try to act uninterested. Sam mysteriously arrived at our school at the start of Year Eleven and took up rowing right away. Nine months later, he's already in the seconds. Usually it takes years to learn how to row.

'I heard he was some kind of mountain biking star,' Penny says. 'But he took up rowing instead. Even though he had sponsors.'

'Man of mystery,' I say.

Secretly I've been collecting facts about Sam, like a bowerbird filling its nest with shiny things. So far I've managed to find out that:

Sam used to live in Singapore. His parents bought a yoga retreat in Byron Bay and they moved back to Australia to run it.

Sam went to an American school in Singapore and that's why he has a twang in his accent.

Sam lives alone in his parents' Docklands apartment with a cook and a cleaner, but no supervision.

Sam's Buddhist. That's why he refuses to go to chapel and instead goes to the library and reads.

Sam can stand on his head. I saw him do it one day in the gym on a crash mat. For, like, ages. Then he calmly got up and walked away.

I'm so busy thinking about my nest of Sam facts that I miss the boys' first eight finishing.

Penny grabs my arm.

'Adam's waving at you,' she says.

There he is. My boyfriend, Adam Langley. Cute, in a generic deodorant commercial kind of way, trying to get my attention. I'm happy to see him, but not thrilled. Lately being with Adam is another chore to add to my workload.

'Aren't you going to wave back?' Penny asks.

By the time I raise my hand, Adam is looking away, his hat pulled down over his eyes.

'Your brother looks like he needs oxygen,' says Penny.

Cristian does look exhausted. He's flushed and breathing hard. By the dark expression on his face, they didn't have a good time out there.

'Do you fancy Cristian?' I prod. 'I think he has a crush on you.'

Cristian's smitten with Penny's quiet beauty.

'Maybe,' Penny says. 'I've never been out with a boy before. I'm not sure what to do.'

'Just be you, Pen.'

It was good advice, even if I'd never, ever been myself with Adam.

Cristian

We're at the start line for the Yarra Classic. I'm nervous because I'm not fit and my hands are shredded from training.

'Ads, you got tape?' I ask Adam Langley.

Adam sits in front of me in the boat. I'm five seat. He's six seat. We're best mates, but it's a strange pairing. He's the third son of Mitch Langley, millionaire property developer. I'm the son of Vasile Popescu, boat caretaker. He lives in a massive Toorak mansion. I live in a falling-down rental in Fitzroy. We are from different sides of the river. Different sides of the planet. The only reason we're sitting

14

in the same boat is because of my sports scholarship to Harley. My sister Leni has one too.

'I don't have tape, Princess. Suck it up,' Adam says. He's joking, but there's a tense edge to his voice. He's as jittery as I am. The Yarra Classic is the first proper race of the season.

I clench my fists and feel the skin tighten with the throb of infection. I should've taped them this morning. It's too late now.

Eights are piled up everywhere, coaches riding their bikes in packs. Organised chaos. Dad's somehow gotten back to see my race. He's riding a clapped-out women's ten speed he got from Vinnie's. I wish he'd get a new one. The pedal keeps falling off and he looks like a goose riding with one leg.

We've got a slot a few seconds in front of Glenon Grammar, Westleigh and Stotts College. It's a handicap regatta, so everyone goes at different times. You could end up rowing along with old masters guys or an elite women's eight. It only makes sense when all the times are crunched at the end. The aim is not to be passed by anyone in your category and to overtake as many crews as you can.

Of course, everyone's checking each other out. I suck in my gut and try to look more of a threat than I am.

'What are those Stotts guys eating with their Weet-Bix? They're tanks,' hisses Adam. Stotts are bulging with muscles and they look fit and untouchable in matching mirrored sunnies and red zooties.

'Girly sunglasses won't help them win the race,' I say.

15

If there's one thing my parents have taught me, it's that flash gear doesn't count on the water. Technique matters. Dad taught me and Leni to row when we were nine and he drilled technique into us from our first wobbly strokes. I can usually out-row anyone my age. Usually. Lately I had the feeling I was getting caught.

The starter gets us into position. It's time for the hurting to begin.

I sit up, breathing in deep. Last chance for air.

'Bring it up a touch Harley Grammar!' shouts the starter.

'Okay, that's a line. Sit forward! Attention! Row!'

We get a decent start and for a few minutes it feels good. It feels like this is our race.

But then it isn't. It's Stotts's race. Stotts and their stupid sunglasses.

Leni

At home, after the regatta, I head straight for the shower and stand under the hot water. After months of wearing tights and shivering in the dark, I finally have rowing suntan marks on my thighs and shoulders. From this angle, it looks like I'm wearing a white skin zoot suit.

Water rushes over the sharp angles of my body. I have no boobs and legs like a horse – all knees and bone. I pinch my stomach and wonder why I don't get a sixpack like the boys do. I want one desperately. My arms are strong and I'm getting defined biceps. I flex one arm in the shower and test its hardness. Not bad.

I resolve to do more sit-ups every day. A hundred at least. Maybe some push-ups, too. But for now, all I have the energy for is to change into tracksuit pants and lie on the couch, watching TV. Our family cat, Banjo, curls up on my feet. I love this tired feeling. My muscles worn out, all my strength left on the river. I put my arms behind my head. From this position, I'm staring at a row of painted trophy oars my parents have won, mounted on our living room wall.

Each oar has a story. European Champs, worlds, nationals, Olympics. All the names of my parents' crews are painted onto the spoon of the blade. When I was a kid Dad would lift me up and let me touch the raised gold lettering and show me the names, Jodie Cummings and Vasile Popescu. Even then I knew I wanted my own painted oar one day. I hope that day is coming.

I don't even realise I've fallen asleep until I wake to my brother tickling my upper lip.

'Wakey, wakey, eggs and bakey,' he says. His traditional morning greeting. Which is better than his other favourite, 'wakey, wakey, hands off snakey'.

We always sit in the same spots for dinner. Dad at one end, Mum at the other and Cristian and I facing each other on either side. Mum insists on family mealtimes if we are at home at the same time. Which is getting rarer. She says the dinner table is where families do their best talking. Tonight, though, the mood is murky.

Cristian eats in virtual silence and refuses dessert.

It's *papanasi*, sweet cottage cheese dumplings with sour cream and jam. A family recipe. Mum learnt to cook all of Dad's favourite Romanian dishes. It was her way of helping ease the homesickness that she says flattened him when he first moved to Australia.

'So yum,' I tell Mum, hoeing in.

'Are you sick?' Mum asks Cristian.

To my knowledge he has never turned down *papanasi* before.

'I'm not sick. I don't want to eat stupid Romanian food all the time. It's making me fat.'

'Don't call your mother's food stupid,' Dad says. 'She work hard. She cook for you. Apologise.'

'Sorry,' Cristian mutters.

'You are a healthy growing boy. You need plenty of energy,' Mum says. 'You're not fat. You're a big boy.'

I caught Cristian looking at himself in the bathroom mirror last week, grabbing a chunk of his tummy. He gets plenty of flack at the river for his size. Always has. Usually it doesn't bother him. But he was flogged badly today.

'Big is the same as fat!' Cristian says.

He pushes his chair roughly away from the table and walks out.

Mum jumps up to follow him.

'Leave him, Jodie,' says Dad, putting his hands on her shoulders. 'He is beaten today. Beaten men do not have celebration.'

Mum nods and we sit down and pick at our dessert in silence. As soon as I can, I leave the table to find out if he's okay. I knock on Cristian's door. Our knock. Three short raps.

'You in there?' I call through the wood.

I hate seeing Cristian upset. It makes me jumpy and unsettled. We've always been close. Twins usually are.

He opens the door a crack and I see he's been crying.

'I'm fine, Leni, go to bed.'

'It's months until the Head of the River,' I say. 'You'll come good.'

'I've got to get fit again, like last year.'

'We'll go for more runs together. Don't worry, there's still heaps of time. You've got a good base.'

'I'm tired, Leni. I might just go to sleep.' He closes the door and I can't help feeling down. When one of us loses, we all lose.

I crawl into bed too, even though it's not even nine. I'm nearly asleep when my phone beeps with a text.

Hey pretty girl, congrats on your race. We sucked tho! Wish we were together tonite. Love u. Adam xxx

He's attached a topless selfie. I send a text back telling him not to worry about the race. But I don't attach myself topless because I don't want to end up on some dodgy website or Adam's Facebook page. I'm not that dumb.

The photo of Adam is hot. But I'm still not sure. Us. Adam and Me. Me and Adam. Six months ago I started to get the feeling Adam was into me. He'd look my way during training. He even got in trouble for it a few times. *Eyes in the boat, Langley.* I was flattered. Adam's popular and good-looking in a wiry, freckled way. He has beautiful eyes that are distractingly light blue with dark edges,

19

a drop-off to deeper water. Word filtered down. *Adam Langley likes Leni Popescu.* I'd never had a boyfriend before so I froze. What next?

Adam texted me one night and I opened it like a present.

Hi. It's Adam. Are you awake?

I was little-girl-on-a-pony excited. We texted until after midnight and I fell asleep, my phone pressed against my cheek.

At school the next day he asked me to sit with his group. I usually sat with my friend Audrey and her knitting circle, but she pushed me to meet Adam instead. Something about it being my *Sixteen Candles* moment. When the popular guy falls for the quiet girl. Perhaps if she'd known a simple seat change would alter our friendship forever, she wouldn't have been so keen.

Adam and I ate lunch together with the whole of Year Eleven watching on. 'See you at rowing?' he said. 'Drink after?' I realised it was probably a date.

After rowing he took me for coffee, bought me a little square of caramel slice and asked me to a party that weekend. I said yes, with the taste of chocolate melting on my tongue. He held my hand across the table and, even though he acted confident and sure of himself, his palm was sweaty and shaking.

At the party we kissed in a dark corner of the garden. Then he held my hand again – this time in front of everyone and when he dropped me home he asked me to be his girlfriend. I said 'yeah, okay'. Even though I didn't know him at all. Because that's what you say when a good-looking, popular guy asks you to go out. Don't you? Especially if you've been plucked from the wall like a creeping vine. The imprint of your body left behind on the bricks.

It was only later that I thought about the kiss.

First kisses should be lingering and exciting. Ours was rushed and awkward. He smelt and tasted all wrong. He kept poking his tongue into my mouth like he'd lost something in there and was trying to find it. It was like he was a piece of Duplo and I was a piece of Lego. Right from the start, Adam didn't feel like the right fit.

I should break up with him, but I don't even know how. Adam's the only boyfriend I've ever had. How do I tell him he's not the one?

Lying on my side I look at my inspiration board – always the last thing I do before sleep. It's a corkboard full of photos, quotes and inspiring things. It keeps me going when my body and head ache and everything feels too hard. When motivation hides from me.

In the middle is a cut-out of the Head of the River cup, which I've coloured in with gold pen. I want it so badly it hurts. I like to touch the cup with my hand and imagine my bow girl going over the line first, thousands of people screaming on the banks of the Barwon River. Thinking about it gives me goose bumps. There's a quote posted up that I think about during training: 'Pain is just weakness, leaving the body'. To the left of that is an old newspaper story I found online and printed out.

Pocket Rockets win Gold!

Aussie double scullers Peter Antonie and Stephen Hawkins were 15 kilos lighter on average than every other crew when they lined up to race for Olympic gold in Barcelona in 1992. Everyone thought they were too puny to take out the race. But they led early, ahead of Austria and Holland and went on to win Australia's first gold rowing medal in 44 years.

Peter and Stephen shouldn't have won, but they did. They stood up to crews that were bigger and stronger than them and took victory. Because they wanted it more.

I smile, flick the light off and crash.

I want it the most, too.

Cristian

Mum comes in after dinner and sits on the edge of my bed, shoving a pile of dirty washing off the end. She doesn't have much time for housework and Leni and I are supposed to hold our own. Leni does a better job than I do. In housework and all things, really.

'Okay kid?' she asks.

Mum has a way of looking into my soul and seeing the black spots in it.

'I'm not fit enough,' I admit, feeling ashamed. I wasted my pre-season dodging training and playing computer games. *Eating.* 'We shouldn't have lost today. It was a shambles out there.'

'It won't be the last time you screw up,' she says. 'Dad and I lost plenty of races.'

'But you won plenty, too.'

'Sure. But in rowing, you've got to learn to take the rough water with the glassy pond. Otherwise it will break your heart. Now show me your hands.'

I hide my blistered hands under the covers and she pulls them back out gently.

'Let me do a little nursing. I like to take care of my babies.'

'I'm 6 feet 4. I'm not your baby anymore,' I say.

'I don't care if you grow to be 8 feet. You'll always be my baby boy. Now come out to my operating table.'

Under a light at the kitchen table she holds my wrists firmly, like I'm three years old and might squirm away. A pale yellow infection has crept in with the dirty river water.

'We need to dry out this infection,' she says. She goes to her heaving medical cabinet and fetches methylated spirits, opening the bottle. The smell of alcohol clears my nostrils.

'I used to look after your father's hands when he was younger. Terrible blisters. He was holding the oar too tight. His teammates called him Jack the Gripper.'

I can see my dad holding the oar too tightly. He's intense sometimes.

Mum dabs the sharp liquid on my hands. It stings the raw skin like the kiss of a dozen bull ants. I draw a breath back through my teeth.

'It's primitive, but it's the only thing that works,' she says. She blows cool air on my burning skin.

Mum's hands are soft now; she prefers walking and yoga studios to rowing. Dad tries to get her back on the water. 'Jodie, you need to get your heels wet again,' he announces. As if she's a sea creature who's drying out on land.

Dad's been relegated to masters crews after a kid not much older than I am now snatched his seat in the Australian eight. He's still strong as an ox, even with two surgeries on his shoulder and one on his knee. His hands are tough and leathery with blister over blister over blister. Like bark rings on a tree.

Mum bandages up my sores with a dab of Friars' Balsam and sticking plaster.

'They feel better already,' I say. 'Thanks, Mum.'

'It's early in the season, Cris, be patient and do your work. Forget about what people expect of you.'

'I wish I was more like Leni. She's so focused.'

'She hates to lose. Do you remember our games of Monopoly when you were kids?'

'Yeah.'

We smile, remembering Leni wiping us off the board and draining the bank of funds. Her tantrums if she happened to lose, which was rare.

'I need to keep my scholarship,' I say, a flutter of panic rising in my chest.

Leni and I have to work hard to keep our full sporting scholarships at Harley. In the summer we row and in the winter, it's rugby for me and cross-country for Leni.

We are expected to excel at both sports and make sure our marks are high and steady. There's no such thing as a free ride. I've got to get my rowing sorted out.

'It was one race, Cris. Your scholarship is safe. Now go to sleep. It's been a big day.'

Lying in bed, all I can think about is our race, reliving the humiliation. It all came apart at the Big Bend. We were pulling hard and Nick lifted the rating, but Stotts was closing in. Then Adam caught a crab. In rowing, a crab isn't something you eat on a seafood platter. It's when an oar gets trapped under the water and you can't get it back out.

Adam stopped rowing for a few strokes and the boat started to flop around. We lost the plot.

'Come on!' I shouted, even though technically I'm not supposed to talk from the middle of the boat. 'Get it together! Sit the bloody boat up!'

That's when Stotts came past us. We were so busy watching them take our boat that we didn't ease off the stroke side. We skewed right and headed for the bank. Charley stood up in the boat, screaming at us to row hard on bow to avert a crash. He tried to help rudder the boat around by sticking his skinny leg in the water.

'Check stroke side!' he screamed.

Everyone on stroke slammed their oars in the water to swing us back into line. Water was flying everywhere. It filled up the bottom of the boat and sloshed around our feet.

Miraculously it worked.

The boat started to creak around the bend. We escaped cracking our boat in two, but the race was lost. Stotts got away, two other schoolboy first eights passed us. Dad's shouting got louder, the worse we rowed. He yells at me in Romanian, which makes it worse. The guys like to mimic his thick accent in the sheds.

'Cristian, more legs! Cristian, quick hands! Cristian, shoulders back!'

'Would he just shut up?' I panted to Adam.

It felt like an eternity but we finally limped over the line at the Hawthorn boatsheds. All I wanted to do was collapse under a tree with a feed. The best part of regattas is getting the love at the parents' picnic. But our coach, Mr West, aka Westie, made us turn the boat around, without even going into the bank, to row all the way back to the city. Another 8.6 ks. Sadistic.

'Bring back Mr Freedman,' muttered Adam.

'Yeah, I miss Freedo,' I agreed.

Our old coach, Mr Freedman might have steered us to victory last year but he wasn't coming back this season. He was on stress leave. We knew something was up when he started turning up for training in his pyjama bottoms. After Freedo left, Dad was in line for the job until some of the parents complained about his 'grasp of English'. It was the first time I was relieved Dad hadn't bothered to master the language.

After a little political manoeuvring Westie was bumped up from the seconds. Around the sheds, he's hated and feared in equal measure.

It was like him to keep flogging us after a humiliating loss. I was sunburnt, hot, exhausted and thirsty. The skin on my hands was tearing apart like tissue paper. Still he kept having Charley call out hard pieces and asking us for more.

Behind me, I could hear Xavier in the bow, sobbing like a baby.

I would've told him to grow up but I wasn't sure I wouldn't join in the blubbering. Instead, I counted the bridges back to the city. MacRob Bridge, Church Street Bridge, Railway Bridge, Punt Road Bridge, Morrell Bridge and Swan Street Bridge. Until we finally pulled past the Henley staging and into the sheds.

'You lot,' Westie said when we pulled the boat in, 'are an absolute disgrace.'

I held a hose up to my head and let the water flow over my scalded scalp. Panting for the liquid like a dog.

'Think this is bad?' Westie said to us. 'You are all up for re-selection trials. Monday morning. Enjoy the rest of your weekend, gentlemen.'

'I didn't think this day could get any worse,' Adam said as we trudged up to the showers. 'But it just did.'

We are never allowed to get too comfortable in our seats; our coaches use a strict algorithm of run times, seat racing and ergo trials to put the whole squad on notice every time we don't do as well as they'd like. Ergs are the worst – seated rowing machines that chew you up and spit you out if you're not fit. You either fight tooth and nail for your seat or face eviction into the seconds or thirds.

'I'm not safe,' I said.

'Me either,' said Adam. That freaky Sam Camero is breathing down everyone's neck for a spot in the firsts.

He's going to have to fight me for it. I'm not rowing in the seconds this year.'

I know that as well as patching up my fitness and losing the muffin top, I've got to get my head in the right place if I'm ever going to feel safe in my seat.

Leni

Most mornings, my hand reaches out to deactivate my alarm before it goes off. In case I ever miss my 5.20 am wake-up call, Dad is a reliable back-up.

'Leni, up!' he calls, knocking on the door.

'Cristian, up!' His voice is always louder for Cris.

I dress quickly and pull on a heavy fleece jumper, throwing my already packed bag onto my shoulders. I jump up and down on the spot to get the blood flowing to my hands and feet. The house is dark so I flick on the kitchen light and grab a banana from the fruit bowl. I eat it, standing up, in three bites. It takes me under ten minutes to be ready to leave. I'm a morning person.

Dad is still trying to get Cris out of his room.

'It's so cold,' I hear Cristian moan. 'Just five more minutes. I'll meet you at the car.'

'Cold? When I was boy we walk to school in minus fifteen. *In snow!* River was frozen solid, so I train indoors, in tank. You not know cold!' shouts Dad. He's irritated now and I wait for the explosion. Dad slams Cris's door.

'We go without you!' he shouts. 'Come Leni!'

I follow Dad out to the car. He threatens to leave Cristian behind on a regular basis. Cris always makes it out to the car, just in time.

The passenger door is broken, so I get in the back and shimmy across the gear stick to the front seat. Our car is on the street because our garage is a makeshift gym. Ropes hang from the ceiling, there's a boxing bag, mats, weights and, of course, an ergo. Training is ever present at my house.

'I leave him behind,' says Dad, trying to start the car. The engine won't catch. He swears at it in Romanian.

In my head I begin a countdown until the front door flies open and Cris runs out, barefoot, carrying his shoes, hair a mess, half asleep.

1-2-3-4-5-6 ...

There he is.

'Wait!' Cristian calls. 'I'm coming!'

We sit in the car for another minute while Dad tries to start it.

'This car is a piece of junk, can't we get a new one?' asks Cristian.

'You have money?' says Dad. 'You buy car.'

Cristian and I hate the family wagon. I hate it even more when I ride with Adam in his family's new BMW with its plush leather seats. In our car all the seats are torn up, springs escaping. The elements have taken hold of the bonnet, eating through the paint. It's missing a front bumper bar and the tyres are always bald. Dad said it's not safe enough for Cristian and I to get our Ps on.

Dad finally gets the old tank started as Mum rides down the street towards us on her bike. She's been on night shift at the hospital and is still wearing her ID around her neck. She waves at us and Dad winds down the window and blows her a kiss.

'Bye, my love!' he calls.

She returns the kiss, but I can see she's knackered. She'll go straight inside, have dinner instead of breakfast, draw the blackout blinds and sleep for hours.

It's 5.43 am. My day has started and hers is finishing.

She'll be sleeping when I'm pushing my crew down the river on the black oily water, watching the lights from the city bounce off the surface in streaks of gold, pink and blue.

I look out the window at the empty streets and listen to the birds chirping and calling to each other. I love early mornings. I feel like I'm seeing the very best of the day.

Cristian

When I make it to the car Dad's humming with anger. But instead of giving me an earful, he's complaining about Westie holding more selection trials. It's our third batch of seat racing in a few months.

'Flogging, flogging, more flogging. Where will that get you boys?' he says. 'Is not only muscle that gets a boat across line first. Is eight oars in perfect time. Like dance. All people working together. Perfect timing. Perfect balance. Cristian, your crew can win, but you have loser coach.'

'Tell me about it,' I mutter.

'He's strangling your confidence. Forgetting technique. What good fitness if you can't row together?'

'Yeah, all right, Dad, can I have some time to concentrate before the trials?' I ask, putting on my headphones in case he hasn't got the message.

Dad was lucky to get me out of bed this morning. He's lucky every morning. When he first bangs on my door I play a head game where I try to get my big toe onto the floor. If I can get my foot out of bed, then the rest of my dopey body will follow. Today, the toe wanted to stay in bed. I sometimes wish I lived a normal life. Get out of bed at 7.30, eat breakfast in front of the TV and take an 8.18 tram to school. That sounds too good to be true.

I look out the foggy window, my eyelids heavy. The only other crazies out at this time are truck drivers, loaded up on caffeine and uppers for long hauls, and cyclists getting in some early clicks. I wish we were going on a holiday, driving up north as far as the car would take us. Up to the beaches and the warm, soft waves. I don't want this car to stop. Because when it does. When Dad pulls into Boathouse Drive, I'll have to face some very loud music.

Nobody ever rowed in the seconds and had the school pay their fees. I could kiss my chances of being rowing captain goodbye, too.

Leni

When the recess bell goes, I run down to the Year Eleven common room to find Cristian. I saw him crying on the bank and rumour has it he's out of the firsts after this morning's racing. As I walk into the room I see Audrey sitting

31

in the far corner next to the windows, beading a necklace. She's with her friends – my old friends. Marion, Yvette, Lucy. The four of them sitting quietly, working on various crafty projects. I fight the urge to drift over to them and sit down. I miss them.

It was only supposed to be a one-time thing. I'd have lunch with Adam, realise we weren't a love match, and return to my well-worn spot in my semicircle of mates. The girls that I loved for their odd quirks and refusal to speak, dress or act like anyone else at Harley. I'd relate my brief crossover to the dark side of popularity and school would go on as it had for the past two years. Handing in our assignments early. Crafting. Laughing. Being spectacularly uncool (and being totally cool with that). Instead, one lunch date with Adam changed the path of my friendships. And I let it.

When it became clear Adam and I were a couple I tried spending recess with Adam and his friends, going back to my old group for lunch. Gradually, at his insistence, I extended my Adam-time to recess and half of my lunchtime, too. But by the time I made it back to Audrey and the girls, I was lost – missing all the threads of conversation and the things that were important to them.

I didn't know Marion's dog Stevie had died, Yvette had a clarinet solo in the orchestra or Lucy was a runner-up in the state fencing champs. I didn't know Audrey had decided she was in love with her boyfriend, Kieren. I started to feel like they were talking about me behind my back. *Traitor. Turncoat. Two face. Wannabe popular.*

One lunchtime, I can't remember now which one, I didn't go back to the girls to sit down. I stayed beside

Adam and listened to him talk. I let the minutes slip away. Trying to be in two places at once was too hard. I gave up.

The next day Audrey gave me a dirty look as I walked past her and Lucy in the front row of the science labs, down to the back where Adam sat.

'You're not sitting with us at all anymore? Is that it?' she asked, jumping out at me as I walked out at the end of class. She was close to tears, her features softening.

'We've been friends since Year Nine, and you dump us for Adam Langley and the beautiful people?'

Year Nine. Mrs Curtain made us partners in English and Audrey let me sit with her group at lunch. Even though she'd cultivated those friendships since primary school and I was just the new scholarship girl. A ring-in. She'd saved me and I'd betrayed her. Slowly and creepily by moving my body from one side of the common room to the other. I was scum.

'Can't we be friends outside school?' I asked, feeling myself burn with shame for even suggesting it. My parents didn't raise me to drop my friends the minute a boy paid me attention.

'Why? Because we're too daggy to be seen with on school grounds?' she spat.

'That's not it at all. Adam just wants me to sit with him. We are going out.'

'And what do you want, Leni?'

She had a good point. What did I want?

'I don't know. I want things to go back to how they were.'

Audrey gave me a hurt look and I realised we were both crying.

33

'Too late,' she said. 'You have your Prince Charming now. Us trolls will leave you alone.'

She did leave me alone. For a while.

I'd look on wistfully as she strode around school on uniform-free day wearing a long flowing green dress with a plaited headband and triangle sleeves. Her medieval look. The rest of the school wore jeans, T-shirts and thongs.

I'd shift through photos on Facebook of her and Kieren charging the field at role-playing weekends, dressed up with chain mail and swords. I'd linger as I walked by her and the girls at lunch and sneak a look at how far they'd come along with their quilts, beanies and charm bracelets.

The ice broke one day at the tram stop. Audrey and I arrived at the same time and got on together. Accidentally choosing to sit in the same booth, our knee caps banging. We looked at each other and Audrey laughed.

'This is silly,' she said.

'I know,' I said, relieved. 'I miss you.'

'Me too, Leni.'

'What are we going to do?' I asked.

'What was that thing you suggested about being friends outside school?' Audrey asked. 'We could try it?'

That was how our 'outside hours' friendship began. We'd meet up after school and on weekends sometimes. She invited me to a medieval party at her house. Adam was at his family beach house and I felt like myself again. We all drank from silver goblets. Audrey sang an old medieval song in parts with Marion. Yvette played the clarinet. Lucy gave a fencing display. I smiled so much my cheeks hurt.

Back at school Audrey would wink at me across the common room and sometimes left a pair of earrings or a bracelet in my locker.

I knew we could make it work, even if I was Adam Langley's girlfriend.

Adam is standing in a rowing group, deep in conversation. I can tell they're talking about Cristian, because they stop when I come near.

'Where's Cristian?' I ask.

Adam rests his hands on my shoulders. It's meant to be reassuring, but I find it suffocating and shake him off.

'Relax, Leni.'

'Don't tell me to relax, Adam. Is he in or is he out?'

'Out. But what did you expect? This morning was a disaster.'

He's right. This morning was one of Cris's worst rowing moments.

'I've got to find him.'

'He's gone home,' Adam says. 'Sit down. I'll get you a MILO.'

'I don't want one.'

'Okay, I won't bother then,' Adam says, hurt. He's always trying to do nice things for me and I'm always pushing him away.

We look at each other intensely for a few seconds. Our relationship is filled with weird, off-key moments like this. In the beginning we papered over the cracks with romance. Flowers, hand holding and lavish dates. After six months it's getting harder to bridge the gap. The only true thing we have in common is rowing.

'I've got to revise for an English test now,' I say.

'See you at the gym at lunch? Weights?'

'Yeah. After my run.'

I'm already in clean gym clothes, ready for more training. I have a T-shirt that says: *Row, eat, sleep. Repeat.* That's how my life is. I run from morning training at the river to lunchtime land training to after school on the river and weekends are back-to-back regattas until April. At least we get Tuesday afternoons off. It's heaven.

On Tuesday I feel like a regular girl.

Cristian

I've been dropped from the firsts. Westie hung me out of the boatshed balcony and let go. I came screaming to the ground and smashed into a million pieces. That's what it felt like anyway. I had a meeting with him, our rowing director and the head of PE. They said it's temporary until I get my fitness and my weight back on track.

I've come home from school early. I was bawling my eyes out in the guys' gym toilets with the door locked. I wasn't about to get caught doing that. I'd rather get suspended for wagging.

Mum's at work, Dad's at the boatsheds. I've got the house to myself.

I'm sitting in the lounge room in my boxers, eating a

pie and a milkshake, hating myself. I eat when I feel like this, trying to fill the empty feelings with sugar and fat. It works for a bit, then more blackness comes in its place. Worse than before.

After Dad dropped me off at training, Westie gathered us in a circle. Eighteen of us were up for re-selection – the first and second crews shuffled like a pack of cards. Everyone was twitchy. There was a smell of fear in the air. We may row in the same school colours, but we're enemies when it comes to keeping our seats in the boat.

The room went so quiet all you could hear was the whir of a guy on the ergo and the patter of rain on the tin roof. The second's coach, Mr Patterson, aka Patto, got out an iPad. Numbers were going to be crunched today.

'Boys, today we are racing in single sculls,' Westie said.

'FFS. I hate sculls,' I muttered to Adam.

The scull is a single boat – light as a wafer and tricky to balance. They make me feel like a wrestler on a tightrope.

'Yes!' Sam whispered loudly and pumped his fist like he'd won lotto.

Sam rocks the scull. He taps the boat along with hardly a splash and rockets along the water. There was something I didn't like about Sam. He may have fooled the girls with his cool, mysterious act, but there was something shifty about him. I didn't trust his yogi Buddhist bullshit as far as I could throw it.

'Group weigh-in before we head out,' said Patto. He's not that much older than me – in his mid-twenties and already an Australian rep in the single scull. His ego hardly fits in the room.

'Weigh-ins? What next, the guillotine?' I said.

'Got a problem with that, Poppa?' asked Patto.

'No problem, sir,' I said.

Most guys in my squad don't care about weigh-ins. They have no problems stripping down in the communal showers. I'm not one of those guys. I've never liked being weighed. It usually makes me feel bad.

Patto dragged out the scales and one by one we stood on them. Charley copped it for being too skinny.

'Fifty-three point four kilos,' Patto said. 'Aren't you a dainty thing?'

Adam got on the scales. 'Sixty-seven point eight kilos,' Patto said. 'A little light on for a six seat, Adam. Time to hit the weights room.'

Adam's dad won't be happy if he's not in the first eight in his final year of school. It's a family tradition. The Langley boys row in the firsts. End of story.

Sam bounded over to the scales and steps on.

'Seventy-six point three. Perfect, Mr Camero,' said Patto.

It's my turn next. There's no escape hatch. No time-travel machine or teleporter to make this all disappear.

'Cristian, let's see how much beef the meat seat is carrying,' Patto said. I glared back at him.

The squad hung around like it was a spectator sport. Any idle chatter petered off to hear my weight. I felt like a circus freak.

I prayed the number wasn't as big as I thought it might be. I thought light thoughts. Patto let out a long, slow whistle and my hopes burst.

'One hundred and seventeen point two kilograms.'

I'd put on 7 kilos since the last weigh-in. The secret bingeing on chocolate bars and trips to the kebab shop weren't so secret anymore. The squad clapped and I took a silly little bow, as if I was actually pleased to be the heftiest man in the boat. My crew might have laughed in the sheds, but on the river, they were hauling my flab along.

Patto patted my tummy. 'Ease off the pies, Poppa. We don't need an anchor in the boat, now do we?'

It took all my self-control not to pick up that iPad and clap him over the head with it.

With the horror of weigh-ins over, I carried my scull over my head down to the staging, flicked the light on the end of my bow and grabbed some oars from a stack on the bank. You'd think it would be quiet this early in the morning, but it was already a circus. Bikes, coaches shouting, street-cleaners beeping, trucks roaring towards the highway, cicadas chirping.

The sky was muddy, but I could see Penny screwing her oar into its gate with the rest of the girls' first eight. She glanced at me, then looked away, pulling her cap down over her eyes. But as she rowed past she smiled at me shyly.

I shivered – not because of the cold wind – but because Penny gives me full-on body tingles. Even from a distance. She's beautiful, graceful and has this way of twirling her hair around one finger and sort of spacing out when we have rowing meetings. What is she thinking about? About me? I doubted it. Leni said she 'maybe' liked me. Was maybe enough to ask her out?

I tried to find my balance, wiggling around on my bum cheeks and taking a few strokes. It felt tippy.

Sam rowed around me. 'We're first, Poppa!' he shouted. 'You, me, Julian and Mal. You ready, fat boy?'

'I was born ready, douche bag,' I said back, full of false confidence. Sam was one of the guys that liked to hang it on me for my weight. Another reason I didn't like him.

We rowed down to the start. The city buildings were dipped in fog and a flock of black birds swooped on my boat. Looking back, it was a bad sign.

Westie lined us up four in a row and shouted across the water. 'Attention! Row!'

Sam got an early lead with a high stroke count. I tried to stay calm and stick to my race plan – long, strong and steady. Loose and confident. Push, drive.

Mal slipped back after the first 250. Julian hung in for a bit longer, but his technique fell apart and it became a two-man race. Me versus freaky Sam. It's what the coaches wanted to see, but I don't think anyone expected me to be sitting on Sam's wash.

At the 500 I took my first proper look over my shoulder to see where I was placed. I wasn't making up ground on Sam – I'd let him pull out to two lengths lead.

Of course that's when Dad started yelling at me.

'Cristian, relax! Don't rush! Listen to the boat!'

I listened to the boat. It was making a clunking sound. I was rushing into the front and my blades dragged along the water. I kept looking over my shoulder and saw Sam was taking more water from me – three, maybe four lengths.

'Time to go, Cristian!' Dad shouted as we passed the 1000-metre marker. 'Time to go now, son!'

I was going already. If I was driving a car my foot would have been on the floor in heavy boots.

I tried to spring from my toes, but I had nothing left. My catches were heavy. Instead of accepting defeat I went for one last effort in the final 500, taking my rating up a few clicks. That's when it happened.

The boat tipped to one side, so fast I couldn't correct it. One second I was dry and the next I was swimming up to my neck in freezing, murky Yarra water. It was so cold my balls shrunk to the size of grapes and I screamed like a girl when I felt something slimy brush past my leg. I tried to get back in the boat but the frame was so small and slippery it kept tipping me back out.

'Come on!' I swore at the boat.

The other guys were racing down the course towards me. I didn't want to become that kid who was cut in half during a training session.

'Cristian! Come to the bank!' Dad yelled. 'Swim your boat across!'

Sam had spotted that I was in trouble and was tapping his boat over to play hero.

'Are you okay, Cris?' he called.

That was all the motivation I needed. I grabbed my boat and with my free arm, dog paddled across the river to the bank and the slimy weeds.

I stood up and my calves slid knee deep into black river goop. Dad gave me his hands and winched me out. I stood there, shivering, my legs covered in sludge. Dad fussed around like an old lady, trying to cover my shoulders with his rain jacket. That's when Leni and the girls' first eight glided past. Close enough to witness my complete humiliation. Penny had a front row seat.

'Girls! Eyes in the boat,' their coach Laura shouted. But none of them listened. It was good entertainment.

A former Head of the River champion fell out of a single scull and got whipped by a mountain biker who took up rowing five minutes ago. A guy in the *seconds*.

And then, goddamn. I started crying.

Leni

I'm heading to the gym to meet Adam for our lunchtime weights session. I'm worried about Cris. I hated seeing him upset this morning. I still can't reach him on his phone and I don't want to call my parents in case they worry.

I'm stinking and sweating from my warm-up run and I can't eat fast enough to squash my hunger, shoving a chicken sandwich into my mouth. I'm almost at the gym, when I hear the clop of footsteps and a hand reaches for my elbow. I turn around and there's Sam, in bike shorts, a tight cycling top and chunky cycling shoes. He's dripping.

'You dropped these,' he says.

In his hands is a small mound of tampons. Oh no. You know those movies where the boy meets the girl and they bump into each other buying the same flavour of ice-cream, or their puppy dogs' leashes wrap around each other or they get assigned to the same weekend detention?

I don't think I've ever seen a movie where the girl drops a breadcrumb trail of tampons for the boy she's crushing on.

'Thanks. How embarrassing,' I say.

I shove the tampons into my backpack, discovering that I left one of the pockets open. Another tampon escapes and bounces on the ground. I pick it up and say bad words in my head.

There's no way to recover from a moment like this.

Sam doesn't seem to care. He's holding back a smile.

'I have older sisters, nothing I haven't seen before. Actually, I'm glad I bumped into you.'

He plops down on a grassy patch next to the gym, crossing his legs.

'Sit down.'

It's more of an order than a request. I'm late for Adam and I don't want him to catch me with Sam, the guy most likely to have stolen Cristian's seat, but I find myself on the ground next to him.

'How's Cristian?' Sam says.

'I don't know where he is. He hasn't replied to any of my texts. He'd be pretty gutted about getting kicked out of the firsts.'

'Westie offered me his seat.'

'Are you going to take it?'

'Dunno. Maybe. I'm happy in the seconds.'

Sam pulls his arms up in the air and stretches. All of a sudden I'm staring at the hair under his armpits. I've never seen a guy so flexible.

'What about all those extra ergos you do? Aren't you trying to impress the coaches? Get a seat in the firsts?'

Sam gives me a puzzled look.

'I'm not trying to impress anyone. I do the ergs because they make me feel good.'

He pushes up on his arms, does a perfectly balanced handstand and then jumps to his feet.

'Tell Cris I hope he's not feeling too down. It's a long season. Plenty of seat changes still to come.'

He holds out a hand and pulls me to my feet. Feeling his skin against mine zings something deep in my groin.

'See you at the river,' Sam says.

By the time I've said a weak goodbye, Sam is heading for the gym, taking his shoes and shirt off as he goes.

I meet up with Adam in the weights room and he's started his program. He's doing chin-ups on a raised bar. He's so light and wiry he makes it look easy.

'Where you been?' he says, dropping like a cat to the ground.

'Longer run,' I lie.

I pull up my strength program on my phone and start with squats, threading a leather belt around my middle. Adam helps me lift the heavy plates onto the ends of the bar. I stand with both feet apart, keeping my back straight. My legs shake as I take the weight off and bend my knees, letting my muscles take the load. I do a few more reps than I would normally, thinking about Sam and our conversation.

'Are you okay, Leni? You're so quiet today,' Adam says as I shake out my thighs.

'I'm worried about Cris,' I say.

Adam touches my cheek and looks at me with a tenderness that makes me uncomfortable.

'He'll be okay.'

How could I tell him I was going over my conversation with Sam in my head. Wishing it had gone another direction. Imagining I had said something different than the stupid comment about impressing the coaches. I could have said: 'Why do you do all those ergos? Because you can't not do them? Because something inside you says you have to? That not doing them makes you feel like you're missing a piece?'

And he would have nodded and said, 'That's exactly it. You really get me.'

Cristian

Leni barges into my room after her afternoon row, peppering me with questions. I've called in sick to Patto. He had a go at me and told me to pull my head in and get back down to the river. 'No time for sulking in rowing. I've been dropped from more crews than I can count. We'll do land training tonight but I'll expect to see you tomorrow morning, otherwise you're wasting everyone's time.'

'Yes, sir,' I said in a dead voice, hanging up my phone.

I've done nothing but sit around, eat, watch TV and sleep. I feel sluggish and bloated. The only high point was getting a text from Penny saying she was thinking of me. I keep opening it and looking at it. It has a heart emoticon.

'What's going on? Why is Sam Cam rowing in your seat?' asks Leni.

I put my hands up in surrender. 'Relax, take a load off.'

Leni flops into a beanbag, breathless.

'Until I drop the weight and improve my fitness I'm rowing in the seconds.'

'What are they thinking? You're the best rower in the squad.'

'I dunno about that. Sam beat me by a mile this morning. Even if I didn't fall in, I wouldn't have won.'

'Everyone's taken a swim in the Yarra. It's a rite of passage.'

'You haven't.'

'There's still time.'

Dad storms down the hall and comes in without knocking.

'Have you been dropped to seconds?' he shouts.

'Dad, calm down!' I say.

'This crazy! Cristian, one day you row for Romania … Australia. Whichever country you choose. You're out because why?'

'Because too fat and too unfit,' I say, feeling overwhelmed. 'They want me to drop 15 kilos. How am I going to lose 15 kay-gees?' I ask him, deadly serious. The coach's scare tactic has worked. I'm terrified I can't do it.

Dad calms down and sits on my bed.

'When I was a young man, like you, I would eat, eat, eat. Eating all the time. My mother was always feeding me. Stews, cakes, bread. So I got fat.'

He puffs out his cheeks to illustrate. 'I not make youth team for European Cup if I don't lose weight. I liked watermelon, so I ate watermelon. For three months. I get skinny. Made crew. Won championship. I never eat watermelon again.'

'You ate only watermelon, every day, for months?' I ask. Some of Dad's stories have to be made up.

'Yes. That's what I say.'

'No offence, but nutrition has changed a bit since the olden days,' says Leni. 'We have a sports dietitian Cristian can go and see.'

'Close your mouth. What's so complicated about that?' Dad says.

Leni and I exchange a glance. Dad means well, but he's out of touch.

Dad pulls over my paper bin. I've tried to hide chocolate wrappers and chip bags in there, but he pulls them out one by one.

'Mars Bars, Pringles, M&Ms. Garbage! Let's show coach what a Popescu man can do. Fifteen kilos. Pffft! Is nothing!' He claps me on the back with more force than I expect. I cough.

'Yeah, okay. I'll try.'

'Good! Is done. Back in the firsts. Stay on scholarship. Win Head of River. We tell your mother only cook skinny food.'

'You could lose a few kilos too, Vasile,' I say.

He laughs and pats his tummy. 'Everyone eat skinny food. Is easier together!'

★

47

We have dinner together and, for a change, Dad cooks. The menu? Skinless chicken fillets, steamed broccoli and potato with no butter. It smells and tastes revolting.

'It's nice, Vas,' says Mum, trying to sound enthusiastic about the bland meal.

'What's for dessert?' I ask, winking at Leni.

'Watermelon pie?' Leni says.

'Watermelon ice-cream?' I continue.

'No respect,' Dad grumps.

Leni and I crack up and he leaves us to clean up the unholy mess in the kitchen.

After I do my homework I lie on my bed, listening to the protests of my empty stomach. Can I get away with creeping into the kitchen to get something from the fridge? A bowl of cereal, a hunk of cheese? Something to keep me going until morning. I grab my rowing bag from the floor and search for a stray muesli bar or apple. Nothing. It would probably be easier to sneak out of my room and down to Smith Street to get a kebab from the twenty-four-hour place. Maybe a baklava, too. Food is literally the only thing I can think about. I'm not sure I can do this. Can I do this?

I chat to Penny on messenger. Most of the rowing squad are on it. We've been flirting lately. Both of us are shy and it helps to have a keyboard between us.

CrisP: *Still up?*

HennyPenny: *Yup. Geog test tomorrow.*

Cris: *So tired tonite.*

HennyPenny: *Me 2. RU OK after today?*

CrisP: *Scared I won't get my seat back.*

HennyPenny: *Don't be scared. Be ready.*

CrisP: *I will be. Night.*

HennyPenny: *Night Cris*

I smile and think about our hypothetical first date. She's wearing a sundress and thongs, her hair pulled out of the hard ponytail she usually wears. We share fish and chips on the beach at St Kilda and then walk along the edge, our toes in the water. My arm rests on her shoulders and she hooks a thumb in the back pocket of my jeans. Afterwards we go to see a band and she sways in front of me, her hips loose.

I snap back to reality. Penny would never go out with a guy like me. A hopeless seconds fatty with love handles. I sneak out of my room and down to Smith Street called by the siren song of barbecued meats.

Leni

My bedroom is never completely dark. Fluorescent light leaches under my blind from the street lamp outside. It's never completely quiet either. Drunk people are always steaming out of the pub down the road, shouting things like, 'Heeeeey! Brutha! Yo! Where ya going?' The guy who lives next door is coughing, so I listen to that for a while. He can go all night long. Coughing so much it sounds like he might throw up from the effort. I see him sometimes lighting up a ciggie on the lumpy yellow chair on their front porch. He looks half dead, but he won't quit. People are so stupid.

I'm getting out of bed for a glass of water when I hear a soft knock at my window and a guy's voice saying my name. Scared, I open the blind and peer out.

Adam's in our front garden, holding the side of his head. Something's wrong. *First* – we hadn't agreed to meet, and Adam, like me, is into planning stuff. *Second* – he looks a mess and there's blood on his T-shirt. I've never seen Adam without product in his hair and matching clothes, even on the riverbank. Even when we are alone together.

'I'll let you in,' I whisper.

I turn the front door latch gently and push him into my bedroom, closing the door behind us.

'What's wrong?'

Adam sits down on the bed. He puts his arms around his body and silently howls, like that painting we studied in school, *The Scream*. I hug him awkwardly. He's cold and shaking.

'Adam, are you okay?' I ask. It seems inadequate.

'Yes … no. I don't know.'

I peel his palm away from his forehead. He has a small gash above his eyebrow and a shiny lump.

I know a bit about head injuries from the time Cristian blacked out during a rugby tackle, got concussion and had to sit out for three weeks.

'Are you dizzy? Do you feel sick? Maybe we should go to emergency.'

'No. I'm not going to the hospital,' says Adam.

'Just to get it looked at, make sure it's not serious.'

'It was my fault. I got kicked out of the firsts. Westie's

doing a cull. First Cristian, now me. I'm not strong enough. Not tough enough.'

'There's no one tougher than you,' I say. Adam will row until he vomits. In the rain, cold, rough water, forty-degree heat. He never complains.

'Can I have a better look?' I say.

I turn my bedside lamp onto his wound. It's not too bad but it might need stitches.

'What happened?'

'My brothers rowed in the firsts, Dad, Granddad. I can't row in the seconds. Not this year. Do you know how many boats my father has bought the school? Do you know what they *cost*?'

I feel sick to my stomach.

'Who did this to you?' I ask, thinking the worst.

'I did,' Adam whispers.

'Why?' I feel confused and upset. Why would anyone do this to themselves? Especially not Adam. He always seems so together. So dependable.

'I was fighting with Dad and he was calling me a pathetic loser and making me feel like nothing. Like I didn't matter. I got so angry I banged my head against the table. He made me feel so bad about myself; it actually felt better to do this instead. I ran away and came here. I didn't know what else to do.'

'The glass table? In the living room?' I picture the designer table with its thick, square edges, magazines stacked artfully on the surface.

'Yep.'

'Adam. You could have knocked yourself out.'

'That was the idea, Leni. At least it shut him up. I couldn't stand it anymore. He is always, always down on me. Something snapped. Haven't you ever snapped?'

I think about it. He wants something from me that I can't give. I've never felt out of control.

'Not like this. You don't want to give yourself brain damage because you're not in the firsts.'

'It's okay for you, you're never going to get chucked out of your crew.'

'How do you know that? Promise me you won't do anything like this again.' I grab his hands and squeeze them.

'I don't think I will,' says Adam.

'Let's wake Mum up. She can take a look.'

'Don't worry about it, Leni. I shouldn't have come here. I'll go home.'

He gets up to leave and I pull him back. He won't look me in the eye.

'Adam. Stay.'

Adam looks pale. 'I have a headache.'

'I gotta wake Mum,' I say. Her home medical kit should sort out a cut like this.

'Don't tell them it was me. Make something up. Tell them my dad's away. Overseas.'

'Okay,' I agree. He lets my fingers slip away.

I wait at the door of my parents' room for a moment, thinking how with one knock, everything would change. I'd be lying to my parents and I always said I wouldn't do that.

Then I knock.

Cristian

I'm sneaking back into the house after a trip to Hasir Kebabs. They know my order now. Doner kebab, extra garlic sauce. I think for sure I've been sprung when I see the kitchen lights are on. We Popescus are early to bed and early to rise and nobody is usually up past 9 pm. It's almost 11 but as I walk towards the light I can see that everyone's up. Even Banjo. Bizarrely, Adam is sitting in our kitchen and Mum is applying Steri-Strips to a cut above his eyebrow.

Dad turns around when he hears my trainers squeak on the wooden floor. He gives me a very sad, disappointed look.

'Where have you been?'

'To Smith Street to get something to eat. Sorry.'

Dad shakes his head at me. He doesn't have to say, *you are a useless prick*. That's what he's thinking. What I'm thinking. Who breaks a diet after five hours? My hand goes to the 7-Eleven chocolate bar in my pocket. It's burning a hole in my leg.

'Don't ever leave the house without letting us know where you are going. This isn't a safe neighbourhood at night.'

Dad turns away from me to the delicate operation in progress on the kitchen table. Mum has surgical gloves on, while Leni holds the light up so she can see.

'Hey Adam,' I say.

'Shhhhh!' says Leni, looking irritated.

'What happened?' I ask the surgical team.

Mum doesn't answer, she's too busy focusing on her patient.

'It was an accident. I walked into a door,' says Adam.

'All done,' Mum says to him in her nurse voice. 'You seem fine, Adam, but I need to observe you for at least a few hours before you can go home. You might as well get comfortable. I'll make tea.'

Walking into a door? Sounds dodgy to me.

Adam says he's fine to drive himself home, even though he shouldn't have been driving in the first place, because he's only just got his Ps and he's whacked his head.

'Absolutely not,' says Mum. 'Can you take him, Vas?'

'Yes, of course,' says Dad.

'I'll go too,' says Leni.

'No, you go back to bed,' says Dad. 'Cristian can keep me company.'

Inwardly I groan. Dad will use the confined space to give me a lecture about willpower and watermelon.

'Thanks, Mrs Popescu,' says Adam.

Mum gives him a hug I know is the top-shelf variety – strong, committed and reassuring. His face looks small and scared over her shoulder. 'Call me if you feel any worse. Right away and I'll take you up to the Royal.'

'I will.'

He closes his eyes briefly and I wonder if he's thinking about his own mum. Wishing she was closer than Sydney.

Adam has driven over in his new Mini, but we all pile into our car.

'You pick up toy car tomorrow,' says Dad, as the engine whines to life. 'Where you live?'

'Toorak,' says Adam. 'Lansell Road.'

Adam's house is famous. One of the most expensive slices of real estate in the entire city, on the most exclusive tree-lined street.

Dad looks blank. 'I not know this place.'

Adam turns on his mobile phone GPS and says 'home'.

A woman speaking in an American accent joins us in the car, telling Dad to drive straight. Two hundred metres. Then turn left. Vasile doesn't like technology and he frowns deeply.

'I have enough women telling me how to drive with my wife and daughter,' he says. 'Tell me direction.'

Leni

'Are you tired?' Mum asks.

'Not really,' I admit. I'm shaken, alert. The sun will be up in a few hours. It's almost not worth going back to sleep.

'Another cuppa?'

'Yeah.'

Mum packs up her kit and makes us both a cup of tea. She always has tea on. A fresh brew clears her head when she is emptied from nursing sick kids.

She hands me a chipped mug and a slice of marbled *cozonac* sweet bread. I'm walloped by memories as I take a bite. I love hanging around the kitchen watching her make it for special occasions. When I was little I'd help her roll the dough and wait impatiently for it to cook in the oven. Wrapped in a sweet cloud of rum, orange peel and cocoa.

'What was tonight all about, Leni?' Mum asks as I blow across the steaming tea in my mug.

'I dunno,' I say, feeling terrible for not being honest.

'I see this sort of injury quite often,' Mum says. 'It's usually caused by someone being pushed into a wall or a table.'

She looks at me intensely. 'Do you think Adam is telling the truth about how this injury occurred? Because if he isn't, I'd have to follow that up through the proper channels.'

I shake my head, and decide to stick to my story and not reveal how Adam got hurt. 'Of course.'

Breaking eye contact is the only way I can stop the story from escaping my lips. I feel a tug of loyalty in both directions. The pit of my stomach swirls with unease.

Cristian

We drop Adam off at home and Dad tries to act like it's not the biggest house he's ever seen.

'Where's your father?' Dad asks. Or rather interrogates.

'Hong Kong. Business. My stepmum Kitty is with him.'

Dad makes a clicking sound of disapproval. He has always loathed Mitch Langley. At regattas Mitch acts like he's head coach, despite the fact that he hasn't rowed since he was a schoolboy. Even then he was a cox. He likes to make crew suggestions. 'That tiny, red man thinks he buys the boats, he picks rowers,' Dad's said, like a hundred times.

'And your other mother?'

Adam's real mother left Mitch when Adam was fourteen.

'She lives in Sydney. I'll call her tomorrow.'

'Yes. Do. Family is important.'

'Thanks, Mr Popescu,' Adam says, politely. 'I'm sorry I woke you all up.'

'Goodnight, Adam,' Dad says. But what he really means is, *I'm onto you.*

We wait with the car engine running until Adam has gone inside the huge steel gates of his house. Then Dad looks hard at me.

'Anything else you'd like to say about tonight?'

'Sorry I broke the diet. I'll try harder.'

'No, not that,' Dad says. 'Why Adam is in our house? Middle of night? Bashed in head?'

'I think you should probably ask Leni, he's her boyfriend,' I say. It's what I'm planning to do.

'All right, I will. Why you sneak out for food, like hungry rat?'

'I was hungry.'

'You hungry, you lose weight.'

That's what I'm scared of. Food is a friend I turn to when I'm down. I'm not ready to give it up. 'Okay. I'll do better. Promise.'

'You're good boy,' Dad says and he puts his hand on the back of my neck. 'Let's go home. This very strange night.'

Leni

I've had about three hours of sleep, and I feel jet-lagged. My movements are slow and my head is thick with fatigue. At least the river is in form. It's sheet glass, no wind. After the nightmare of last night, these are the conditions I dream of. The air smells like summer, too, perfumed with eucalyptus.

I'm standing to one side of the gym, quietly warming up. Swinging my right leg back and forth under me, holding onto the wall for balance. I'm thirsty and a headache bangs behind my eyes. Switching sides, I notice Rachel and Millie on yoga mats across the room. They're teasing each other about their morning hairdos. Millie messes up her short hair so it's Mohawk style. Rach pulls her wet ponytail across her top lip, like a moustache. They fall about laughing.

I'd join in, but my crew doesn't expect me to be silly. Somehow I've got a reputation for being 100 per cent serious, 100 per cent of the time.

Rachel lies down and lets Millie push her legs over her head in a stretch.

'Stop!' Rachel shouts. 'I'm not a circus freak.'

I sit on my own, pulling my head down to my knees. Pretending I'm not interested in the morning chatter and gossip of the other girls.

'Girls, let's go!' says Laura, running into the room. 'We have three timed thousands to do this morning. Chop, chop!'

Now I start to feel part of the group, filling up our

water bottles, pulling on caps and arranging the blades neatly on the grass. I know how to do this. The stuff off the water is more confusing.

'Hands on!' says Aiko as we file around the side of the boat and lift it off the racks.

We walk the boat down to the bank, expertly flipping the fibreglass shell off our shoulders and above our heads, rolling it down to sit on the water.

'Blades in, let's get out there,' says Aiko.

I like the routine of rowing. Everything has a place to fit. I know my seat and what to do when I'm told.

Pretty much as soon as the warm-up starts, Rachel is in my ear about how tired she is.

'Ugh. I need a coffee. Actually I need a bucket of coffee. Actually I need a slab of Red Bull.'

'Shut up.'

'What did you say?' Rachel bites back.

I'm trying to push aside my lack of sleep and focus on the row. But I feel murderously cranky.

'I don't need you in my ear complaining, okay. Back me up.'

'I always back you up.'

'Do you?'

'I don't like your tone of voice, young lady,' Rachel says, trying to lighten it up.

I sit forward, wishing that today of all days I didn't have to sit 20 centimetres from Rachel for two hours. She reluctantly joins me with her blade ready to start.

We are rowing out by the docks, closer to the ocean. The air has a salty tang and the river widens up. There's room to breathe. On either side of us are old docks and numbered shipping yards.

'We will row from dock number three to nineteen,' says Laura as she zooms up on her tinny. She holds up her stopwatch.

'It's roughly a thousand. You're on the clock, so I expect hard strokes all the way.'

We take off and the balance is tipping to stroke side. I struggle to get my blade off the water. I lift my hands up violently and try to right the boat. It only makes it worse.

'Relax Leni,' says Rachel. 'The balance will come.'

I grunt in frustration as the boat slides back onto stroke side, trapping my fingers painfully between the side of the boat and my oar handle.

'Come on!' I yell, my finger throbbing in pain. 'Sit the boat up!'

It's not only the boat that's feeling wonky. I'm rushing the slide and slow around the back turn. I'm not setting up a nice, easy pace for the girls to follow. I feel breathless and queasy.

'Find the rhythm, Leni,' says Aiko. 'Everyone else, relax and let the boat run!'

We find twenty decent strokes and then Aiko calls the finish.

'Well that was utter garbage,' says Rachel behind me as we check the run off the boat.

'Rachel, can you for once be positive? We had twenty good strokes, let's focus on those,' says Penny. I silently thank her. She doesn't speak up much, but when she does it makes perfect sense.

'The good news is, kids, we have two more of those to go,' says Aiko into her microphone.

There's a groan from the seven bodies behind me. Laura idles nearby in her boat, looking disappointed.

'What. Was. That?' she says, looking down at her stopwatch. 'Let's not row like that again, ladies. I thought I was back coaching the Year Eight sevenths. Leni, mate, settle down the rating and let's get some rhythm going. It's all over the shop.'

Dad skids his bike into the sheds. He's back from coaching the thirds and looks like he's about to blow up.

'Uh-oh,' I say to Penny as we tinker with a few minor changes to our seats, the boat out on slings. 'Watch this.'

'You take strongest rowers out of boat and replace them with novice?' says Dad to Westie, who is looking at crew footage on his iPad as his crew washes down their boat.

'Good morning to you too, Vasile.'

Dad points at Sam, who's quietly circling the boat with a big yellow sponge.

'This boy fit, yes. He has talent, yes. But technique? Not as good as Cristian or Adam. He needs more time in second boat. Is too early for him.'

Sam looks embarrassed. He stops cleaning and listens in.

'It's not about technique, Vas. It's about potential.'

'My son has potential. Why else would he be on scholarship?'

'He's also unfit, unmotivated and overweight.'

'We see. He show you.'

61

'In case you hadn't noticed, I'm the coach of the firsts. It's my decision who's in and who's out. And this boy,' says Westie, motioning to Sam, 'has the potential to go all the way to Olympic gold medals. Don't tell me you don't see that too.'

'I see he's not ready,' says Dad.

'I see a parent who needs to take a step back,' says Westie.

The two of them eye each other in cold silence. Dad puts his hands up and takes an exaggerated step backwards.

'Fine. Don't come crying to me when you lose Head of River.'

The seconds come in and I wait for Adam to get ready for school so we can go in together. I need to see he's all right. As he walks over to me I notice he's not wearing red socks anymore. He's already been stripped of that first crew honour.

'Hi Leni,' he says. As if this is any morning. Not the morning after last night.

'How are you?'

'Fine,' he says with a tight smile. 'A bit tired.'

'Really? Are you okay to row?'

He's wearing the dorky straw hat that's part of our school uniform. Tipped at an angle, it hides his injury perfectly. I want to tell him not to pretend there's nothing wrong.

'Yeah. No worries.'

'I'm worried,' I say.

I reach for his arm and he lets me look him in the eye for precisely three seconds, all the hurt and pain from last night bubbling up. Then he puts the fake smile back on.

'I have a plan to get Cris and I back into the firsts. You'll see. It won't be long. Come on. I'll treat you to an egg and bacon roll from the deli. To say thanks for last night.'

Just like that, Adam is back in control. All the frayed bits pulled together with his pressed blazer and perfectly aligned tie. He holds my hand and laces our fingers so tightly it's uncomfortable. I wiggle my fingers free and put my arm around his waist.

'Egg and bacon roll *and* a chai latte.'

'Deal,' he says, leaning in and kissing my neck lightly.

Cristian

Adam's waiting for me in the common room at recess. Both of us are still stinging from our training row with the seconds. The crew might have been hot stuff last week, but with two new rowers in the middle of the boat, everyone has to find their feet again. We were out of sync and didn't get their in-jokes.

'Let's walk, Poppa.'

Adam steers me out the school gates to the street.

'Hey man, is your head feeling okay?' I ask.

Adam has hidden his wound under his school hat, but I still know it's there. Underneath all the school-prefect, straight-A front, he seems unhappy. Stressed.

'I don't want to talk about that.'

'Sure?'

'Positive.'

This is how it was with Adam. He was the leader and I was the puppy dog.

'The seconds are okay, but they're not our crew,' says Adam flatly. 'We belong back in the firsts. You know what the other schools are saying?'

'No, what?'

'There's trouble brewing at Harley. Westie is chucking out star rowers for novices.'

'What are we supposed to do about it? This isn't musical chairs.'

'I know someone who can help us.'

'Who? Jenny Craig?'

'Guy at my gym. The one I go to with my brothers and Dad.'

Adam works out at a private club on his side of the river. Shiny, brand-spanking new equipment and wall-to-wall pumped-up AFL players and gay guys. Lots of fluffy white towels and personal trainers pushing an agenda.

Adam took me there once and I couldn't wait to leave. It was the antithesis of the shabby, zen yoga studios around my area. Everyone was watching me lift, then watching themselves in the mirrors.

'He can get us some stuff,' says Adam.

'Stuff? Like protein powders? Aminos?'

'Nah, like real gear.'

I know what gear is. Also known as juice, sauce, slop, product. Gear is steroids. And it's not the first time I'd been offered a taste. A team from South Africa came out on a school rugby tour last year and a few of the blokes were into it. Told us it was the best way to get bulk. I ignored them, but maybe Adam was listening.

'I gotta get back in the firsts, Cris. This is the only thing I can think of. I've talked to this guy. He gets it for the footy players. Anything we like. Good gear.'

'Where am I going to get money for that?'

'I can pay for it.'

I feel uncomfortable. Our family isn't well-off but I don't like my cashed-up mates paying my way, either. If I pulled a few extra shifts at Bunnings, would it be enough?

'I dunno, Adam. Don't they, like, shrink your balls or something? Make you Incredible Hulk aggro?'

'Nah. This guy has good product. That weight you have to lose, will be gone in like, a month. I can get big. I'm too skinny. The more I lift, the skinnier I get. The protein shakes can only do so much. I need this. We can stop, way before the Head of the River. There's no testing, right? So no one has to know. Everyone does it now anyway.'

'Isn't it cheating?'

'Clean sport is a myth, my friend. You either get smart or you get beaten.'

We walk in silence, each of us weighing up the risk. It's minimal, our school doesn't drug test for performance-enhancing drugs, and it would be so easy to say yes. Rowing had gotten too hard. There was too much at stake now. We'd worked our way to the senior crews, but now we both needed a shortcut. The quickest point from A to B.

'Will you do the talking?' I ask.

Adam smiles and slaps me across the shoulders conspiratorially. He doesn't like to do things on his own. It wasn't just about helping out a friend, he wanted a partner in crime.

'We'll go see this guy after school. He'll hook us up. So, you'll come?'

'Only to talk to him? I'm still not sure I want to do this.'

'No-obligation, free quote,' says Adam.

We change the subject and talk about our biology assignment as we head back for more classes, but all I can think is *should I? Shouldn't I?* Like I'm tossing a coin in my head. On the shiny side is easy entry back into the firsts and holding onto my scholarship. On the tarnished, green side is a voice that's asking if I'm a drug cheat.

It's the dumbest of dumb ideas, but I imagine taking my shirt off in front of Penny at the river. Imagining her face when she sees how ripped I am. It tips me in the wrong direction. The shiny side falls up.

Leni

Audrey and I take the 86 tram home and get off at Sunny's bakery on Smith Street. She orders a Vietnamese pork roll, extra chilli.

'Same,' I tell the girl behind the counter. This is our Tuesday special. It never changes. That makes me happy.

While we wait for our rolls to be assembled, I pour a sachet of protein powder into a container of water and shake it up.

'Let me taste that,' asks Audrey.

I hand it over. 'You won't like it,' I warn.

She swigs and makes a face.

'My tongue. It's burning!'

'It's not that bad.'

'It tastes like hell. Here, take your Satan shake.' She hands it back to me. 'You are dedicated to drink that.'

The most exercise Audrey gets is using her mouse hand to play *World of Warcraft*, working up a sweat on a new earring design and running around muddy paddocks pretending to be a warrior queen. She's not the slightest bit interested in my training.

'I wish Harley would spend half the cash that they do on the rowing program on fencing gear for Lucy,' she once mused. 'Rowing gets all the attention and all the funding.'

I couldn't really argue with her. Everything else did seem to pale in comparison to my sport.

Audrey pays for our snack – we take turns shouting each other – and we walk towards her house. We've got an English essay to do, but we take it slow, chewing on the fresh coriander, strips of carrot, the tangy mystery pate and hot fatty pork.

We stop and look in the window of her favourite second-hand shop, 'Release the Hounds'.

'Should we go in?' Audrey asks. 'Get a little something pretty?'

'Best not. I'm broke. Let's go back to yours and make a start on *The Kite Runner* essay. Due tomorrow, don't forget.'

★

We're studying in Audrey's bedroom. It's like being in an enchanted forest. She's painted the walls dark green, and hand-drawn wood animals with big eyes, creeping vines, forests and snow-capped mountains. She's got a fish tank with two Mexican walking fish called Weasley and Dumbledore. Audrey says you're never too old to love Harry Potter. She has a quidditch broomstick in one corner.

My head's not in my work. I keep reading the same paragraph over and over, the words losing focus. I put my book down, wondering if I should betray Adam's trust and spill the details of last night. Would that make me an even worse girlfriend? Some things aren't for sharing.

'Do you think I'm the sort of girl who shouldn't have a boyfriend? Lately I've been thinking maybe I should be single,' I say.

Audrey looks up from her book, puts her glasses on. She's horribly short-sighted.

'You are torturing that poor Adam Langley. You still haven't put out, have you?'

'I do put out. In certain pre-specified areas.'

Adam and I were engaged in an exhausting sexual tug of war. I held onto my virginity on one end of the rope and he pulled his in the other direction. The direction he was used to.

'What's sex like, Auds? Worth doing?'

'Of course it's worth doing. But only when you're ready. And when you're ready *with the right guy*.'

'I shouldn't make such a big deal of it.'

'It's the biggest deal,' says Audrey, sitting up and looking at me intensely. 'Look, technically, it's just sticking something in a hole, but it changes everything. Like EVERYTHING,' she says. 'You're not kids anymore. Boom. Like that.' She clicks her fingers. 'You gotta worry about the babies and the diseases and taking the pill. Before sex, you're playing. After, it's business.'

'So, Kieren, he's like the one? How do you know?'

'I don't know. But he makes me feel safe and beautiful and we look out for each other. He gives me the *jtzooum*.'

We talk about the *jtzooum* a lot. That weird, tingly, floaty feeling that some guys give you. Adam doesn't. Sam does.

Audrey and her boyfriend have been together since she was in Year Ten. He's just finished Year Twelve. In high school years that's a long time.

Audrey sighs. 'I told Kieren to dump me for schoolies' week.'

'Why?'

'I doubt he wants a little Year Eleven girlfriend who can't even go to clubs on the biggest party of his life. I told him we should break up for a week, and he can do whatever he likes. Then we can get back together.'

She looks miserable. 'I think I made a huge mistake.'

I give her a hug.

'Get back together with him. Kieren is awesome and you guys are like vegemite and toast. Not as good apart.'

She nods and wipes her nose on my sleeve.

'Yuuuk,' I say. 'We're not *that* close.'

I decide to confess something murky and secret to Audrey because we tell each other almost everything.

'I'm crushing on someone at school.'

Audrey leans forward and widens her eyes.

'Might this have something to do with you wanting to be single?'

'Promise you won't tell anyone.'

'Pinkie swear.'

'It's Sam Camero.'

'Bike Pant Guy? He's in my ceramics class. You should see him handle a piece of clay.' She makes a lewd gesture with her hands and laughs.

'What do you think of him?'

Audrey shrugs. She hasn't spent a minute thinking about Sam. Unlike me.

'Doesn't talk much, comes in, does his thing, leaves. Obviously he's very lovely to look at, but I reckon he's well aware of that. Oooh. Want to look him up on Facebook?' she asks.

I've already googled him, but I let Audrey feel like a detective.

'I'll log in as you. Password?'

'RowingGirl.'

'Of course.'

'Sam Camero, Samuel Camero Jr, Samantha Camero. There's heaps of them.'

I look over her shoulder at the profiles. 'Cut out all the Samanthas and all the ones overseas. There he is.'

Sam's profile photo is of him riding a mountain bike over a huge cliff and taking air.

'Let's see. Photos first,' Audrey says. 'Photogenic character, isn't he?'

Sam's photo bank is like an action adventure catalogue. Mountain biking, rowing, snowboarding, bungy jumping and one of him in an insane yoga pose. There's a cute one where he's holding a baby I assume is his niece or nephew.

'What can Facebook tell us about the elusive Sam?' Audrey says, reading his profile.

'One hundred and eighteen friends. Interested in women. *Lucky*. Birthday, September. Dating status: It's complicated. Hmmm. What does that mean?'

What did that mean? It's new since I last stalked his profile.

'Favourite activities: Bikram yoga, whatever that is, rowing, mountain biking. Yawn. He likes Discovery Channel, Nat GEO, *Breaking Bad*, *Dexter*, favourite movie *The Lord of the Rings* ... okay, maybe I have a crush on him now.'

I'm too busy looking at Sam's page that I don't notice Audrey has moved the mouse to hover over the 'Add friend' button. She looks at me, smiles and clicks it.

I scream and try to wrestle the mouse away from her.

'You did not do that!'

'It's sent, Leni!'

'You are the worst best friend ever!' I scream, falling backwards onto her bed and covering my face with her pillow.

The next time Sam logs into Facebook he will see a big fat 'Friend Request' from me.

'He probably has a crush on you too. You're gorgeous,' says Audrey.

'You think?'

'Don't fish.'

'I'm not!'

I knew I wasn't Year Nine Leni anymore, painfully skinny, with a faint moustache and greyhound legs. I looked good to guys. I'd seen them staring.

'I can't believe you sent Sam a friend request from my account. What's he going to think?'

'That you want to be friends? You'll thank me when you and Bike Pant Guy are doing Bikram yoga poses together.'

'What am I going to do about Adam?'

'Have you gone off him?'

'I dunno. He's sweet and good-looking, but not much *jtzooum.*'

'Wishy-washy. Break up with him,' Audrey advises.

'You make it sound so simple.'

'Why are you making it so hard?' says Audrey.

The question burns at me. Why wasn't I calling it off?

On my way home for dinner I come up with two answers. One: I was worried what Adam might do if I did break up with him and two: Adam made me feel special. He chose me, when he could've had any other girl at school. That was worth holding onto, wasn't it?

Cristian

It's Tuesday so we have a precious afternoon off training. Adam drives us to his gym after school. He's edgy and driving badly – tailgating and going through orange-red lights. He plays angry rap music and we don't talk. If we did, we might renege. Or at least I might. He seems resolute.

'I'm nervous,' I say, turning the sound down on Adam's stereo. 'How does this work exactly?'

He turns the music back up, even louder. 'I have no idea! Relax Cris!'

The air-conditioned room smells like sweat and perfume. A bouncy soundtrack makes the lycra-clad receptionist jiggle as she swipes Adam's membership card and he pays for a guest visit for me. Putting down thirty bucks as if it's paper money. The timber floors squeak with the impact of expensive running shoes and machines whir quietly. I eye a guy with no neck and hulking shoulders in the free weights room. Is he using? He catches me staring and I duck my chin to my chest. I don't want any more trouble.

'Is Doug here?' Adam asks one of the trainers.

'Finishing up a spin class,' says the girl, nodding towards the pulsating darkened room.

We stand near a wall, painted up with inspirational sports quotes. One of them says: 'Pain is temporary. It may last a minute, or an hour, or a day, or a year, but eventually it will subside and something will take its place. If I quit, however, it lasts forever.' — Lance Armstrong.

Underneath someone has scribbled 'cheat' in very small letters – surely a sign for Adam and I to heed. I nudge Adam and point to the quote. He gives me his 'shut up Cristian' stare. I'm close to pulling the pin on the whole shady deal when Doug strolls towards us, shiny with sweat. He looks at us standing there all jittery and high schoolie and wisely decides to exit the building.

'Boys. Let's adjourn to the café,' he says smoothly.

Doug's wearing a 'Fitness Now!' uniform and looks pretty normal, which is reassuring. He's slim and toned. Like a regular personal trainer.

'Next time, wear casual clothes, you look like preschoolers in those uniforms,' says Doug.

Doug orders us three coffees, his is skim with Equal so I order the same, even though it tastes so awful I can barely drink it.

'Don't look so guilty,' Doug says to me.

I don't bother to answer him. This is Adam's deal.

'Okay, let's do business. What do you boys want?'

'What have you got?' says Adam.

'Everything.'

In ten minutes flat we are walking down the street, our schoolbags loaded with gear and guilt.

I'm sitting in my bedroom, the door locked. The pills are in a plastic bag in my desk drawer. I've got to find a better hiding spot. But I don't have a fake air-con unit or a loose floorboard and my parents aren't prone to doing room searches. They trust Leni and me. Maybe they shouldn't. If Dad found out I was using performance-enhancing drugs he would sell me to the highest bidder or ship me back to Romania in a crate with air holes. Make me live with my dotty grandparents in their tiny apartment in Bucharest.

This goes against everything they believe in. They've talked about how much they detest drug cheats. How unfair it was to race against athletes who were chemically enhanced. Mum lost out on gold in the worlds because of a rower who looked like a man, except for her ponytail and the inch of make-up she wore to race. The next year, Mum won the Olympic gold in Seoul because that girl had been caught. Incidentally, Seoul was when yellow-eyed sprinter Ben Johnson was disqualified for drug use. Photos of him should be enough to put me off. He's half human, half science experiment. Fair and square. That's what my parents believe in. They like to think I'm the best of them, but maybe I'm the worst.

I take out one of the drug packets and open it, reading the fine print. I hit up Dr. Google and type in the name of the drug. 'Increases aerobic capacity, blood pressure and oxygen transportation. Increases the rate at which body fat is metabolised. Prescribed for people with breathing disorders such as asthma.'

Not so bad.

'Also prescribed for the treatment of horses.'

Horses? Damn.

There are some other scary side effects of steroids which I skim over. Mood swings, aggression, testicles shrinkage (not good), reduced sperm count or infertility (I don't exactly want kids yet, so whatever), baldness (plenty of hair, no big deal), development of breasts (will I have to get a sports bra?), increased risk for prostate cancer (don't old dudes get that?). The diet pills that Doug gave me aren't much better. Google says they cause anxiety, dry mouth, sleeplessness and rapid heart rate.

Scared, I click off the pages and clear my search history.

They have to put in all the worst side effects. Most of the time that stuff never even happens. I'm young. I'll be fine.

I grab my water bottle and press a pill from each packet, wash them down before I chicken out.

Maybe I'll wake up looking like Sam.

I text Adam.

Took them. U nxt

He replies straightaway.

Already done it.

I feel scared, excited and guilty all at once. It's not the worst feeling in the world. But it's not the best, either.

November

Five months to Head of the River

Leni

It's family dinner but there's not much talking. Cris and I are so tired from training, we can hardly lift our forks. Everything has stepped up a notch. Our mileage on the river, school, exams. The end of the year is in sight. The air is warmer, purple flowers are blooming on the jacaranda tree, summer is close. I'm scraping my plate clean but I notice Cris hasn't eaten a thing. Even though it's a healthy meal with lots of vegies. So does Mum.

'Cris, what's up?' she asks. 'You've hardly touched your meal.'

He bristles and lets out an irritated sigh.

'I'm not hungry.'

Mum looks at Dad as if to say 'get involved'.

'Leave the poor boy alone, Jodie. He's not four years old. He doesn't have to finish everything on his plate.'

'Thank you,' Cristian says to Dad. He gets up, dumps his full plate in the sink and goes to his room.

'Hey!' Mum calls out. 'You're on wash-up Mister Teenage Angst.'

We all jump as the door to Cristian's room slams shut.

'What's gotten into him lately?' Mum says.

Dad and I shrug.

'Seconds syndrome?' I say. 'May I be excused? I've got to study. Exams.' I've been cramming hard and there's so much left to learn. I'll be pulling a late one tonight and every other night this week. You can't get straight As and not lose sleep and your social life.

Dad eyes off the mess in the kitchen and sighs.

'Go.'

As I head down the hall Dad calls out.

'Tell Cristian to hit book, too!'

'Cris, do some study!' I yell at his bedroom door, which is shut and probably locked. He's been acting so strange lately. All secretive and withdrawn.

I study for exactly an hour before my phone beeps, giving me a ten-minute break. I call Adam, but the call goes to message bank. I'd been speaking to his recorded message more than him lately.

'Hey, it's Leni. Want to panic about exams together? I could not be more stressed about chem.'

I wait for the phone to ring or maybe a reassuring text. But there's nothing. I'm not imagining it. Adam is backing off. Maybe I'd gotten too close to knowing what his perfect life is really like behind those iron gates.

I fire up Facebook and check my friend request status. Still nothing from Sam in over a week. I refresh the page.

Nothing. I'm embarrassed and I want to explain that Audrey sent the request, not me, but then I would also have to admit I was Face-stalking him in the first place.

Audrey reckons I should withdraw my offer of friendship.

'Who waits ten days to reply to a friend request? What a tosser.'

'Maybe he doesn't check it that often,' I say.

'Maybe he's not worth your time, doll.'

Doll. Only Audrey could use that expression and get away with it.

Cristian

In my room I try to blow off the simmering anger from dinner by doing pull-ups on the bar Dad installed for me from the doorframe. I can do five before my arms start to wobble. I fall to the carpet and lie with my feet up on the wall, panting.

I feel weird since I started on the drugs. I have too much energy and not enough focus. I don't feel like studying, even though I need to. I'm already behind and soon I'll have to sit a barrage of three-hour exams. I need to talk to my teachers, fit in extra study, but all I can think about is getting back in the firsts and dropping this weight.

My stomach makes a weird gurgling sound. I should be starving, but the pills have dulled my appetite. Mum's suss. I need to work out a way to put her off the scent. She's smart though. It will take some dodging.

I pull my scales out from under the bed. They're dusty. I've hidden them there because just looking at them makes me anxious. I never know what they'll say and how the numbers will make me feel. Usually this is where I'd shove them back under the bed and ignore them for another few months. But I'm curious what's happening to my body. I stand on them. Hoping for the best.

I've already lost.

'Yes!' I say to myself, pumping my fist and shadow-boxing around the room. I've taken back control of my weight. It feels good.

'In your face, Westie,' I say.

Lost 3.3 I text to Adam.

Gained 1.1 he texts back.

Winning! I text.

Leni

I catch up with Adam at his locker after morning assembly, but he seems cagey. I tap him on the shoulder and he jumps, slams his locker door shut and looks at me like I'm trying to spy on him.

'What's up, Leni?' he says.

I look at his school blazer. There's literally no space for any more achievements. He has a prefect pocket, house colours, rowing colours, six sports badges. When you look at him, Adam seems like the model student. Closer in, I can see he's struggling.

'Get my message?' I ask, sounding more hurt than I thought I was. What is it about someone backing off that makes them more interesting?

'I did. Sorry I didn't get back to you. I was studying and had my phone off.'

'Want to meet at the gym at lunch?' I ask. 'Weights?'

We hadn't been training together lately, study had taken precedence.

'Mmm,' Adam looks distracted. 'I can't today. Cris and I are lifting together. It's a heavy session.'

'I'll come too.'

'No. That's okay. I'll see you later, at the river.' He traces a line under my bottom lip, which fails to give me the *jtzooum*. 'I'm going to take you out to dinner. After exams. When everything settles down. Would you like that? Vue du Monde?'

I have absolutely no idea what Vue Du Monde is, but judging by the other hatted restaurants Adam has taken me too, it'll be amazing.

I put my finger gently on his scar. It's healed beautifully.

'Yes. Let's do that.'

Maybe I would break up with Adam after we went to Vue Du Monde. Maybe I wouldn't.

Another morning session and it's muggy. A gust blows across the water, along with a flurry of rain. The wind is pushing the boat around. Behind me, Rachel is at it again.

'I'm freaking staaaarving,' she moans as we wind up another hard piece. We are racing short-burst 500s against the seconds and they've pipped us twice. Morale is low.

I finish the piece and bend over my knees, breathing hard. Feeling the blood burning and coursing under my skin.

'I forgot my water bottle,' Rachel says. She doesn't even sound out of breath. 'Does anyone have any spare H_2O?'

Every comment she makes scratches at my gut.

'This isn't junior rowing!' I snap. 'Someone give Rachel some bloody water.'

Aiko passes her bottle down the boat and I turn around and virtually throw it at Rachel.

She's fixing a clip in her hair. I roll my eyes and sigh.

'Don't be so passive aggressive, Leni,' Rachel says, smiling. 'Say what you really think.'

'I think you should stop doing your hair and put in a little effort on the blade.'

'I am making an effort.'

'Enough chatter girls!' shouts Laura from her bike. 'Sit forward!'

I blast off the first few strokes with all the anger and frustration I feel towards Rachel. It works against me. I catch a crab and totally lose it. The boat swings sideways and we have to easy oar or risk slamming into the bank.

'Really?' I shout at the sky.

Rachel comes after me in the change room.

'What's your problem with me, Leni?'

'I'm here to win, Rachel. That's all. I don't know if that's why you're here too.'

'I want to win. But it's not so easy for the rest of us mere mortals. I don't have *Olympians* for parents.'

'That doesn't guarantee me a spot in the firsts, you know. I have to work for it, too.'

When I was eight and I won the 800 metres at Little Athletics one of the parents said of course I had won, considering who my parents were. I cried and Mum told me that from then on, every victory was mine. I owned them. She and Dad had absolutely nothing to do with it.

'Nothing's been handed to me on a silver platter. I don't have a trust fund and unlimited pocket money.'

Rachel laughs. 'And you think I do?'

'Why wouldn't you?'

'My dad works two jobs to keep me at Harley, so he never, ever sees me race. Neither does my mum because she's got more than enough on her plate without having to worry about my rowing schedule. You want to know about my life? How easy it is? Do some research. I think you'll find it isn't such a pleasure cruise.'

'Join the club.'

We stare at each other for a few seconds. Totally unresolved and in a worse place than before.

Rachel shrugs.

'See you at land training. Hopefully I can put in a little more *effort*.' The word is loaded with sarcasm.

With wet hair and my backpack on I fly down the stairs of the boatshed towards the Swanston Street tram stop. I need to get away from Rachel, the teeming boatsheds and the rank smell of river water.

Laura stops me. 'Wait! Leni!'

'I'm late!' I say, backing off. 'My tram leaves in three

minutes.' I'm looking for an excuse not to have to talk about my terrible row this morning.

'I'll give you a lift to school.'

'Oh, okay.' I can't turn it down.

Laura's Mazda is full of training gear, bike parts and uni papers. She's studying to be a PE teacher. It's fair to say she's my idol. If I could somehow be her, I would probably take the option. I'm nervous and tongue-tied in her company. Especially outside of training. I surreptitiously check her out. Her legs are comically long, completely hairless, tanned and thick with muscle. Her arms are sculpted and lean, shoulders wide, hips narrow and stomach flat. I'd bet she has a sixpack under her tight T-shirt. She makes me feel like a weakling.

Laura throws an Australian team cap on her head and heads out on the road. I feel sick with anticipation. What does she want to discuss? I stay quiet as we navigate the atrocious morning traffic, inching like a river of honey towards the school.

'Have you been worried about exams?' she asks.

'Yeah,' I admit. Who doesn't worry about exams? I'd been flat out for weeks colour-coding, spreadsheeting, revising, researching, reading. I'd worked so hard some nights it felt like my eyeballs were bleeding. That, on top of my rowing training, had made for a full-on end to the year.

'Feeling the pressure in stroke?'

'No,' I say, sharply.

'I could move you down the boat you know. Give you a time-out?'

'I like my seat. I don't want to switch.'

Part of my dream is to be sitting in the stroke seat when we win Head of the River.

'It wouldn't be permanent, just to give you a little breathing space to get back in the game,' Laura says.

When did I leave the game?

'You know, I didn't win my Head of the River,' she says, changing the subject. 'Didn't even make the semis. Got knocked out in a repechage. I thought it was the end of the world. Bawled.'

'I couldn't handle that,' I say. 'Not this year. We've worked so hard.' *I've worked so hard.*

I can see no future where I don't have that medal in my hand. Losing is not an option.

'I don't even remember who won it that year,' says Laura.

What's she hoping to achieve with this chat. It's not even a little bit inspiring.

'You know what I do remember?' she says. '*My crew.* We had so much fun. I had more laughs in that boat than any other I've been in since. I loved those girls. Still do.'

'I don't even think my crew likes me,' I admit.

'They look up to you,' says Laura.

'That's not the same thing.'

'True. But respect is the basis for any friendship. Let them in a little, okay? This is your last season as a school-girl, Leni. Enjoy it. It gets a lot tougher when you leave school, trust me.'

'I want to win so badly,' I say. I'm nearly in tears.

'You might win, but you might not. You're very hard on yourself. Don't forget, rowing is what you do, not who you are. If you fail from time to time, that's part of learning.'

'Do I have to give up the stroke seat?'

'Yeah. Sorry, kid, that's my call.'

I'm fighting back tears when I get out of the car but Laura punches me lightly on the arm.

'Hey, don't forget to love it out there. No matter where in the boat you're sitting.'

I bump into Sam in the library during my double free. We are the only people in the Ethel Jillaby memorial study room. It's a small room. He notices me. My eyes are still red from crying. I feel fragile and wobbly. I try to back away, but he's already clearing a space opposite him at the table.

'Sorry. Taking over the joint,' he says. 'There's plenty of room.'

'How's your boat going?' he asks. Stretching his neck from side to side and taking a study break.

I shrug, tears welling up. I wipe them back with my fist, but he sees them.

'What's wrong?'

'Nothing. I've got heaps to do. Let's study.'

Sam gets up from his side of the table, walks around to mine and crouches down so we are face-to-face. So close I can see he has a light monobrow and the beginnings of a cold sore on his lower lip.

'What's wrong, Leni?'

'I got dropped from the stroke seat.'

'You like it there? Up the front?'

'Yeah. I don't know what's going on. Last few sessions it's been struggle street.'

Sam nods. 'Me too.'

'Seriously?'

He sighs, drops down to the floor and crosses his legs. 'It's tough in the firsts. My technique is sketchy. The boat isn't moving well. Our coach is an absolute tosser. To tell you the truth, I wish I never got moved up.'

'Can't go back now.'

'Guess not.'

We stay like that for a minute, looking at each other closely. Curiously. It's not often you find a moment of absolute truth during a double free.

'You'll get back in front,' Sam says.

I try to believe him. It'll be hard to go out training and not be leading my crew.

'Thanks, Sam. You will too.'

He jumps to his feet and heads back to his laptop.

'Hey, Leni,' he says, looking over the top of the computer. 'Why'd you send me a friend request?'

'Because I want to be your friend, I guess.'

'Oh. Good. 'Cos I want to be yours.'

We put our heads down and silently study together. Later in the day I get a notification on my Facebook page. *You are now friends with Sam Camero.*

It gives me a head-to-toe thrill and I instantly forget he took his sweet time replying to my request.

Cristian

It's a hot morning on the river. Nobody's had a good night's kip. Especially not me. I've been so racy and jumpy it's hard to get more than five hours a night. I was the first out of bed at our house, agitated and ready for a big session. When Patto breaks us into pairs and starts doing boring catch drills I want to explode. I'd rather be smashing out 10 kilometres on the ergo or running the tan. This isn't a workout. Adam feels the same.

'Bor-ring,' he groans in front of me.

I jiggle my knees, waiting for my turn to row. It's agonising. Usually I would drift along, half asleep. Lulled by the drag of my blade over the surface of the river. This new pepped-up me doesn't like to sit still.

Finally I get a turn and Adam and I go for it, bashing it along. Pulling heavy on the blades.

'Relax guys,' says Patto. 'It's technique work. No need to break any oars.'

We drop it down a notch but later we have a real crack at the hard pieces. Doing power twenties as if we can lift the middle of the boat out of the water. Patto is pleased.

'Nice work out there you two. Keep rowing like this and I won't be able to keep you in my boat.'

'That's the idea,' says Adam.

I head for the showers and Westie calls out to me across the room. He's giving Sam an extra erg session. Looks like fine-tuning of technique issues. Word is Sam's having trouble with his catch. He certainly looks miserable with all the extra coaching attention lasered on his back.

'Poppa! Over here!'

One good thing about rowing in the seconds is I don't have to see as much of Westie. I drag my feet over to him.

'Yes, sir?'

'Relax Cristian, it's good news. The school wants to name the new racing eight after your father. The *Vasile Popescu.*'

'That's amazing. He'll be so happy.'

'It certainly is an honour. We've had our issues, but he's achieved great things in his own rowing career and has a long service here at the club. Take this for him. I was going to give it to him personally, but he disappeared off down the river with his crew.'

Westie hands me a thick cream-coloured envelope with my dad's name on it.

I know what's inside. An invitation to a boat-naming ceremony. I've already been to a couple. We dress up in full uniform and stand around as the boat's new name is unveiled and a bottle of champagne is smashed over it for good luck. There's usually pretty good food and, at the last one, Adam and I nicked off with a couple of beers and sat on the roof of the gym, watching the sun set. This time it's our name on a boat? It's hard to believe.

Westie looks me up and down. 'You're looking trimmer. Patto says you and Adam are rowing well, too. Keep it up.'

It's the closest to a compliment that I'd ever heard from Westie.

'I will. I want my seat back.'

'Earn it and it's yours.'

*

Penny exits the girls' change rooms and we make eye contact. She's showered and dressed and I'm stinky and blotchy.

'Good row?' I ask, trying to keep my distance so as not to overpower her with my guy stench.

'Nah, not really. Too much drama.'

'Rachel and Leni drama?' I ask. Everyone in the boatshed knows they're not getting on.

Penny nods, lowers her voice. 'They had a massive fight just now. I hope they sort it out soon. It's starting to affect our rowing.'

'I'll talk to Leni. Try to get her to back down a little. You know what she's like.'

'Talented, intense and always right,' Penny says, and I nod in agreement.

Penny puts her hand on my arm and my next sentence catches in my throat.

'You look fit, Cris. You'll be back in the firsts soon. Everyone thinks so.'

She pulls a loose strand of hair behind her ear and keeps her hand on my arm a little too long to be just friendly. I'm about to ask her for a before-school coffee when Aiko bounces over.

'Come on, Pen. We'll miss the 8.22!' Aiko says, dragging Penny away.

'Bye Cris,' says Penny, giving me one last, possibly interested look, before being swept off to the tram stop.

I clap Adam on the back in the change room as he adjusts his tie in the mirror. The other guys in the crew rag on him about how much time he spends on his looks. He's always fiddling with hair, skin, uniform. Even his socks have to be pulled up the right way. He's always been a bit obsessive.

We're alone and it's safe to let our guard down.

'Westie told me I'd lost weight. Penny said I look fit, too.'

Adam grins. 'I told you. It's working.'

Adam flexes his arm, showing off a growing bicep.

'Check this out. Pure muscle. Extra erg at lunch?'

'Hell yeah,' I answer.

At home, I give Dad the invite to the boat-naming ceremony. He pretends he's not very excited. Later on I catch him moving all the takeaway flyers from the fridge to stick it up with a magnet. I'm proud of him. So is Leni and Mum. It's a big moment for our family.

Leni

We're racing today – a smallish GPS regatta to see how everyone is placed before Christmas. Exams are done and dusted and we're all back on the job. Ready for a big fitness haul over the summer break. Rachel sits in front of me in stroke. I watch her blonde ponytail bounce up and down as we take the transit lane to the start. I don't like the view. Sitting behind her in training has been tough. I feel demoted.

'Let's smash this race!' says Aiko, pumping us up. 'Forget about training. Racing is a different ballgame.'

'Good luck,' I say to Rachel's back. It's the first time I've spoken to her since we had that big fight after training.

She turns around, looking surprised. It's been super tense between us, but I want to make it right before we race together. Laura keeps hammering into us that we're a team.

'Thanks, Leni. Back me up?' she says, smiling.

'I'll be right behind you.'

'I know you will.'

We row okay, better than expected. We come second in the heats and third in the final. St Ann's gets us again, as well as Melton Girls. I hate to admit it, but Rachel is a natural in stroke seat. Her rowing is neat and precise and her rhythm is relaxed and unhurried, a bit like her. I'm keen to get back in the front seat, but a part of me feels like a weight has been lifted now that I'm not setting the pace.

'I don't know how Melton got away from us in that race,' I say to Rachel as we head for the school tent after our final. We have bronze medals around our necks. It's nice to have jewellery, but it's the wrong colour. I take mine off and shove it into my backpack. 'We should have been well ahead after the effort at the 500-metre mark.'

Rachel bites into her medal and grins. She's in weekend mode, having changed into a flippy skirt and cute singlet. 'Who cares? We got ourselves a bit of bling for the trophy cabinet. You heard Laura, third is good for us at this stage of our training. We just had a major seat change. Enjoy it, Leni.'

I try to relax and forget it, but I can't let it go. It's hard for me to enjoy being beaten by two other schools.

Mum waves at me from a bike. She prefers to ride along watching races, than sit in a deckchair with the other parents.

'Third! Fantastic, Leni!' she shouts. 'Just going to watch Cris, then let's meet at the trailers.'

'Your mum is amazing,' Rachel says. 'Have you ever worn her Olympic medal?'

'It's framed.'

'Oh. Still, having an Olympic gold medal in your house. Must be inspiring.'

'I suppose so.'

I see that gold medal every day. It makes me feel like I have so much to live up to.

'Don't take it for granted that your olds are here. My little brother has behavioural therapy on Saturdays. It's expensive, so my dad works weekends to pay for it.'

'Therapy for what?'

'He's autistic.'

'Oh. Sorry.'

'Don't be sorry. Riley's awesome. I love him heaps.' She smiles. 'I don't tell many people though.'

So this was Rachel's life. An autistic brother and parents too busy to watch her race. Maybe I should let her in on some of my problems. Tell her about how those medals in my house really make me feel. How unsure I was about Adam. I think about what Laura said to me in the car. *Let them in a bit.* Was this what she meant?

We sit down together and watch a few races from the bank, cheering on Cristian and Adam as they easily win the second division in their eight.

'Smart Snax?' Rachel says, handing me a bag of nuts and fibrous bits.

I take a handful and make a face. 'Tastes like tan bark,' I say.

Rachel laughs. 'Exactly.'

I take another handful and chew hard. We smile at each other.

I like the sharing bit more than the eating bit.

The first crew trails over the line fourth. A disappointing result for them. Sam looks upset and bangs his blade on the surface of the water. I guess he doesn't like to lose either. He looks towards the bank and I feel like he's staring straight at me.

'Firsts have some work to do,' comments Rachel. 'But I do like to watch them. Sam Camero is hot.'

Adam comes up behind me and gives me a hug. He and Cristian are on fire. Both of them seem so determined to get back in the firsts. It's all they ever talk about and they train together in the gym every day.

'Do you want to come to my beach shack for the weekend? Would your parents let you stay over? Kitty and Dad will be there.' Adam's family owns the biggest beach house at Portsea. So big it has stables.

'Stay over?'

We've never had a sleepover before. It makes me nervous.

'Yeah. Separate rooms, of course.'

'I can't,' I say, relieved. 'I promised Dad I'd help him with the boats.'

I was glad to have an excuse to avoid Adam's house with its dark media room and endless bedrooms. The cold, beautiful pool that no one ever seemed to swim in.

Adam seems irritated.

'More time on the river? We've been here all morning. Come over. You won't regret it.'

The last part he whispers sexily in my ear and it gives me the shivers, but not in a good way.

'I can't. I promised. Sorry.'

'That's okay, Leni, go be a grease monkey,' he tries to make the moment light, but I feel like I wrecked it. 'I've got to go and boat load, I'll call you,' he says.

My body relaxes when he retreats. The weight of sexpectation lifting.

I love tinkering with the boats and being around Dad when he's so focused and still. When he stops to explain things to me in a quiet, patient way. Passing on knowledge he's learnt over decades. Secret rowing business. I love the smell of the sheds – oil and WD-40, mixed with sour possum piss.

The boats are up on slings after racing, washed and ready for their pit crew.

'Run your hands over the boats,' Dad says to Cristian and I.

I jump up to start, but Cristian lags behind. He hates this as much as I love it.

We go through the boats carefully, checking for tiny holes, squeaky slides or loose bolts. Most of the team doesn't know about the fine-tuning that goes on behind the scenes. They get in the boat and expect it will be tweaked to perfection. They have no idea Dad has been adjusting so the equipment matches their legs, arms and body weight, even their rowing style.

Dad knows these boats. Knows their insides the same way a surgeon knows guts, veins, hearts and weak valves. There's no boat he can't make sing. Even the heaviest, waterlogged old tub.

'Can I go upstairs?' Cristian says in a whiny voice. 'I'm knackered. I need to lie down.'

Dad looks up from his screwdriver. Frowns.

'Go.'

Dad and I are used to Cristian bailing on the hard work, playing with his phone and then passing out on a training mat.

'Good racing,' says Dad.

'Beating second crews? Big deal.'

'It's still a win,' says Dad. 'Lift your head up. Smile.'

Cristian looks glum. 'Can I go now?'

'Yes. Dismissed.'

We work better without Cristian's sulky, negative vibes hanging around.

'I don't understand. He's up. He's down. Happy, angry, sad. I worry, Elena. I want you and Cristian to be happy. Are you happy?'

I shrug. The honest answer is not really, but I don't want to worry him.

'Of course. Cristian's fine. He misses being out of the firsts. It's hard for him.'

'Talk to him. Make sure he's okay. Sooner he's back in the firsts, the better,' says Dad.

I sit on a sling and watch as Dad measures out the rigging, tinkering with the pitch, height and gearing.

Dad's smudgy glasses have slipped down his nose. He takes them off and lets them dangle round his neck on a makeshift string holder. He has a tool belt around his belly, and his shirt is full of holes. Mum tries to make him throw out his old rowing clothes, but he sneaks them out of the 'For St Vinnies' bags and back into the closet.

'Elena, come here,' he says in Romanian. I can understand, but not speak the language. 'Hold this.'

He gives me a fistful of rubber washers. 'What I'm doing now is rigging the boat higher. This crew does their training in rough water, and this will allow them to sit up higher, their blades to clear the water.'

I'm reminded again how precise this sport is. Most people think we get in and heave the oar through the water with our arms. They don't get the tiny measurements that count for everything in a race. I look over Dad's shoulder as he gets out a screwdriver and moves a foot stretcher to accommodate a tall rower's daddy long legs.

Dad lets me screw all the loose bolts back in, coming back to give them the final, heavy tighten. I like knowing my dad has been the last person to touch my boat and his strong, tough hands have made sure nothing will come unstuck.

'Knock off?' Dad says. There are sweat patches on his back and under his arms.

I get us both a drink from the vending machine and we sit on the bank and look at the water. There's not a ripple of wind and the light is a soft gold.

'This reminds me of the day I first got in a boat,' Dad says.

I let him tell the well-worn story again, enjoying the familiarity.

'I was supposed to go to soccer training that afternoon, but my cousin was short a rower and he convinced me to go down to the lake and row with his crew. It was like this. Perfect spring day. No wind. I had no chance. The minute I got in the boat I was hooked. It was almost the same way I felt when I met your mother.'

'... and you never played soccer again,' I finish.

'Silly,' Dad says. 'Could've made a fortune if I'd kept kicking a ball.'

Cristian

I hate boat maintenance. It's grimy, messy and fiddly and I don't get it. All the little pieces are a complicated puzzle. It hurts my brain. Everything hurts my brain. For sure I've screwed up my end-of-year exams. I'm enjoying the calm before the storm of results coming out.

I'm lying on a mat, in the dark, quiet shadows of the gym room. Everyone's gone home after the regatta so I've got the place to myself. It's spooky here. A possum scratches in the ceiling somewhere, its paws screeching as it runs along the iron beams, leaving behind telltale drop-pings. There's beer behind the bar and I'd love one, but it's locked up so I'd have to commit a felony to get at it. I'm breaking enough rules already.

I had my first kiss here. A few steps away, sitting on the bench press table. The girl was Sally Naylor – daughter of Dad's old crew member, Ferg Naylor. She's better looking than her old man.

We were both thirteen, tall and stocky like the kids of rowers are. I was showing off and pushing a barbell off my chest. The weight was too heavy and I ran out of muscle, the bar collapsing on top of me. Sally had to rescue me by pulling it off my ribs. I pulled up my T-shirt and there was a red mark that would later become an impressive bruise. She ran her hand over it and said 'ouch'.

I took the opportunity, even though her dad was a few metres below us manning the sausage sizzle, to kiss her. I used my tongue, because that's what I thought you were supposed to do, and she reared back like a scared pony and ran off. She wouldn't look at me again until we were fifteen, then we went out for two weeks and she dumped me for being too keen. Didn't she want me to be keen?

I don't get girls. Still.

Thinking about Sally I get wood. I consider going into the men's to do something about it, but I can't be bothered so I picture Westie's ugly mug until it subsides. Instead of stroking myself I take a few lazy pulls on the rowing machine. Then I rev it up to full power, to see what's there. The readout is better than anything I've been doing for months. I sit up taller and let it rip for 1000 metres, amazed by the time. Smiling, I put the handle back, letting the wheel spin out, my heart beating hard. I get up for a look around the room.

This boatshed is a shrine to Dad and his rowing mates. On the wall is an honour roll of past Australian champions. My dad's old crew takes up six lines. His name painted in gold ink. I stare at it and run my hand over his name. Vasile Popescu. Will my name ever make it onto a wall? I doubt it. The space is for Leni, one day.

I look at a framed photo of Dad's crew sitting in the grandstand after winning worlds. The nine of them look so young. Dad has sideburns and long hair. His biceps bulge and his legs are massive. He's wearing a green singlet studded with the Australian crest and he's looking off camera with a slight smile. The others are grasping a trophy and have medals slung over their necks. They're a tight group. Mates.

'The friends I'll keep until the day I die are oarsmen,' Dad tells Leni and I. 'If it wasn't for rowers I would never have made it out here in Australia. They took me into their hearts. Into their homes. That's why I want you to row. You'll meet people who'll stick by you no matter what. Who will show you more kindness than you can stand.'

Right on cue, Adam calls. Ads is a mate I'll have forever and always. I know it.

'Your sister is doing my head in,' he says, without even saying hello.

I laugh because Leni does everyone's head in. She's a slippery fish. Hard to pin down and even harder to catch. Adam doesn't stand a chance.

December

Four months to Head of the River

Leni

We're walking towards school for Dad's boat-naming ceremony. It's been a perfect, blue-sky day, which is tailing off into a warm, still summer night. Dad's dressed in his best pants and shirt, Mum is in a pretty floral sundress and sandals. The plan is to go out for a special dinner afterwards. ThaiTanic, kids' choice. The school has displayed the new eight on the front lawn in front of the chapel. The pearly white fibreglass is gleaming – untouched by scuff marks, mud or rust. Mum holds my hand and Dad's as we walk as a family over to it. Cristian is a few steps behind.

On the bow Dad's name is printed in block letters, *Vasile Popescu*.

'Dad! It's totally awesome,' I say. Excited for him.

Dad runs his calloused, knobbled fingers over his name. I've never seen him cry, but he's looking misty. He looks at me and then at Cristian. I can tell his heart is bursting, like mine. Not everyone gets a boat named after them. It's rowing's highest honour.

'This is night to be proud of your name. Where you're from,' Dad says.

'We are, Dad,' I say.

Popescu. Usually I had to spell it out to people. Then answer the question: where are you from?

'When I came here I had nothing,' says Dad. 'So far from home. So homesick. To me, Australia was Opera House, kangaroos, sheep. I didn't speak language. Had no friends. I start again. This,' he gestures to the boat and thumps lightly on his chest, 'shows me I make something of my life here.'

'Come on, Vas, let's get you a champagne,' Mum says, squeezing his arm.

I hang back for a few seconds, soaking it up. To get into the '92 Olympics Dad trained for three hours, then worked all day at a factory job, then trained again for three hours, then went home, ate, slept and did it all again the next morning at 5 am. 'It wasn't easy,' he told me when I once tried on his old team jacket, its bottle-green sleeves hanging past my skinned knees. 'But nothing worthwhile ever is.'

My parents are swept up in the crowd of rowing parents. Tonight, the mums have swapped their regatta outfits for swishy cocktail dresses. The dads for suits and ties. Standing next to them Mum's outfit now looks drab and worn. I notice Dad's jacket strains around his bulging tummy. It's missing a button.

Everyone wants to talk to Dad. Tonight he isn't the crazy European fix-it guy on the old bike. He's the star of the show. The guest of honour. VIP. People get him beers and fancy canapés and want to chinwag about the season ahead. About the old days too – Barcelona and was he really mates with the Oarsome Foursome? Mum doesn't try to tip in her own resumé. She lets him take the full ray of the spotlight. The way she does with us.

Cristian and I stand together on the soft lawn as the sun starts its slide behind the sandstone chapel building, listening to the tinkling of champagne glasses. Adam joins us and I'm pleased to see him. We've spent so much time apart that I may actually be starting to miss him. He looks so handsome tonight. He takes my hand and I don't wriggle away.

'You look pretty,' he says.

'Thank you.'

'Everything's all set for the party at mine later,' says Adam. 'You guys are coming, right?'

Adam's putting on an 'end of the world as we know it' pre-Year Twelve Christmas party. Everyone's been talking about it incessantly for weeks.

'Of course,' says Cristian. 'Got dinner with the parents, but we'll come later, won't we, Leni?'

'Yeah. Can't wait, Adam.'

The last thing I feel like doing is going to a Langley party, but as the official girlfriend it's expected that I'll be there.

'Dad's loving this,' Cristian comments.

'What's not to love? I say. 'Wait until we get to the speeches.'

Cristian

I'm watching Dad soak up his moment of glory. Everyone wants to be close to him. He's surrounded by people clamouring for his attention. Mum's been squeezed out to one side. It makes me realise what a hero he is. I'm always embarrassed by him, always trying to block him out or avoid him at the sheds. Why? He's a hundred times the man I am. He got his medals the hard way. Up at dawn, out on the water, smashing it up and down until his fingers bled and his back gave out. What have I done? Given up on my body and let that shifty gym rat push pills into my hands.

Looking at my family name on the bow of the boat, I'm so proud of Dad – and so ashamed of myself.

'Hey, Leni, I've gotta piss, I'll be back before the speeches,' I say, taking off.

I try to walk off the guilt, breathing up and getting away from the crowds, but I'm sinking in regret. I wander past the new boat, gleaming so white and clean. I never think of boats as beautiful, but this one is.

Sam is standing next to it, running his hand over the curved fibreglass skin. Tenderly, like it's the back of a girl he wants to sleep with. It's obvious how much he loves this sport.

'Hey, Poppa, you must be proud of your old man tonight,' Sam says.

Sam earned his place in the firsts the same way my dad snatched his seats. Through relentless discipline and mental toughness. I was a weakling compared to them both. I didn't even deserve to be here.

'Yeah, he's a bit of a legend.'

'That's an understatement.'

Later, Miss Rutlege, our Head of Sport gets on the microphone.

'Could I gather everyone around the *Vasile Popescu* for the official naming ceremony?' she asks.

I hang back from the crowd until Dad finds me with his eyes and waves me over to him. He's holding a small hammer to break open a flow of celebratory champagne.

'Come son!' he shouts. 'I want my children around me!'

I stand by his side as he represents good, honest sportsmanship and hard graft. If only he knew what his son was doing. He'd take that hammer and bring it down over my knuckles.

Leni

Dad smacks the champagne bottle several times with a hammer, but nothing happens.

'Come on Vas, put your back into it!' shouts Westie.

Dad flexes his muscles and goes again, harder. This time the glass breaks and bleeds bubbly liquid from its stocking casing over the side of the boat.

He laughs and hands the hammer back to a student.

'Come on up here, Vasile,' says Miss Rutlege on the microphone. She looks down at a set of reading notes. 'Officially, I'd like to name this eight the *Vasile Popescu* and wish it all the best of luck on the water in the coming season. For those of you who don't know Vasile's story, he came out to live in Melbourne in 1989 after the fall of the Communist rule in Romania to marry his Australian wife, Jodie, also a highly accomplished oarswoman. They had two children, Cristian and Elena, both of whom are valued members of our Harley rowing squad. Vasile's rowing history is extremely impressive. He rowed for Romania at the Seoul Olympics in 1988. He was then selected in the Australian team and rowed at the World Championships in 1991, winning gold, and at the Barcelona Olympics in 1992, winning silver. He is our valued boat caretaker and a respected coach of the senior thirds. Please welcome him to say a few words.'

Dad walks up to the microphone. Everyone's ready to hear his wisdom. Bask in a little of his reflected glory. I start to panic for him. He should have written a speech. How come I didn't tell him to write a speech?

Maybe it's the beer or the excitement or maybe Dad looks out and realises how many people are hanging on his every word. But he is silent for a long time. The only sound coming from the PA is feedback. Eventually he mutters an embarrassed thanks and then starts speaking in hybrid English-Romanian. Nobody can understand him. It's gibberish. I feel a push at my back from Adam and somehow I'm taking Dad's place at the microphone, and giving the speech for him.

'This is a great honour for Dad and for our family,' I say. My voice sounds too bright and polished. I don't want this moment. It's not mine to take. 'Dad's career as an oarsman is so inspiring and Cristian and I hope to row in his boat, possibly to victory in the Head of the River next year.'

Everyone claps when I say that. All their hopes raised.

I turn to usher my dad back to the microphone, hoping he's ready to take over, but he's slipped away. I search the crowd but can't see him. Mum's also vanished. Cristian makes a cutting motion across his throat as if to say, 'Enough. Stop, Leni. Stop trying to make everything perfect.'

'Thank you, Elena,' says Miss Rutlege. 'Now to another order of business. Your outgoing rowing captains, Gill Kentwell and Paul Rosen, will now announce the new Captains of Boats.'

Where are my parents? I'm desperate for them not to miss the rowing captain announcement. The announcement I've waited years for. I search the crowd for them.

'Where are they?' I whisper to myself.

Gill's talking and everyone's looking at me. Why are they looking at me?

'There she is! Leni Popescu, the new girls' Captain of Boats,' says Gill. 'It's quite a night for the Popescu family.'

Even though my insides feel churned up I keep smiling and faking it.

The announcement of the boys' captain is next and I hold up crossed fingers and give Cris a smile. He doesn't smile back.

'Alongside Leni is our new boys' Captain of Boats for next year,' says Miss Rutlege. 'I'll ask Paul to name his successor.' Paul Rosen takes the microphone and I silently repeat Cristian's name in my head, willing my brother to walk up and take his rightful place beside me.

'The next Captain of Boats is a rower with enormous potential,' says Paul. 'He only took up the sport a year ago and is already rowing in the first eight. Congratulations, Samuel Camero.'

Hearing Sam's name, instead of Cristian's, feels like a punch to my throat. I can't imagine how Cris feels. All my joy at being named girls' captain drains from my body. The other rowers pat Sam on the back as he makes his way to the microphone, grinning. I ignore him and see Cris pick his way out of the crowd, pushing through the clapping, wolf whistling idiots in the first eight.

Cris looks like a thunderclap as I approach him, slumped against the gym wall.

'Cris, I'm so sorry you didn't get … ' I start.

He glares at me, his face stony.

'You had to win, didn't you?' he snaps. 'Bloody golden girl strikes again. Is there any way you could make me look worse? Straight As, Captain of Boats, stroke of the first eight.'

'I wanted this for both of us,' I say, hurt.

'Nah, I don't even think that's true. You want all the glory. Nice job highjacking Dad's speech by the way. Good one.'

Stung, I go to defend myself, but Cris is already leaving. He strides across the lawn, ripping off his blazer and kicking a rosebush as he walks out the front gates. Scattering the petals across the bitumen.

★

It should be the best moment of my life. Sam Cam and me – co-Captains of Boats. A photographer has us pose together with a pair of crossed oars and Dad's new boat behind us. He stands us back-to-back like some cheesy catalogue photo, arms folded over our chests.

'Congratulations, Leni,' Sam says as we smile for the camera.

I should return the kudos, but I'm angry at how this night has turned out. It should have been glittering and it ended up lumpy. All I can think is how gutted Cristian is. How he had a go at me for making him look bad. Do I do that? Soak up other people's glory like a sponge.

'First you take my brother's seat in the firsts? Now you have his captaincy too?' I say. It's not fair of me. I'm taking my disappointment out on the nearest target.

'I'm hardly going to turn it down,' says Sam.

'That's it guys, thanks,' says the photographer and Sam and I push apart.

'Hey, what's with the attitude? I thought we were officially friends now,' says Sam. 'What's up?'

'Nothing. Enjoy your moment. Congratulations, I guess.'

I walk away and hear Sam shout, 'Say it like you mean it!'

'Captain Leni!' Adam says, grabbing my waist from behind as I try to leave the scene and find my fractured family. 'Ready for a massive party later?' He kisses my ear. 'Let's get crazy.'

I should be excited. They'll be a dance floor over the pool. DJ. Catered. Everything too much money can buy.

I can't do it. I don't want to hang out with a bunch of people who don't really know me.

'I don't feel like it. I'm so tired. I might find my parents and head home.'

Adam sighs, drops his hands from me like I'm hot.

'Why do you always put me last?' he asks.

'I don't.'

'You do. I'm so far down the list of your priorities I might as well not bother.'

'Maybe I can come later, with Cris,' I say. We both know I won't.

'Nah, it's too late. Forget it. Do what you want, Leni. You usually do. Tell you what. Let's forget about us too. It's not working.'

As he walks away I wait for the feeling of relief to come, but all I feel is a knot of hurt working its way up to my throat.

Has Adam just broken up with me?

Cristian

I'm sitting on the banks of the Yarra. It's dark and there are booze boats floating up and down, full of pissed office workers having Christmas parties. Cheesy music blaring. I'm drinking too. By myself. Leni is Captain of Boats and I'm captain of the loser squadron. I'm finishing up a six-pack I got from the slack bottlo down the road from school. Making myself numb. You only get one chance to be a rowing captain and I blew mine. It's not like I didn't need it on my exit letter. Leni's got her uni plans stitched up. She'll be a doctor. I'll be, what? I don't even have a preference.

I feel awful because instead of congratulating her, I snapped at her and stormed out on her big moment. Told her she was a golden girl. I only said that because I felt like Captain Evil.

My phone rings. Adam. I pick it up.

'Yeah?'

'Where are you? Come to my party. I need to talk to you.'

'Can't do it, comrade.'

'Why not? Get off your arse and catch a cab. I'll pay for it when you get here. Where are you anyway? Still out with your parents? Is Leni with you?'

'Family dinner was cancelled. I'm at the river. By myself.'

'Why?'

'I dunno. Maybe I'll have a swim.'

The black river meanders past. I imagine falling into it and letting the water rush up my nose. Sinking into the mud on the bottom.

'Don't be stupid. Penny's here. She looks hot and she asked me where you are. I reckon it's going to happen for you two lovebirds tonight.'

I should go home to bed and sleep it off. I'm not in the right headspace to go to a party. But the thought of seeing Penny changes my mind.

'Penny's there?' I can hear the keenness in my voice.

'Yes, loverboy. She's in my back garden wearing a mini skirt she *really* has the legs for. You do know Nick has a crush on her, too. You best get here before he cuts your grass.'

'I'll be there in twenty.'

'Atta boy.'

I lie back, close my eyes and feel my body lose touch with the ground. My insides whirl and spin. It's like being on a whizzy ride. I think about Penny taking me into her long arms. Letting me kiss her. Letting me touch her soft skin. Letting me undress her. Letting me inside her. The last thought gets me off the riverbank and lurching towards the nearest tram stop.

As is tradition with Langley parties, everything is laid on. I check my name off the guest list with two bouncers stationed at the front gates and wander into the enormous house. There's a marble staircase and posed glamour shots of the master and mistress of the house. Ugly, but no doubt priceless, art hangs on every other available wall. Kitty, aka MILF, is greeting guests, sipping from a pink straw dipped into a mini bottle of Moët. She's changed and is now dressed like one of the schoolgirls in a short, bejewelled kaftan that shows off her shapely brown thighs.

'Cristian!' Kitty says warmly. She clasps me in a booze-soaked embrace, a little unsteady on her heels. 'Let me look at you.'

Kitty stands back and gives me a once over, like I'm a show dog. I'm surprised she doesn't check my coat and behind my ears. She's immaculate. Frozen, botoxed brows, an unlined forehead and make-up that looks sprayed on.

'You are more handsome and grown up every time I see you,' she says, flirting. She leans in and squeezes my arm aggressively. 'How come you don't have a little girlfriend?'

'I don't know,' I say, backing away from Kitty and her cougar paws and heading outside where the music is thumping at high volume and most of the girls are putting pockmarks in the purpose-built dance floor.

I grab an expensive foreign beer from a silver ice bucket. I'm drinking too fast, but it's one of those nights that you have to erase as you go.

'Look who made it!' shouts Adam. He's beefed up and showing it off in a white singlet. A random Year Ten girl hangs off him adoringly.

'Who's this?' I ask, feeling protective and giving the girl a death stare. I wasn't going to stand there and let Adam cheat on my sister with some bimbo.

Adam lets the girl loose. Comes over to me, dropping the act.

'Leni and I broke up. It wasn't working.'

'Sorry, man,' I say. 'Maybe it's for the best. You're off to Aspen for Christmas, right? Don't want to miss out on the snow-bunny action.'

Adam drops his shoulders and runs a palm across his forehead. 'Between you and me, your sister broke me. No matter what I did it wasn't good enough for her.'

'I doubt that's true.'

'I don't think she ever loved me. Not like I loved her.'

I want to tell him Leni did love him. That they have a shot at getting back together, but it would be lies. I never thought they were a good match. Something was off. Leni became less herself around him. The keener he was, the more she retreated.

He looks bereft and we both sink into a bummed-out silence.

'Come on,' I say, trying to cheer him up. 'This is a party. Where's Penny Mission? I was promised a mini skirt.'

Adam points across the pool to the barbecue area, where a hired chef is whipping up seafood skewers and gourmet hot dogs.

Looking at Penny chewing on a prawn, I suddenly feel shy. The booze has turned me thick and stupid, not invincible like I thought it would.

'Need to get this into me first. Dutch courage,' I say, sculling from the beer.

Adam clinks his bottle against mine. 'To getting back in the firsts,' he says. 'That's all that matters now.'

'The firsts.'

I lose count of the beers it takes to approach Penny. All on an empty stomach, too. By the time I make it over to her, I'm concentrating very hard on walking in a straight line. She notices.

'Woah, Cristian, had a few?' she says.

One of her friends giggles. I try to act sober and lean heavily against the pool fence to keep me from falling over. 'Penny. Would you do me the honour of going for a walk around the garden?' I ask.

Penny's friend gives her a look, but she nods.

'Sure. If you can still walk.'

I offer her my arm, but as it turns out, I need propping up more than she does. She guides me to a pair of pool lounges and I fall back into one, gratefully. I could easily pass out, snoring, but I try to focus on what she's saying. She is so pretty. I think about reaching out and stroking her thigh.

'Are you okay? About Sam Cam getting Captain of Boats?'

'Fine. Totally fine,' I say, not wanting to relive the awful moment. 'Now can I get you a drink, young lady? Anything you like. My shout.'

Penny laughs. 'I'm not drinking.'

'No?'

'I've got my dad's birthday breakfast tomorrow morning. We're going out to this place by the beach. Besides, I don't like the taste.'

I'm disappointed I can't get her a little tipsy. I stagger out of my lounge and squash in next to her.

'We don't fit,' she says, giggling.

I sit up and put my arm around her, leaning in for a kiss. She pushes at my chest and turns her head away.

'No, Cris.'

My head spins wildly and an eject button is pushed in my guts sending a rush of saliva into my mouth. I don't have time to stagger to the nearest fancy soft-close toilet and in a spectacular romance fail, I vomit all over Penny's lap.

Leni

Mum comes into my room and shuts the door.

'Am I in trouble?'

'Of course not.'

'I wanted to help Dad.'

'Yes, I know. Vas had so much to say. Too much probably. This meant quite a lot to him.'

'Is he upset with me?'

'No. Just himself. He feels he let us down. I told him to forget about it, everyone gets nervous. Sometimes we say the wrong things. Sometimes nothing at all. The end result is the same. There's a boat, with your father's name on it. Soon, that boat will get rigged up and taken out onto the water. Nothing can take that away from him. What about you, Leni? Are you okay? You seem down.'

'Adam and I broke up.'

Mum pulls me into a hug. 'Oh, sweetie. I'm sorry to hear that. I like Adam.'

'He dumped me and I was voted rowing captain, but Cristian wasn't. I always thought it would be us together. Cris and I had a fight. He told me I always had to win.'

Mum looks at me seriously.

'When you were a toddler I couldn't take you to parks without fences. Cristian, he would happily sit by my side, but you would take off like a rocket. I'd turn my head and you'd be running into the distance. Gone. You've always been an adventurer. Someone others follow. You'll be a great captain. Just don't forget to trust your teammates to make it work in the boat. Let them help you achieve your dreams.'

116

'I will, Mum.'

I might have photos of other athletes on my wall, but Mum is my true sports hero.

'And who is the boys' captain? Sam?'

'How did you know?'

'That one's easy to pick. He's like you, Leni. Out on the water you have the same look in your eyes.'

'What look?'

'Like a fire has started that you can't put out.'

She looks into my eyes until I blink and we both laugh.

'Yes. You have it. I had it. Your dad had it.'

'Cristian?'

'Maybe a flicker. Walk a little taller at the boatsheds. You are Elena Popescu, Captain of Boats. Not bad, kid.'

'Yes, Mum. Don't you start early tomorrow? You should be in bed.'

'You? Telling me to go to bed? Boy, my job is done, hey? I have a grown-up woman now. Not a little girl.'

'Mum, can I go round to Audrey's? I need a friend tonight.'

'Sure, you want a lift?'

'I'll ride.'

'Okay. Not too late.'

I chain up my bike and knock on Audrey's door, holding a plastic bag with a tub of melting cookies and cream ice-cream. I can see the TV light flickering through the frosted glass, but there's no answer. I dial her number from my phone and hear it ringing in the house somewhere. I knock again on the windowpane through the security bars.

'Who is it?' Audrey asks.

'It's Leni.'

She opens the door, looking sleepy in boxers and a boy's T-shirt.

'Did I wake you?' It's barely 8 pm. What's she doing in bed?

I hold up my ice-cream. 'Got spoons?'

Audrey gives me a weird look. 'Um. Can we maybe do this tomorrow night?'

'What's wrong with tonight?'

'Audrey! Get back here my sexy wench! I'm not done with you!' booms a guy's voice from inside the house.

'Kieren's here? Isn't he on schoolies' week?'

'He was but he came back early. He missed me.'

'Sorry, Audrey. I'll go.'

Audrey walks onto the front verandah. 'Are you okay, Leni?'

Why does everyone keep asking me that?

'I thought we could hang out. Never mind.'

Kieren lumbers out of the house, a towel wrapped around his waist and his hair messed up. It could not be a more embarrassing moment for all three of us. I feel like the squeakiest third wheel.

'Hi Leni,' he says, looking at his bare feet and pulling his towel up higher.

For some reason I start crying. I fumble with my bike chain, practically ripping the lock open. As I speed off down the street, Audrey shouts, 'Wait! Leni, come back!'

I finally slow down at a park in the shadows of the housing commission flats on Gertrude Street. I'm not ready to go home. I scroll through my phone's contact list. Could I call someone in my crew? Penny maybe? No. She was at Adam's party with Cristian. Besides, we weren't close. I wouldn't let her in, no matter how hard she was knocking. Aiko, Rachel, Millie? All I really talked to them about was rowing. Erg times. Weights. Runs. Who were these girls I spent so much time with?

What was it that Dad always said? 'You'll meet the best friends of your life on the river, Leni.' Wasn't happening to me. Outside of rowing, there was a distance between me and my crew. Had I put it there? Pushed them away like I did to Adam? I sit down on the swing set and push my legs back and forth, gathering momentum.

A group of women watch me from a nearby picnic table. I kick my legs harder, throwing my head back and looking at the outlines of the graceful ghost gums and the sun draining out of the sky, leaving behind a fingernail clipping of moon. Feeling my stomach drop away. I put my headphones on, listening to music as I let myself go completely. I miss this. Being a kid. Thinking if I kicked my legs a bit harder I could go the whole way round.

'Hey girl, you like swings? You a big kid, are ya?' laughs one of the women as I pedal past them. 'Got any money?'

'I wish I was a kid,' I say, handing the woman a few gold coins from my purse.

I cycle past the shop that sells only cookbooks, Trippy Taco and a Bar called Barry. Swerve in and out of the statues of three oversized matryoshka dolls on the foot-path. That's what I am – a matryoshka doll. Too many layers hiding the real, smaller me.

Cristian

As it turns out there's no apology big enough for emptying the contents of your stomach into a girl's new mini skirt. I'm trying to clean Penny up by taking off my school shirt and mopping around her lap area. This is making the situation considerably worse.

'Get away!' screams Penny. 'Ugh. This is the most disgusting thing that's ever happened to me.'

I back away with my sodden, reeking shirt as her friends swoop in, whisking her away to one of the eight marbled bathrooms for a complete hose off.

'I have a spare outfit,' says one of them. 'You can have a shower, Penny. Get that filth off you.'

'You are a complete pig,' says the other.

'I'm so sorry, Penny,' I plead.

One of the bouncers grabs me by the arm in a grip so tight I'm sure it will leave a mark.

'We've called you a taxi, son,' he says. 'We suggest you take it.'

I look for Adam, but he's out of sight, so I let myself be led out of the garden, head down and shirtless as if I've been collared by the police.

I want to break away, find Penny. If I wasn't such a mess I'd tell her that I haven't ruined something so perfect since I crashed my Revell Super Hornet model plane by throwing it off the roof, when I was eight. I shake myself free of the bouncer as we reach the wide, quiet street outside. I slam my fists into the high hedge lining the Langley property. Ripping and pulling at the perfectly trimmed branches.

'Oi! Settle down!' shouts the bouncer.

My hands nicked and bleeding, I leap into the waiting cab and tell him to drive. Now. Fast. Back to where I come from. Back to the other side.

Leni

I'm sneaking in round the side of the house, trying to avoid more parental advice. Our back garden has always been a magical place. There's a weathered cubby Dad built when Cristian and I were preschoolers which still has our chalk marks, a trampoline where Mum taught me how to back-flip and a Tarzan rope hanging from the jacaranda tree. When he was ten Cristian could shimmy up it in seconds and fling himself into the air, hooting like a monkey. I used to spend every spare minute here. Now, I barely step foot outside unless to grab my bike from the shed.

I'm slow to notice the light flashing in the tree house. When I do, it's too late.

'Leni?' Dad calls from his hidey hole in the trees. 'Come see your father.'

I climb up the ladder, crawling into the small space. He's wearing a miner's light strapped to his forehead and lying on one of Mum's yoga mats with a triangle pillow for his head.

He pats next to him, flicks off the light. 'Look at moon. Hardly there at all.'

'Why you up here, Dad?'

'Jodie told me go to man cave until calm down.'

121

Mum often sent Dad out to the tree house in frustration. Where she was calm and level, he was irrational and quick-fused.

'What are you reading?' I ask, picking up the book he has draped in a V-shape over his knees.

It's an English language textbook. Nearby is a pile of my old primary schoolbooks with large print and simple storylines.

'How else will I get to coach first eight?' Dad asks. 'If English isn't better?'

I remember that Dad also likes to win. He wants to lead the top crew as much as I do.

'How come you didn't learn English when you first came to Australia?'

'Jodie organised literacy courses in city,' says Dad. 'I thought waste of time. Why study when I can row? The guys in my crew taught me swear words, how to order beer. Enough to get by. I never made effort. Not like you. You good girl, Leni, you work hard. I'm proud of you.'

'Your speaking isn't too bad,' I say. Trying to make him feel better. 'You do get by.'

'What's the saying? Can't teach old dog new things?'

'You're not an old dog yet,' I say. Although he has more grey hair than black these days.

'I'm sorry, Dad,' I blurt out. 'I didn't mean to take over your speech. I was only trying to help.'

'You saved me from looking fool. Too much I wanted to say. Most of all thank you to my family for putting up with me.'

'We don't put up with you. We love you.'

Dad holds out an arm and I slide in under it, feeling safe. It's nice to get close again. He smells the same as I remember when I was a kid. Like soap and boat grease.

'Mum say you and Adam broke up?' he says. 'Are you broken heart?'

'No. Just, disappointed. I don't like it when I can't make things work.'

'Adam good boy. But he have complicated life. Plenty on your plate next year rowing in firsts and final year. You'll be a fine Captain of Boats.'

'Thanks.'

'Go inside now. Your mum not relax until all kids back home. I've got reading.'

He opens his book again, turns on the miner's light and squints at the page, sounding out the words.

Cristian

My mouth is talcum-powder dry and there's not a single drop of water in my room. It's the Sahara and I can't bring myself to leave the room to look for an oasis. I'm trying not to move my head, willing someone to arrive with a bucket of drinkable liquid. I've slept in last night's clothes and my room smells like last night. Awful. My eyes hurt. Even the hairs on my body hurt. Some of the night comes back to me. Shards of it piercing my brain. I make a fist and wince. My hands are ripped up. Oh dear, the hedges. Penny. Oh my God. No.

I scramble for my phone in the bed sheets and read the messages on it, all my worst fears confirmed.

Adam: *Gotta learn to hold your piss Poppa! Call me when you've slept it off.*

Charley: *You are going to hate yourself tomorrow.*

There's a photo attached of me doing something unspeakable with a swimming noodle. I'd laugh, but I feel more like crying. There's a knock at my door.

'What?'

Leni opens the door a crack, peers in. She looks nervous and I remember how big a dickhead I was to her last night. Another apology to make.

'It stinks in here.'

Leni holds her sleeve up to her nose.

'Big night?'

'You could say that.'

'Is it true you barfed on Penny Mission?'

'Affirmative.'

'That's too bad. Penny's a good chick. She might even have liked you before she was anointed in your leftover lunch.'

'Have you heard from her?' I ask.

'It's not good news, bro.'

I groan and pull my pillow over my face.

'She hates me.'

'Well, maybe *hate* is too strong a word. But she doesn't want much to do with you after last night. You know she's never been kissed before?'

'No. That makes me feel so much worse.'

'I think she was hoping it would be a bit more romantic than some dude chucking up all over her.'

'I wanted it to be romantic. That's it. I'm never drinking beer again.'

'Yes, you will.'

'I'm a loser.'

'No, you're not. You got drunk and acted like one,' says Leni.

She leaves the room and returns with a big glass of water. She puts it on the table next to me and I grab it and drain it.

'I'm so sorry about the things I said last night. I'm glad you got Captain of Boats. I'm proud of you. I was just gutted I didn't get captain too. It's bad enough being in the seconds.'

'You should've gotten boys' captain.'

'No. Sam will be good. He's a better choice than me.'

'You think?' Leni asks, looking unsure.

'Yeah. I personally don't like the guy, but he loves rowing and he wants it so hard. So I heard you and Adam broke up. He's pretty cut up about losing you.'

'I deserve to be dumped. I was a terrible girlfriend.'

'Not terrible. Misunderstood.'

'Feel like a run later?' she asks.

'Not a snowball's chance.'

'Might head out on my own then. Get some salt and grease into you.'

I need the world's longest shower and to take last night's clothes to the laundry and disinfect them. But having a shower means leaving the four walls of my bedroom and I won't do it. Instead, I lie in bed with my laptop and try to reach out to Penny via messages on my Facebook wall.

I update my status.

Sunday, 12 December, 10.47 am.

Cristian Popescu *is so sorry.*

I'm hoping for an inbox message from Penny and I obsessively refresh the page. I get eighteen replies from guys at school saying what a loser I am. One from Adam telling me to turn my phone on.

I rifle through my playlist trying to find the right words. The right mood. No song is right. They can't possible say what I feel when I see her glide past in her boat, when she kneels down to screw in her oar or ties her hair back in a ponytail. How much I want to hug her, not even do anything X-rated. Well, not yet anyway. Just hold her and feel her chin rest on my chest and smell that girl smell. Have her whisper something, just to me, and to feel that everything might be okay.

Desperate, I make up my own poem.

Cristian Popescu *Beautiful girl/ stupid boy/ A big mistake/ I take it all back/ will you give me another chance?*

I regret pressing the update button immediately. I might as well have posted **Cristian Popescu** *is hopelessly in love with Penny Misson, who hates his (weak) guts.*

My friends, and I use that term loosely, send eleven messages in rapid-fire succession. Most of which go a little like this:

Nick Jamison: *Cristian you sad, sad prick.*

Adam Langley: *Awww, babycakes. I think you're beautiful too. Meet me later?*

I type 'Inbox?' hoping Penny will contact me privately.

Adam sends me a private instead. *Forget it Poppa. She's never going there again.*

I sigh, hoping Penny will show up. Nothing. Is she out there, looking?

I get another message on my feed.

Jodie Popescu: *Cristian, I'm coming in.*

Thirty seconds later there's a knock at the door and Mum bustles in. She crinkles her nose as she's hit by the rank stench of my BO and stale alcohol. She opens up the blinds and the window, letting light and a fresh, welcome breeze into the room. It's sunny out. I wish it was raining.

'Mum, can you not spy on me on Facebook?' I ask, pulling my covers up to my chin.

She collects my filthy clothes and dumps them in my hamper and then pushes it out to the hall.

'I will spy on you for the rest of your life,' she says. 'What happened last night? You came crashing in at 1 am. Woke the whole house up. I don't know if you remember, but you were very drunk. Very sick. I had to put you to bed.'

That bit of the night floods back to me. Oh God. It'd been a while since Mum had to help me take my shoes off. I brace for a lecture on the evils of alcohol.

'I'm not crazy about you drinking, Cris. You're underage, for starters. Why did you go overboard?'

'I dunno. I didn't have enough to eat, I was trying to impress a girl, I guess.'

'A girl? Which girl?'

'Penny, you know, she's in Leni's crew. I like her and I chucked up all over her.'

Mum rests her face in her hands and looks at me. She sighs.

127

'And?'

'And now I feel like a complete idiot and I want to die. I can never leave this room. Seriously, don't make me.'

'First of all, you will leave this room. Because you need a shower. You stink. Second, I didn't raise you to vomit on some poor girl and then not properly apologise. So get up, scrub yourself, go and buy Penny some flowers, take them round to her house and tell her you are very sorry. Got it?'

I want to tell Mum to get the hell out of my room, get out of my life and stop treating me like I'm not about to turn eighteen, but I find myself agreeing. That's the power mothers have over their sons.

'And next time, don't drink so much. Or better still, don't drink at all. You should see the state of some of the intoxicated teenagers we get at the hospital. Would put you off drinking until you're fifty.'

'That's already happened,' I say.

After a cleansing cold shower, I put on my best jeans and the lucky T-shirt I usually pick up in. I walk over to Aztec Rose, the florist on the corner. The place Leni and I go to buy flowers for Mum on her birthday. I'm overwhelmed by the explosion of blooms, the stench of their perfume. I stand there, stunned, until a lady asks if I need help. *Yes, I do, in so many ways*, I think. *Help me.*

'I want to, um, buy some flowers, for a girl.'

'What's the occasion?' the lady asks. She has a nose-ring and is wearing spotty purple gumboots. She looks nice so I blurt it out.

'To say sorry for being a dickhead last night.'

She laughs. 'We get that a bit around here. You're on the right track.'

She plucks a bunch of small pink roses from a bucket, water beading on the petals. They're sweet and old fashioned. I sniff at them.

'They smell pretty good.'

'These are a winner with the ladies,' she says gently. 'Shall I wrap them up? Here. Write something.'

She gives me a free card and a biro and I think about what I'm going to write for ages. The lady doesn't seem to mind. Finally, I use my best handwriting to say: 'I'm sorry. From Cristian.'

'Off you go,' she says, as I pay her in gold coins. 'Good luck.'

I stand on the road looking at Penny's house for about twenty minutes. She lives in the most perfect chocolate-box house, in the most perfect tree-lined street in the quietest, most drug-addict-free neighbourhood. It took me over an hour to get here on two trams. Even though I ache to see her, I can't make myself walk up the leaf-free brick path with its abundance of pink roses. Why, why did I pick roses?

As I'm dithering, I miss my window of opportunity. The door to her garage rumbles to life and I hear the voices of her family and the bark of a dog. Panicked, I chuck the flowers as hard as I can towards the verandah, like a morning newspaper, and hope she finds them. I run away like a scared little boy, ducking behind a tree for cover as her family's Subaru four-wheel drive glides past. Roses or no roses, Penny is not about to forgive me. That's fine and understandable. But I think I love her. I do. For real.

Leni

When I don't know how to sit with myself and my skin feels a size too small, I run. I lace up my shoes, strap music to my bicep and close the door behind me. The house is too quiet. I can practically hear it breathing. I need to break out of the silence and let my whole body scream. My plan is to run to the river and do an ergo. I pound the sticky footpath, past beautiful, surreal graffiti walls, Asian nail joints and hipsters eating eggs in cool cafés with industrial lighting and uncomfortable stools. People wasting time. I don't like sitting in cafés.

As I run I imagine a number in my head. Big, bold, black type.

7.20

That's my number. Or it will be in January on rowing camp. I'm writing everywhere. On my inspiration board, above my bed, next to the toilet, on my mirror, the fridge door. Everywhere I turn, there it is staring back at me. Daring me to achieve the impossible. No female student at my school has ever rowed that fast in a 2000-metre ergo time trial. I would be smashing the current record by ten seconds. As I run I imagine what the time will look like on the ergo readout. Flashing up in digital as I pull my final stroke and collapse like a deflated balloon over the handle.

The number thing was champion runner Cathy Freeman's idea. She wrote her dream 400-metre time down *before* the 2000 Sydney Olympics. Put it up everywhere to remind her. On 25 September 2000, Cathy snatched the 400 metres in a time of 49.11 seconds. She was the first Aboriginal athlete to win gold. I'm not old enough to remember it, but I've seen the YouTube clip. The entire country went nuts.

Mum reckons if I write the number down, my body will follow.

'If you want something, you have to see it in your mind first,' she said as we peeled potatoes elbow to elbow one night before dinner.

She waved her hand at the framed photo from the Seoul Games that hangs above the TV. It's a little faded and dusty, but there she is. An Olympic champion. Young and strong, her face lit up with joy and relief. A gold medal hangs around her neck, an Australian flag draped around her shoulders. She stands next to her pair partner, Veronica. The Han River is hazy in the background.

'I thought about winning that gold medal in Seoul every day for four years,' she said. 'When I finally did it, I was fulfilling a promise to myself and to Veronica.'

I'm preparing to fulfill my own promise as I spring from my toes, down the leafy wide streets of East Melbourne, past the Punt Road footy field and Melbourne Park. Over Swan Street Bridge to Adam's side of the river. I take my cap off and tuck it into the back of my shorts, letting the breeze hit my wet hair.

I look down at the fancy Garmin watch Adam bought me for my seventeenth birthday. It's telling me how fast my heart is beating, how many ks I'm eating up, where I'm going on a map and whether the ground is rising or falling. What it can't measure are the thoughts racing through my head. Why can't I stop thinking about Sam when I should still be cut up about Adam?

A thin strip of path curls by the river, down to the boat-sheds. The Sunday scullers and veteran crews are out. I don't want to stop when I reach the sheds, so I turn left to the Tan's sandy running track. I cruise past the mums pushing prams and the fun runners in training. Counting them as I pass. *One little Indian, two little Indians, three little Indians.* I hurt. All over pain that begs me to stop. To sit down. To drink at the air. But I don't. I can't. I'm not there yet. If I stopped now, everything would be ruined. Besides, when I push into the pain zone, I'm the best version of myself.

As I head down the steep slope of the Anderson Street hill I really let myself fly. I feel strong and fearless now, digging deep into my reserves to find more heart, more courage, more strength. It's like mining for gold in a vein that's been scraped dry. I scrabble in the darkness for my precious nugget and take it up to the surface. The metal is bright and hard, and finding it makes me more determined not to stop.

'How far down you can dig when you're really suffering makes the difference,' says Laura, 'between losers and winners.'

Winners find gold, every time, no matter how dark it gets underground.

★

At the sheds I run up the stairs to the gym. I ignore the searing pain in my thighs and chest. When I hit the top, I'll fall to the ground and lie still, listening to my heart slow down. I reach the final step and beep my watch to signal I'm done. Thirteen point two ks. Later, I'll sync the numbers into my laptop. Compare them to my last run. As I gasp for air, hands at my hips, I see there's a lone rower hunched over an ergo, dripping fat drops of sweat onto the wooden floor.

Sam.

He's got headphones on and can't hear me. He's totally lost in his own tunnel of pain. He drops the erg handle and swigs at a water bottle behind him. He has to turn around to reach it, and as he does, he sees me. We look at each other – both red faced, wet, exhausted and unable to speak from lack of oxygen. He takes his headphones out, the music still blaring from the little buds.

He seems dazed and clears his throat, wiping down his arms and face with a towel.

'Leni, hi. I was doing a quick 10 k.'

Nobody does a quick 10 k. It's a thankless slog and we both know it.

'You're in better shape today than most of the rowing squad,' I say, assuming Sam was out drinking last night too.

'You mean Adam's party? I wasn't invited. Besides, I don't drink alcohol. I was at home by myself this morning. Thought I'd come down to the river and, y'know, hang out with the boats. Did you go? I guess so, you're Adam's girl, right?'

'We broke up last night.'

'Oh, I'm sorry.'

I watch for a change in his face. Any indication he feels the same way about me. There's not much to go on.

'I was going to do an erg too,' I say, changing the subject. 'But I might have killed myself on the run down here.'

He waves me over to the ergs and I sit on the one next to him. Rolling up and down on the slide.

'I'm sorry I was a bitch last night. You'll be a good captain. I was disappointed for Cristian.'

Sam holds up his hand for me to stop talking. One of them has a big blister that's raw and infected.

'Don't worry about it. Last night was always going to be weird. Mercury was in retrograde.'

'Mercury in what?'

'The stars.'

I go to laugh, but he's deadly serious. Sam's into astrology. Another shiny thing for my nest.

'Is it just me or is there a weird vibe between us?' he says. 'I like you, you know that, right? Actually it's more than that. I admire you. I'm looking forward to being co-captains together.'

We're still breathing heavily, looking at each other with the same intensity of the library. Except today it's a romantic moment that can't be denied. It hangs in the air – hot and urgent. I know for sure if Sam decides to kiss me, I won't pull away. I shiver as the sweat cools on my skin.

'Are you cold?' Sam asks.

'A bit.'

134

If I get up from the ergo, the moment will shatter. Sam knows it too.

He leans in closer, his lips touching mine. I taste his sweat and he tastes mine, and there's a hunger between us that I've never felt before. He kneels down in front of me and brings me into him.

Radiating heat from the training and from each other, we, close up the shed and walk together towards the city. Past the club insignias and balconies with rowers enjoying a beer after a light row. Sam tries to hold my hand but I shake it off, worried one of my parents' mates might spot us. The river is a hotbed of gossip.

'Not here,' I tell him.

We walk towards the Swanston Street tram stop, looking up the skirts of the Arts Centre. The 86 clacks down the road towards us as if to break things up. I want to hold on a bit longer. Like a kid who hasn't finished playing with their toys, being dragged off to bed. Sam holds my hand again, and this time I let him. I squeeze it and he winces. He swaps sides and offers me his non-turning hand. It's smooth and blister free. I trace my finger in a circle on his palm.

'This is my tram.' I say, regret in my voice. I have enough money to get back home, tucked into a pocket in my shoe.

'Don't get on it. *Please*,' Sam says as the tram stops in front of us. 'Come to my place. We can watch a movie.'

I'm still in my running kit. It's damp and turning festy.

'I should go home and change.'

With Adam I would've made an excuse, slipped away. With Sam, I was caught. I was thrashing in his net.

The driver dings the bell twice and the doors close violently.

'I think I missed it,' I say, knowing this is much more than a missed tram.

Sam opens the door to his apartment. It's so empty it practically echoes. Floor-to-ceiling windows look out to a point blank view of Docklands, boats bobbing on their leashes. A white leather couch and a glass coffee table are the only furniture in the room. Garish paintings overcompensate for the grey sea outside. The only sign a teenage boy lives here is the gaming console on the floor and Sam's running shoes kicked off next to it.

'You live here by yourself?'

'My parents are down every month and I have a house-keeper who leaves me food to eat and checks on me. My sisters come by. Sometimes.'

'So you, like, look after yourself? Is that even legal?'

'Yeah. You can leave home at sixteen. Besides I don't need looking after.'

He motions to the white granite kitchen.

'Would you like a drink?' he says formally.

This whole play date suddenly feels like a bad idea. There's no buffer between us. No one to stop things going too far.

'Can I have a shower?' I ask. I can smell myself, sweat drying in the folds of my skin.

His eyes widen. With what – surprise? Excitement?

'Don't get any ideas.'

'Of course, let me show you,' Sam says.

He pulls a clean towel from a cupboard and disappears into a room I assume is his bedroom. I linger outside the door, shy now. The room gives nothing away. No photos, no posters. His bed is a thin camping mat on the floor and a sleeping bag. He doesn't seem to use the king-size bed, studded with dozens of fancy Asian silk cushions. A mountain bike is propped in one corner, a small silver statue of Buddha beside it.

'Where's your stuff?' I think of Cristian's room with its mess and boy stench. This room smells like incense.

'No point getting too comfortable here,' Sam says. 'I'll be gone at the end of next year. Besides, my parents expect it to look like a showroom when they visit. It's their stuff. They decorated it. I'm staying here temporarily.'

He throws me a pair of tracksuit pants and a T-shirt. 'Too big, but they're clean.'

He leads me to a bathroom so white it hurts my eyes.

'You'd better go now,' I say, gently pushing him out and shutting the door. Maybe because I don't trust myself, I use the lock.

I turn the shower to the highest temperature I can stand. Too hot for most people, it feels right to me. My skin turns pink and I trace the glass shower screen with a bar of soap. Twirly, dreamy letters. Leni loves Sam and a heart. I look at it for a moment, then wipe away the evidence with a soapy sweep of my hand.

Something Sam said nags at me.

I'll be gone by the end of next year. Gone where?

Sam is lying on the floor when I come out of the shower. As I get closer I see he's asleep, his head resting on the crook of his elbow. I should leave. It's the perfect opportunity to slip out of the apartment and back to my normal Sunday. Help Mum with some gardening or get a jump on my holiday reading. I wander around the living room, quietly looking at things. I run my hand along the sleek silver line of a music player and pick up a CD case from the shelf.

It's a mix tape. Old school. Someone has written *Sammy's Birthday Mix* on the cover. I pull out the paper tracklist tucked inside like a love letter. I look back at Sam, he's still out cold. I once searched Adam's phone when he was out of the room and this feels the same. Forbidden. There's a line I'm crossing.

The music is my taste, indie, but not particularly cool. It's the writing that bothers me. Flowy purple letters with hearts instead of dots. Girl's writing. Whoever she is, she's taken a lot of effort to search for the exact right mix of music. It's familiar, full of in-jokes, sunny summer anthems and triple j hottest 100 contenders. I feel a flash of jealousy and then remember Sam has sisters. Sisters who could easily be music lovers. Sisters who probably call him Sammy.

Feeling silly I slip the CD case back. I look at the front door, and then at Sam lying peacefully on the floor and make a decision that surprises me.

I walk over to Sam's slack body, lie down behind him on the soft carpet and put my arm over him. My tummy fits in the arch of his back, breasts pressed between his

138

shoulder blades. I stare into the curls at the back of his head and a small mole on his neck. His hair smells damp and woody. I can hardly believe Sam is right here for me to touch. How did this happen? So fast? All of a sudden we smacked into each other, like cars colliding on a road. I press my lips to the raised brown circle on his skin and he stirs, but doesn't wake.

My breath finds the rhythm of his, a calm, deep rise and fall. His heartbeat is so slow it's barely there at all. I've never fallen asleep with a boy before. Even though I've done things that other people might think were more intimate, to me, it's the closest I've ever felt to another human being. Even as I fall asleep, I don't want to wake up.

Sam wakes up first. The light outside is fading, lights blinking across the bay. I feel his breath on my face, my thoughts rising to the surface of a long, black unconsciousness. I open my eyes halfway. We are looking at each other at close range. Only a few centimetres separate my mouth from his.

'Thank you,' he says, his voice a few tones lower from sleep, his breath sour.

'What for?'

'For staying.'

'I wanted to.'

He stretches, breaks away from our eye contact and puts his arms behind his head.

'Sundays are the worst day.'

'For what?'

'Being alone. Being … lonely.'

He reaches down and holds my hand. We kiss again. Then we do other things. Things I couldn't stop, even if I wanted to. And I don't want to.

Cristian

After my failed flower drop, I go home and try to reach Penny by text.

I seriously can't stop thinking about you.

I feel happy when I see your beautiful smile

Forgive me? Please?

Do you even know how amazing you are?

I wait for something in return, but there's only cold silence. I miss our flirty messages. The possibilities. By the end of the day Penny has culled me from her Facebook friends list and blocked me from social media. It makes me even more desperate to reach her. Mum just left for work, Dad is potting herbs in the garden and Leni has been gone all day.

The house is too quiet. I feel panicky and stressed about my messed-up life. My messed-up head. The drugs I'm taking and what damage they're doing. Everything. Outside my window, it's starting to get dark. I text Leni, worried. *Where RU?*

I shouldn't be surprised.

When we were kids on a camping trip up north, Leni borrowed a canoe and paddled it to a nearby island, thinking it was close. She was planning to get there and back before anyone even noticed she was gone. By lunchtime the water police were out looking for her and Mum was crying. She turned up, halfway to the next town, exhausted and burnt to a crisp. No hat, no water, no sunscreen. Taken downstream by the current and totally out of her depth. My parents didn't know whether to shake her or hug her. In the end they did both. 'Don't do that, ever again!' I had yelled at her, furious. But she did. Over and over again. Disappearing into the ether. Thinking about no one but herself.

Sometimes I think she's selfish, but mostly I know that's how Leni is. She gets lost sometimes.

Leni texts back and I grab my phone, relieved.

Sorry! Nearly home.

She shows up a few minutes later at my bedroom door, flushed and happier than I've seen her in ages. Wearing men's tracksuit pants and a baggy T-shirt.

'Nice threads.'

She looks down at her outfit like she'd forgotten she was wearing it.

'Did you and Adam get back together?' I ask. Hoping I won't have to do the make up break-up ride with my bestie and my sister. It's been awkward enough already.

'No. But there is someone …'

'Don't. Adam's my best mate. If you tell me, I'll have to tell him. Best you don't mention any names.'

'I wasn't going to anyway. It's probably nothing.'

Leni falls into a beanbag. 'You might not want my advice, but maybe you should take a cooling-off period from the Penny situation. I've seen all that Facebook stuff. Stop sending her messages. She's going to get creeped out.'

141

'I think she already is. I went round there. Chucked some flowers at her house. It was Mum's idea. I'm like a proper stalker.'

'*Stop*,' says Leni, giving me her sister eye.

'I'll stop,' I agree. Sometimes I need Leni to pull me into line.

I put music on and we sit and listen to it for a while. Both absorbed in our own thoughts.

'Leni, you ever think about not rowing anymore?' I ask in the darkening room.

The dark always makes me feel like I can say anything to Leni. When we were little we shared a bunk bed. Leni below, me hanging my head over the edge. We would talk and talk after lights out until one of us would fall asleep mid-sentence.

'*No*. Do you?'

'Sometimes.'

'You have four months to go, Cris. Just hang in there. You'll get back in the firsts. Win the Head of the River. Win Nationals. You've done it before. Wait 'til the next erg trials. You'll smash Sam. You'll smash everyone. Have you looked in the mirror lately? You've lost so much weight. You've got guns. Everyone's talking about it.'

'Are they?' I perk up a bit. It's been a while since I've had guns. All my muscles have been lost in a thick layer of fat.

'Yeah. You and Adam both. What have you guys been doing in the gym?'

I glance at my desk drawer. Still inside it is the zip-lock bag with enough 'roids and appetite zappers to last me a month. After we ripped through the first supply of drugs, Adam went back to Doug and got us a top up. I wish I didn't have to take them, but they're my only hope. I've promised Adam I'll get back into the firsts with him and to do that my spare tyres have got to go and I've got to train harder, faster and better than superfreak Sam. If I stop now I'll be forced to row out the seasons in the seconds and probably lose my full scholarship. I might have regrets but there's no going back. The results make the guilt easier to bear. At least the drugs are doing the job.

'Don't worry, I'll finish this season. I have to,' I say, avoiding her question.

'Dad's been asking me to check in with you. He thinks you're all over the shop. Are you okay, bro? Really? You do seem a bit on edge.'

'Tell him I'm fine.'

'Are you?'

I wasn't okay. I was agitated. I couldn't focus. My nerves were jittery. One minute I felt like I was flying. Invincible. The next, I came crashing back to earth in a depressed heap. But I could stand it; the side effects were temporary. The Head of the River cup I'd keep forever.

'No. Tell him anyway.'

She will, because we cover for each other. Always have, always will.

Leni

I heat up some leftover pasta in the common room micro-wave and wait for it, glancing around the busy room. Where do I go now?

143

On my left is Adam and his crowd. I couldn't sit with them, even if I wanted to. There's something to be said for space, and Adam seems to want it from me. On my right is Audrey and Marion. Audrey has her back turned to me, head bent over a plastic container of beads and trinkets, sifting for the perfect droplet to hang on an earring or necklace. She'll sell them to the beautiful people for a hefty mark-up.

Marion passes her a silver chain and Audrey takes it, threading on an arrow and a red ceramic pendant. She holds it up to the light, asks Marion what she thinks.

'A feather?' Marion says.

'Yeah, good idea. Pass me a yellow one.'

That would've been my job – before I screwed everything up. The girls laugh and I feel a sting of regret. Why was I so quick to take the easy option? To choose Adam, when I wasn't even sure about him? I long to go up to Audrey, plonk down on crossed legs and lean into their conversation, but I made my choice. There's no going back now.

Across the room Adam catches my eye. I smile at him, hoping we can be friends, but he glazes over and turns to Aiko next to him, giving her his full attention. Just like he used to do with me. I put my head down, anxiety rising. At least Sam is absent. I spied him heading down to the library with his laptop.

The microwave dings, finally, and I grab my hot container and head for the gym. I'll be friends with my weights program today. And every other day until the Head of the River.

★

I fast-track to the tram stop after school. Audrey's there, waiting. Like always. I feel my spirits lift. At least out of school grounds I still have some friends.

'You okay?' Audrey says. 'Kieren and I were worried about you the other night. How come you didn't call me back?'

I feel sheepish for making a scene at her house the other night. I've made a big drama over something I should be able to handle. I'm eighteen next year. An adult. How come I still feel like a baby? Audrey's so far ahead of me, having real sex relationships with boys who drive and have chest hair and are almost at uni. I feel left out and lagging.

'Sorry I ran off,' I say. 'I guess I didn't want to intrude.'

'You could have stayed. We would've put clothes on.'

'I shouldn't have dropped in like that.'

'You should *always* drop in like that, Leni,' Audrey says. 'You don't need to announce yourself. Hey, I heard you and Prince Charming broke up. Did you do the dumping?'

'Actually, he dumped me.'

I feel miserable.

'Well, there's only one thing that will make you feel better. Sunny's pork roll?'

'I dunno. I've got study,' I say.

'Come on. This is our last hang out before Kieren and I take Doris to Queensland for the summer.'

Doris is Audrey's family campervan.

'Don't go. How am I going to survive the summer of sales without you?'

I'm dreading my summer job – check-out chicking at Target. Six weeks of black polyester slacks, scratchy shirts and lost name tags. Endless beeping of sporting goods, sunscreen and cheap T-shirts, my feet aching and my cheerful 'how are you today?' greeting straining to breaking point. The only thing that made it bearable was seeing Audrey on a nearby register. Meeting up during our twenty-minute break for warm cinnamon doughnuts and bad coffee from Donut King.

'When do you leave?' I ask. Missing her already.

'Friday arvo. Right after our last class.'

'Oh. Not staying for Christmas?'

'Nuh. Mum's chucking a fit, but she's releasing me from my daughterly duties. Sure you can't meet me on the road? We'll be at Summerdaze after New Year's.'

'Gotta make some cashola,' I say.

I needed to save every cent while school was out. Unlike my classmates, my parents couldn't stretch to pocket money. Cristian would be at Bunnings in a green apron, hauling heavy stock and mixing up paints. We would both work the longest hours possible and the worst shifts, so we could have some funds during the year, when we were loaded with training and study.

We hop on the tram and sit facing each other.

'How's that rowing thing going?' Audrey says.

'I made Captain of Boats.'

'Legend. And what of Bike Pant Guy? Now that you and Adam are off, are you guys planning a Bikram yoga session together?'

I put my hands over my face and groan.

'We kissed.'

'No.'

'We did *more* than kissing.'

Audrey gasps. 'More *what* than kissing? What about Adam? What exactly have you been up to, young lady?'

As we inch towards Fitzroy on the hot, smelly tram I tell her the whole story. All of it, except the bit about falling asleep with Sam. That part is mine to keep. Replaying it in my head when I need to.

'The big question is, does Sam give you the *jtzooum*?' Audrey asks.

'He gives me the *jtzooum* times a thousand.'

'Oh dear,' says Audrey. 'You've got it bad.'

Cristian

Some things are easy to predict: I'm the laughing stock of the boatsheds. As I walk into the sheds, Nick pretends to vomit on Charley's head next to him.

'Where's Penny?' says Charley.

He's younger than me by a good two years and he's a foot shorter. I could squash him with one hand. 'Are you going to give her another spew shower?'

'Shut up. Or I will hurt you both.'

Adam puts his hand on my shoulder in solidarity. Or maybe to stop me smashing the guys' faces together. I'm usually pretty laidback, but lately I've been exploding at small things.

'As if you blokes are any better with the ladies,' he says. 'Nick, I saw Elissa Clarke palm you off on Saturday night. Charley, I don't even think you've managed to kiss a girl or reach puberty for that matter. How about you blokes stop shooting your mouths off?' Adam moves towards them aggressively, and Charley and Nick scuttle off in the direction of the boats.

'Thanks, man,' I say.

When we were fifteen and sat together in the thirds, I was chubby and awkward. The older rowers were constantly ragging on me. Telling me to lose the love handles. Sort out my bowl cut. I got so self-conscious I'd get undressed in the locked toilets, instead of the change room. Adam would go in to defend me every time – straight in, scrapping and giving it back to them. Even though I was tall enough and strong enough to stand up for myself.

'Forget them. Imagine what we are going to look like after summer holidays? Built. Nobody will bother us then.'

Adam does look meaner and more solid these days. The scar above his eye adds to the effect.

'No worries. Listen, I've got some more, um, vitamins for you. Enough to last us until the Head. Come and get them after our row. They're in my car. I'll give you a lift to school.'

'Cool. Hey, Ads, are you having any weird side effects?'

Adam shrugs. 'A few.'

'What ones?'

Adam pulls up his shirt and turns around. Angry, pus-filled acne peppers the skin across his back.

'Clearasil doesn't even touch it,' he says, pulling the shirt back down.

'I feel a bit weird. Angry or something,' I admit.

'Of course you do, you're pumping a shitload of extra

testosterone into your body. Don't worry too much about it. Just try not to pull down any more hedges, okay?'

'Sorry about that.'

'No worries, mate. It's just a few more months.'

Leni

It's the last day of school, thank God.

It's hot and everyone's acting a little crazy. Rachel's wearing a uniform that's completely taken over with graffiti. The white collar painted pink. As soon as the final bell goes the Year Elevens are in charge. We've finally reached the top of the heap.

We get our exam results back, and everyone gossips about them for a few hours. Mine are as expected: straight As. The same results I've been getting my entire school life. Anything less would be devastating. I work my arse off to make sure they never, ever slip.

We watch some supposedly educational DVDs, clean out our lockers and mooch about waiting for the day to time out. At lunchtime I take a break from the gym and walk down to the uniform shop to order my embroidered Captain of Boats pocket that I'll sew onto my blazer.

It won't be the first time I've worn the blazer. Our outgoing captain Gill Kentwell was in the shower after a training session and I took the opportunity to try on hers. The room was empty, but anyone could've walked in, so I only kept it on for a few seconds. I put my hand to the loops of gold thread outlining the crossed oars and the lettering underneath, imagining my own name there. *Elena Popescu, Captain of Boats.*

Sam will have a rowing blazer too. Just like mine. *Sam.* He's all I can think about. In quiet moments he fills all the spaces, cracks and holes in my head. I spotted him back at assembly this morning, my heart doing a cartwheel. He's been gone most of the week volunteering with the *HelpingHands* school program. They get time out from classes to visit old people, deliver food to shelters or plant trees. I've done it the last few years, and I regret not putting my name down this time. I've missed out on all that time with Sam.

In the shop there's a pile up of recently awarded kids putting in their orders before we break. Prefects, sports captains, house captains. It's an orgy of over-achievers. I inch forward in line. The room is stuffy and suffocating.

I feel a tap on my shoulder and turn around.

'Getting your captain's pocket?' Sam asks. His voice has none of the softness from the weekend. He's standing very upright, his hands in his pockets. Not looking me in the eye. Classic bad body language.

'Yep. You?'

I'd expected something different after we spent the afternoon together. I wasn't with Adam anymore, he could ask me out. Why wasn't he asking me out? Instead of changing the channel we seemed to have resumed normal programming. Co-captains. Friends? Friends with benefits?

'Same.'

As I get to the front of the queue, I hand the lady my filled-in form.

'Captain of Boats. Congratulations, Leni. I hear the team is looking good again this year. So you want to pay for this now, my dear?'

I take out my wallet. 'How much is it?'

'That's ninety-five.'

'Dollars?'

'Yes. Want to put it on your account?'

Ninety-five dollars is too much. I backtrack, embarrassed.

'No, it's okay. I'll hold that order until next year. Sorry.'

I leave the woman and run out of the shop, mortified.

'Where you going, Leni?' shouts Sam behind me. 'Hey!'

Sam catches up with me at my locker. I'm cornered against a row of steel. There's no one in the room. I'm trapped.

'What's up? Why didn't you get your pocket?' he asks, frowning.

'I just didn't,' I open my locker and grab my bag to keep my hands busy. There's no way I'm admitting I can't afford it.

'But why? It'll look weird if we both don't have them.'

'I'll get it next year.'

I go to leave the room, but Sam stops me.

'Would you mind if I bought it for you? He pulls out a shiny credit card. 'My parents don't check this card, especially school stuff. Let me do this.'

I feel a flash of anger and frustration. Is this chivalry or pity? How did I bounce from one benefactor to another so quickly?

'Just because we did that stuff on the weekend, you don't owe me anything.'

'It's not because we kissed.'

'We did more than just kiss.'

'I was trying to help. Fine. Do it your way.'

He walks away, but then spins around and comes at me with an intensity I'm not ready for.

'My parents dumped me in an apartment, by myself, to go and do yoga in a rainforest. One of the small ways I can get back at them is to spend their money, you'd actually be doing me a favour.'

I laugh and he joins in, the tension broken.

'I need to do this myself. I've got a job this summer.'

Sam sighs with his whole body. 'You still don't get it, do you?'

'What?'

He leans against a locker and puts one foot up, rests his head back. I look at his Adam's apple with pure lust. If this wasn't a locker room, in the middle of school, I'm not sure I could stop myself pouncing on him.

'Want to know why I took up rowing? When I had all that sponsorship in mountain biking?'

'Yeah.'

'Because it meant I didn't have to do *everything* by myself. On the trail it's me, a bike and some hills and trees for company. But on the river, eight guys have got my back. And I've got theirs.'

For all my obsessing over Sam, I hardly even know him at all. Rowing makes him feel less lonely? I didn't even think he needed other people. But letting him pay goes against everything my parents have taught me. They are proud people, and so am I.

'We're not on the river now, Sam.'

'It doesn't matter. I've got your back, too. We're part of the same team. Co-captains.'

'It wouldn't feel right.'

He walks away. 'See ya at training,' he says over his shoulder.

I'm left hanging, the taste of disappointment in my mouth. I slam my locker shut, nicking the corner of my thumb in the door. I cry out in frustration and pain as a group of obnoxious Year Sevens walk in. I suck on my thumb and they laugh nervously.

'What the hell are you laughing at?' I shout.

Cristian

It's the third-last period of the school year and I've been called to Mr Forrester, my year level coordinator's office. When I get there, Westie is sitting in the room. I know what it's about.

'Cristian, sit down,' says Mr Forrester.

'Is this about my marks?'

'Yes,' says Mr Forrester.

I got them back earlier in the day and shoved them into the bottom of my bag, hoping they would stay buried.

153

Knowing that, like a dead body in a shallow grave, the horror of them would be dug up soon enough. Four Ds and a C.

'Mr West tells me your rowing is back on track, but you need to lift your game academically,' says Mr Forrester. 'Part of being on sporting scholarship here at Harley is to maintain a good average in your studies alongside high achievements in competition. You've slipped from a B average down to ... ' He consults a piece of paper. 'D+. You need to work hard next year to improve overall. The good news? We are here to help. Extra tutoring. Study skills sessions. What do you need, Cristian?'

'We want our heavyweight star back in the firsts and doing well at school,' says Westie, who seems to be sucking up to me. It doesn't suit him.

All I need is to take off my school uniform, grow a beard and earn some proper money. All I need is to get the hell off Harley's grounds.

'I dunno, sir,' I say, shrugging. 'You tell me.'

The final bell does at last ring. Students pile out of every available exit. Carrying art projects and Secret Santa gifts, cellophane bags of shortbread and homemade chocolates. Weighed down with bags full of our year. Part of me wishes I could crawl home, but we have our last row before we get broken apart for summer with our training schedules and a promise to our coaches not to get unfit.

Traditionally it's a 'fun' session. No tests, heavy weights sessions or soul-destroying runs. Just a cruisey row and a barbecue with the parents and coaches after. When I get down there, all the girls are dressed up in Santa hats and face paint. All the girls, except Leni. I head for her. She seems relatively sane in all this Christmas merriment.

'Help me?' she asks, throwing over a bundle of tinsel. As captain she now has to be a joiner. Being part of a group doesn't come naturally to Leni. I dump my bags inside the sheds and drape red and green tinsel over the bow of an eight.

'How'd you do in your exams?' she asks.

'Don't ask. Don't tell. You?'

'Same as last year.'

The same means perfect. Leni would freak if she got anything less than ninety-nine. She stresses herself out every year working until 2 to 3 am every night, flogging herself. Then she pulls out a row of top marks.

'Why are we doing this? Can't we have a normal row?' she says.

I tape a Christmas bauble to a rigger and smile. Leni might find this painful, but I love the fun side of rowing. I miss the junior crews. When we would row hopelessly out of time and no one cared. When we laughed our way up to the start line and it was irrelevant if we won or lost.

I'm jealous of the Year Nines all gangly and unco in their Christmas gear. Mucking around and singing a song together.

Adam walks down to the river, wearing an elf's costume.

Leni looks up, sees Adam and then throws the rest of the tinsel at me to finish up. It's been strained between them. It seems the break-up is final.

'See you upstairs,' Leni says to both of us.

'Don't say a bloody word,' Adam warns me as I give his outfit a slow clap. 'The Year Ten girls forced me to wear it.'

Sam and Leni are choosing random crews for the day and giving us a pep-up speech before summer holidays. Penny is sitting with the firsts. She's got her head down, picking at a thread of cotton on her zootie. Her plait is threaded with silver tinsel and she's got angel wings on. She's a few feet away, but I can smell her. Flowers and coconut. The same as she did the night of the party.

I've backed off but I'd love to ask her where she's going for her holidays. I've heard she's going overseas with her family. If I knew I could look up the maps and photos of exotic countries and imagine her there. I wish it were me leaving. Getting on a plane, wheels pulling off the tarmac.

'You all have your training diaries so write in them, every day,' says Leni. 'Stick to your training schedules. Get together if you can. Don't get sucked into lying on the beach doing nothing. Oh, and if anyone needs to borrow an ergo over the summer, speak to Mr West after the row.'

'A weekend rowing camp will be held 21 to 24 January in Sale,' says Sam. 'Boat loading is at 7 am sharp here. After that the buses will leave. We will be right into ergos, seat racing and long, training rows. Bring your A game and you'll have a good time. Come with a gut from too much Christmas pudding and you'll suffer.'

Everyone groans. Rowing camp is a festival of muscle aches and early nights.

Sam puts two boxes out on a table. 'For fun we're going to mix up the crews today. Pick a number from box one and that's your crew. Choose a piece of paper from box two and that's what you have to think about during school holidays.'

I pull out the number five and a piece of paper.

In Leni's writing is the quote: 'Our greatest weakness lies in giving up. The most certain way to succeed is always to try just one more time.' – Thomas Edison.

Did Leni rig it so I got this piece of paper? Does she know how much I long to give up?

Leni

Adam grabs me before our last row. We haven't spoken since we broke up. Not even a text message. He's good at silence. 'Leni, can we talk?' he says, pulling me into an empty bay of the shed.

We sit on stretchers, facing each other.

'I'm sorry I haven't called. I've wanted to, but I think it's better if we get a clean break from each other.'

Part of me was a little hurt Adam hadn't tried to get in contact, even if I didn't want to be his girlfriend anymore.

'Yeah, that's okay,' I say. 'You don't want me to text?'

'Maybe next year. For now, I might just try to move on.'

Adam gets up, gives me a kiss on the cheek. Still no *jtzooum*.

'Bye, Leni. Merry Christmas.'

'Bye, Adam. You too.'

★

I'm rowing with Year Tens, a few guys in the thirds and, naturally, Sam. The universe keeps throwing us together. Thank you, universe. Everyone's wearing Santa hats and costumes. But I refuse to. Rachel is coxing and tries to make me change my mind.

'Come on, it's Christmas! I'm coxing, for goodness sake. The end of the boat might snap off. Have some fun. Don't be such a grinch.'

'I don't do silly hats,' I say. 'And I'm not a grinch.'

Sam and I ferry an armful of oars to the bank. There's so much I want to say to him. So many loose ends. But in an instant we're enveloped by the rest of the crew, chattering, laughing and singing Christmas songs.

'Hands on!' shouts Rachel.

Sam sits behind me in seven seat. He reaches forward and shoves a hat on my head, before I can protest. Because it's him, I let it sit there. Feeling ridiculous. I set off as I always do – rowing hard and with purpose. No point wasting a session.

'It's a fun row, Leni!' shouts Laura from the bank. 'Let's try to keep the rating down okay?'

We row like hacks, the boat tipping wildly and everyone laughing and mucking around. Laura asks us to do a drill where we all swap seats by walking down the sides of the boat. At one point Sam and I swap and he has to crawl over my head, his crotch literally millimetres from my face.

We do some fun races against the other crews, but nobody cares who wins. Nobody, except me.

As we head in, there's a moment where Rachel asks for silence and tells us these are our last thirty strokes for the year.

'Make every stroke count,' she says.

We roll forward on the balls of our feet. As I lock my blade on the water, I feel seven other bodies, all different shapes, sizes and ages, right there with me. We push together, gliding towards freedom.

All the boats are put away. Later, Dad will tune them up and make sure they're all clean as a whistle and ready for the onslaught of rowing camp. But for now he's turning sausages on a barbecue set up on the balcony. A line-up of hungry boys wait impatiently with plastic plates in their hands. 'Are they ready yet, Mr Poppa?' asks Tom Kendrick, for the hundredth time.

Dad waves his tongs to shoo him away. 'Get back locust,' he laughs. 'Don't rush chef.'

Sam and I have drifted to each other's side, we can't keep away. I'm trying not to show everyone how much I want to be with him. Half listening to my crew's summer plans. Beach houses. Summer internships at magazines. Trips overseas.

They've tried to keep it quiet, but Aiko is having virtually the entire crew down to her parents' farm near Woodend after Christmas. They'll all swim in the dam and share secrets and get even closer to each other and further away from me. Not being with Adam had made my stocks dive at school. I felt it the instant he broke it off.

'Who wants food?' Dad shouts across the room.

Sam jumps to his feet. 'Want a vegie burger?' he asks the group. I feel like he's talking just to me.

'Vegie? No freaking way, mate, give me meat!' says Nick. The boys like to tease Sam for being a vegetarian. It's all part of the Buddhist thing.

'Yeah, I will,' I say, although eating is the last thing on my mind.

Sam comes back to the group, his hands full.

'You catching up with your older woman during the break, Sammy?' asks Nick.

Older woman?

'Don't know what you're talking about, Josh,' Sam says. But he looks furious.

'When you going to admit you have a woman? Mate, Bee Henry is gorgeous. How old is she anyway, nineteen? Does she buy beer for you?'

Who is Bee Henry? Does she have swirly handwriting and call him Sammy?

'Shut up, Nick!' shouts Sam. He throws one of the burgers at Nick's chest. It splats down the front.

'Food fight!' Charley shouts.

It's only because he's surrounded by people that I don't walk over to him and demand an explanation, push one of those burgers into his mysterious face.

'Relax, Camero. We're all jealous, mate,' says Nick, taking off his T-shirt. 'What's your secret?'

'If you don't shut up right now, I will throw you in the Yarra,' says Sam.

It's the closest I've seen Sam come to losing his cool. Meanwhile I feel sick thinking of all the things we did on Sunday. How much I had trusted him. I swallow hard, saliva rushing into my mouth. How could Sam think it was okay to be with me, without telling me he had a girlfriend? I feel so stupid. So used. I look sideways at Sam, who hands me the burger with an oily squelch. 'Sorry,' he says. We both know he doesn't mean spilling tomato sauce on my hands.

I blink back tears. 'It's not okay,' I whisper. I'm sure it's not loud enough for anyone else to hear.

I walk with as much dignity as I can down the stairs and burst into tears. I chuck the burger violently into a bin, run a hose over my hands and wet my face. I try to collect myself. I don't want to be seen crying by anyone. Especially not my crew. I can't go back to the barbecue so I find a hiding spot down the back of the shed. Pulling myself into a small ball on the concrete floor behind the boats.

I stay there for a while, listening to the scuff of feet on the floor above. Hearing a song being turned up and then turned down by a teacher. Footsteps creak on the wood stairs and I cross my fingers. *Be Sam, be Sam, be Sam.* He can make it all better. Just by saying he chooses me. *Choose me, choose, me, choose me.*

The instant I see the green thongs and thick calf muscle, I know it's not the guy I want. But it might be the right guy.

'I'm down here, Cris,' I say.

My brother can read me. Read my moods. Be there, even when I don't know I need him.

'Leni. Are you okay?' he asks.

'No,' I say. Knowing he will listen, not judge. It's time I came clean to him about Sam.

Cristian coaxes me back upstairs. I'm wearing his sunglasses over my red eyes and he's making sure I'm laughing with really bad jokes. He offered to confront Sam and have it out with him, but I didn't want a scene. I choose to ignore Sam and focus on breathing in and out.

Mum arrives from the hospital and I hug her tightly. We sit on the balcony as a family.

'Everything okay?' Cris says.

'Yeah. Everything's fine.'

After Sam leaves I search for Bee Henry under Sam's friends on Facebook. There's nothing. She's obviously the last person on the planet without a profile. I shift through Sam's photos and find her there. She's wearing a fifties-style yellow sundress and a straw fedora hat. Underneath the brim, she's got a wide smile, freckles and brown curly hair. She looks like a girl version of Sam. Absolutely gorgeous.

Closing my eyes I imagine him beside me on the balcony, his hand closing over mine, resting my head into his shoulder. I think back to that afternoon in his apartment when we rolled sleepily into each other. The beautiful, raw newness of it has faded and gone. The aftertaste is bitter. Nobody has ever let me down the way Sam did today.

I stare out at the river, at a couple walking down the path, holding hands. Even though my family is around me, I feel a loneliness that seeps right through to my bones.

★

I'm unpacking my rowing bag at home when I find the receipt.

Leni Popescu. Captain of Boats. Blazer pocket.

Order: $95.00. PAID.

The signature and the credit card details are Sam's.

He's scribbled a note along the bottom.

I've got your back. Love, Sam.

Love?

January

Three months to Head of the River

Leni

It seems like a blink and summer holidays are over. I'm on the bus, on our way to rowing camp in Sale. I look around at the squad. We've only been apart for six weeks, but everyone looks different. The boys have the beginnings of beards, longer hair and beach tans. The biggest transformation is Adam and Cristian. They are both 100 per cent ripped. Cris has dropped all his puppy fat and Adam's body has gone from sinewy to brawny.

Sam isn't here. No one has seen or heard from him since our final row. And he missed the bus and boat loading. Maybe he's decided to drop out in Byron with Bee. Have a bunch of kids on a farm, form some springy dreadlocks, smoke too much dope and turn his back on his private school past.

Part of me is relieved not to see him today. The other part put on foundation and waterproof mascara. That part is disappointed and pathetic.

The fifth crew are singing about falling in love, screeching the chorus at the top of their lungs and pretending they have microphones.

'When will it end?' Penny says, putting her hands over her ears. She's wearing an exotic silk sari, her fingers decorated in yellow-brown henna. Her time overseas is written all over her body. She seems older, more worldly. What has she done that I'm too scared to?

'How were your holidays?' asks Penny.

'Boring. I worked,' I say, looking out the window at the passing paddocks.

What did I achieve with my months of freedom? Just 3784 Target dollars in my bank account. Every dollar soaked in boredom, aching feet, pants that didn't fit and dug in around my waist and a borrowed name tag that didn't even say my name. All summer I was, 'Hello, my name is Sandiya'. The nice customers would say, 'Sandiya, that's a lovely name, unusual.' I'd nod and say thanks. It was a spare that I found in the break room. It used to belong to a silent Indian girl who lasted two weeks on the register before moving to Gloria Jeans on the second floor to sling coffees.

I should have more to show for my last summer holiday before Year Twelve. Penny's seen the Taj Mahal. What have I seen? The 86 tram and a fluorescent department store. The inside of a gym, the river, the Tan. I feel boring and quiet. To feel bigger I put on my rowing captain rugby top that says: *Leni Popesu – Captain of Boats* on the back in white lettering.

Funny thing is, wearing it makes me feel smaller.

'Are you nervous about camp?' Penny asks. 'I'm so scared. It was hard to do my training while I was travelling. Not too many ergos in India.'

'It'll be fine,' I say.

Truth is, I'm scared to death too. I can't eat properly. Even my morning bowl of cereal was a struggle. Soon there will be ergo trials. And there's no hiding from those. The rest of the camp will be hard yakka. The principal aim of taking us away from the city seems to be to flog us until we can barely stand.

Cristian

So here we are – rowing camp.

The place is bleak. We're staying at a Catholic college in Sale, on an isolated river in the middle of pretty much nowhere. There's nothing around. No shops. No trains. No buses. Nothing much else to do but row, row, row and row some more.

This year I'm not as nervous and unsure as past camps. Adam and I have our secret weapon and if everything goes to plan, it's unlikely anyone will beat us on erg scores. It's a matter of time before we're back in the firsts. Once I get back in I have to put my head down and row like hell until March. That's my ticket to freedom.

'Bloody hell, Poppa, you've dropped some weight,' says Charley as we get on the bus.

I'm swimming in my old clothes and had to spend some of my Bunnings money on getting new training gear.

It's hard not to notice I've become the incredible shrinking man. Mum keeps frowning at me and asking me if I've eaten a good breakfast.

I don't even recognise my body anymore and I don't know how to be in it. Sometimes at night, I run my hands down my front, feel the hip bones poking out and count the ribs appearing on my chest. Funny, I thought getting skinny would make me happy, but I've never been this unhappy.

'Laid off the pies,' I say, playing it down. 'Did some running.'

The last thing I need is too much attention.

On the bus I sit a few seats back from Penny and wish I was Leni so I could sit next to her. She looks different. Older. Her hair is longer and lighter from the sun, pulled up in a messy ponytail. She's carrying a sling bag on her shoulder embroidered with small green elephants. It's a long bus ride up, but I think about kissing the back of her neck for about 97.5 per cent of it.

Nick, Damo and Julian work on rigging up the boats in pastel boardshorts and no tops. Showing off the kind of tan you don't get working ten-hour shifts at Bunnings. I feel a pang of jealousy at their freedom. It's my first day off work since Christmas. At least, for once, I have money in my pocket.

'Fark, how good does Rach look this year?' says Julian, giving Rachel a slow wolf-whistle as she walks past in a skintight zootie. 'Wouldn't mind a piece of that.'

We've been assigned rooms. Boys in one wing and the girls in another. The coaches and their torches will patrol the perimeters. We might be horny now, but in a few hours we'll be too knackered to try any funny business. It's face plant after face plant into the musty single beds. All of us passed out like caterpillars in our sleeping bags.

'How was your Chrissy?' Adam asks. He's only just come back from the States and looks even more cut. He's passing off his thickly muscled thighs as a by-product of back-country skiing.

'Okay,' I say, remembering the way Mum insisted on hanging up stockings for Leni and I, even though we are far too old. The heaving table of Romanian food I had to bite my knuckles not to scoff down. The stray rowers and friends that came along afterwards for strong coffee and pastries. The few that stayed too long, laughing into the warm night. The traditional confusing call home to my grandparents Bunica and Bunela on a dodgy line.

'The same as always. Yours?'

'We had a sad lunch at a hotel in Aspen. Dad forgot to buy me presents, and then gave me his credit card as if that would make up for it. I missed my mum. Usually we spend Christmas with her.'

'Yeah, but you got to go skiing, didn't you?'

Adam looks at me, like maybe I missed the point entirely.

I'm attaching my riggers to the second boat when Westie taps me on the shoulder.

'Weigh in, Poppa.'

Adam shoots me a look and I nod at him. Sam Cam is late for camp. We are in prime position for a hostile takeover. Everything is going our way.

'Sure, no problem,' I say, without a hint of fear. My diet is monastic. Protein shakes, egg whites, skinned chicken, rice. It's so boring and repetitive I can hardly stand to put it in my mouth. All I can think about is the day after the Head of the River. When I can put away my zoot suits, let my blisters heal and never ever get up before light. Eat all the food.

We walk silently to the weights room and he places a small digital scale between us.

'Have a good break, sir?'

Mr West looks up from his clipboard, surprised. Informal chit-chat isn't his strong suit.

'I did, thank you,' Westie says. 'I became a granddad for the first time. Precious little baby boy. Can hardly believe I'm old enough. Seems like yesterday I was in the first boat myself.'

'What's his name, sir?' I ask.

'Arlo. Not crazy about the name, but I'm crazy about the kid.' He pulls his phone out of his pocket, shows me a picture of a squashed baby, its face wrinkled, eyes closed. I have no idea what to say.

'Cute,' I mumble.

Westie shoves the phone back into his pocket.

'On you get. By the look of you this is a formality. I've never seen such a dramatic transformation in such a short time. What have you been doing?'

'Not eating. Obviously.'

Westie frowns. 'You need to do this the right way, Cristian. One of my daughters faded away around your age. Had to be put in hospital. Drip fed. Took her ten years to recover. Tore our family to bits.' He pauses, then clears his throat. I'm stunned by the sudden revealing of Westie's family life and a shred of concern for my wellbeing. He pulls his feelings back in sharply. 'Make sure you're doing it the right way is all I'm saying. Nothing too crazy.'

'Sure,' I mutter.

I stand on the scale and don't even bother taking off my trainers. I know what I weigh. I'm obsessed with the numbers. I weigh myself every day, sometimes twice a day. I've been on a tasteless high-protein bodybuilding diet for months. I finally have the body I've always wanted. Narrow hips, a flat sixpack, wide shoulders, pecs, amazing biceps. On the outside at least, I'm perfect. Pity my head is such a mess.

'Don't want to remove those first?' asks Westie.

I shrug and look down at the number between my feet.

'Don't think I need to, do I?'

'Cristian Popescu. Welcome back to the first boat.'

'That's it, I'm back in?'

'The five seat is rightfully yours, son. Fair play. You earned your way back to the top boat. You look fit.'

I won't be satisfied until Adam is back in the first eight, too. He won't get his chance to show off his radical improvement until erg trials. I can't wait.

Leni

I'm sharing a room with Rachel and Penny. Rachel was disappointed not to be rooming with her besties, Millie and Aiko. I was happy we didn't have to choose sides.

'What did you do this summer, captain?' Rachel asks as we ferry boats from the trailer, string them out on stretchers and re-rig.

'Not much. Worked. You?'

'Same. Maccas. I had New Year's off, but the rest of the time it was "Can I take your order? Want fries with that? Would you like to try our new McFlurry?"'

'How are you today? Would you like a bag with that? Cash or card? Have a nice day,' I say.

We share a look of complete understanding of minimum wage existence.

'And now we've gone from the frying pan to the fire, literally,' says Rachel. 'Hot enough for ya?'

It's hot. Of course. The same cruel rowing camp joke. It rains when we're all at the beach. Then as soon as we arrive at Sale, the sun rises, high and unforgiving and the temperature becomes unbearable.

'Weather report says rain later in the week. We should enjoy the sun while we can,' Penny says as she screws in a bolt.

'You're a glass half full sort of gal, aren't you,' says Rachel, tweaking Penny's cheek.

Rachel and I work opposite each other on the eight. Slotting seats back onto slides and fitting riggers. We get it done quickly and without fuss. Usually Rachel would be trying to get someone else to boat rig for her. She's different this year. Less lazy. More present. Summer has changed her too.

'Mr Poppa? Can you check our boat?' Rachel calls.

Dad arrives to look over our work, checking the heights and making sure every bolt is tight.

'Lovely work girls, keep this up and I lose job.'

He's wearing a floppy cricket hat, zinc on his nose. He hasn't stopped all day. Dad's in hot demand on rowing camp. He can barely walk a few metres without getting stopped with a 'Mr Poppa! Can you help me?'

In contrast, Westie peers into an iPad in the shade, scrutinising footage and data. Barely even laying a finger on the boats.

'What did you do for New Year's?' Aiko asks across the boat. She seems put out that Rachel and I paired up for rigging.

'Hung out at home,' I say.

'You spent New Year's with your parents?' Aiko asks.

Everyone looks at me like I have two heads. Waiting for me to explain such a massive lapse in coolness.

'I was with my parents, too,' says Penny, rescuing me. 'We were in India. It was the best night of my life. Actually my parents went to bed later than I did.'

I smile at Penny and she winks at me. I can see why Cristian can't let it go with her.

'Come on, let's go for a row.'

Two rows and a good sleep under our belt and it's time for the real testing to begin. Laura assembles us under a shady tree next to the river, a cooling breeze skimming off the water. We've only been here a day but I feel dirty already, dust has infiltrated my luggage and I'm damp with sweat.

Laura sits down, cross-legged. She's wearing a wet rag around her neck and has a bucket full of extra bandannas soaking in cold water. She hands them out.

'Tie them around your necks. You won't win any fashion awards, but I won't have you falling out of the boat with heatstroke. Also sunscreen, hat, long-sleeve tops. No sunburn please. It will sap your energy and you know what always starts rowing camp.'

Everyone groans, except me.

'That's right, chicks. Erg trials.'

'A general piece of advice,' says Laura. 'Don't smash out the first 500 metres. It's counterproductive in this heat. You'll lactate up and fall to bits. Stay within yourselves for the first half. Work into it. Settle early and keep a nice steady pace.'

I look around the group and clock the cold terror on every face. I'm terrified too. I've trained, but work knocked me around. My back is tight and sore from standing all day and the last training piece I did on the erg was slower than I expected.

'Don't look so scared,' Laura says. 'Let's get them out of the way and move onto the important stuff – getting on the water. One more thing. US scouts will be out here again this season, looking at rowers for their college program. I won't let you know when they're here or who they're interested in. Mr West and I agree you shouldn't have that added pressure. But for any of you in Year Twelve who might be looking to study in the States, it's a good opportunity. I have a few friends on scholarship over there and they have great sports facilities and coaching.'

Penny and I line up at a tap to fill our water bottles. She puts her ponytail in her mouth and chews on it, looking worried. Nobody will relax until the trials are done.

'You interested in the US?' she asks me. 'Wouldn't it be amazing to study overseas? You should go for it. You're the best rower in the firsts. Easily.'

'Maybe,' I say. But in truth I hadn't even considered it. Everything in my life was so locked down already. My plan if I didn't get a scholarship to the Australian Institute of Sport for rowing was to study medicine at Melbourne Uni. I'd row for Mercantile rowing club – that was my dad's club. Trial for the Under-19 Youth crews. Maybe even snag my way into the junior Aussie team. America was too far away, wasn't it?

Dad catches up with me en route to my trial. He's got grease smudged under one eye and his T-shirt is covered in it. I reach out and wipe the mark from his face.

'You girls trialling now?'

'Yeah,' I say. I've gone from anxious to sweaty panic. I feel exhausted and floppy. So much rests on a good result here.

'Row it hard from start. Don't leave anything behind. You're tougher than other girls. The AIS, they look erg scores.'

The Australian Institute. They were looking for rowers too. Like I need any more pressure. I feel like my head's going to blow up thinking about it.

'But Laura said to ease into it,' I say.

'Nah, let them chase you. What's PB?'

'Seven forty.'

'Break seven minutes thirty today. Easy.'

'I dunno, it's pretty hot,' I say. But Dad claps my shoulder and pushes me towards the ergos.

'Go for it.'

I run to the toilet for a nervous wee before it begins. In the cubicle I use a black marker to write my dream time on both of my thighs. My hand shaking as I trace out the numbers. **7.20**.

Every time I take a stroke I'll be able to see that magic number. I'll be fulfilling a promise to myself.

Eight ergs are lined up in the gym, waiting quietly for their next victims. This is the worst part of rowing: the sheer, awful and undeniable pain from your toenails to your scalp. There are no shortcuts. You have to hurt if you want to do well. I sit down to stretch.

'Ready girls? Let's go!' says Laura. I wish I were her. Standing next to the machines and not rowing them.

'I *hate* erg trials,' Rachel mutters as we walk to the gallows.

'Me too,' I agree.

We get on the machines and Laura clears each monitor, ready for a start. The ergo vents circulate hot air around the room. Every trial is 2000 metres long. Two hundred strokes. Two kilometres. We used to be tested over 1 kilometre, but we're senior squad now. The screws have been tightened. The whole painful ordeal takes just over seven and a half minutes.

Seven minutes might not seem like much. It's three tram stops, half a recess break, or the time it takes to cook and eat a packet of instant noodles. But seven minutes can change everything. You can have sex for the first time, jump out of a plane, step in front of a speeding train and die on impact or write a song or a piece of code that captures the world. In my case I could row an ergo score that could change the path of the rest of my life. It could determine where I end up next. University? The AIS? In an Aussie crew?

As I hold the handle and breathe up, the bad thoughts come.

You're tired, Leni. Your back is sore. It's hot, you don't feel good now; imagine how you'll feel at the 1000-metre mark?

Another voice chimes in. This one is my good fairy.

You're fine, Len. Relax, it's only a few minutes. Breathe. Suck it up. You can do this.

I want to feel unbeatable but I'm sapped of energy. I'm so tired I let out a huge yawn. I could crawl away and sleep for hours. I don't want to be here. I'd even rather be on the check-out. On Boxing Day.

Rachel is on the machine next to me. She lets out a sharp breath, looks at the ceiling and closes her eyes.

'You ready?' I say, a little more aggressively than I expect.

She's lost her tummy over the summer and looks fit. Is she a dark horse?

'Too bad if I'm not,' she says, managing a smile. 'Good luck.'

'You too.'

We sit forward on the machines and enjoy our final pain-free seconds.

'Attention! Row!' shouts Laura.

I plan to follow Laura's advice and work my way into the trial, but then I hear Dad's voice behind my ergo after my first twenty strokes. He's speaking in Romanian. No one else can understand what he's saying, but I can.

'Go, Leni. Don't be timid. You're cruising. Bring up the rating. Go now. Harder.'

I change my race plan and push my legs down with force, spinning the handle quicker round the back turn. Rachel seems to be sticking to Laura's advice, her strokes are smooth and controlled.

Smooth and controlled won't get me back the stroke seat, I think, going for an effort for ten. *Smooth and controlled won't get me a scholarship to the AIS.* Each stroke feels heavy and doubt creeps back in.

You're exhausted now. How are you ever going to make 2 ks, Leni? You've got so far to go. You've stuffed it. You should've listened to Laura. It's too late now.

My breathing is raggedy and out of control. A stitch gathers in my shoulder and stabs between my right collarbone. I focus on the readout in front of me, willing for the numbers not to creep up.

Vooum, vooum, vooum go the machines as we pull on the chains. The 750-metre mark slips by. Still so far to go.

You can't keep this up. Take a light stroke, just one, then get back into it.

Usually I can block out the negative and push through the pain, but today I'm hanging on by my finger tips. I sneak a look at Rachel's readout and panic. She's a few seconds under my time and in control. When I turn my head back, I've taken a couple of light strokes without realising. I speed up to make up ground. My stroke rate pops up to thirty-two. I'm taking one and a half strokes for Rachel's one. She looks amazing. So strong.

Focus on your own bloody erg! I berate myself.

Laura comes up next to me. 'Breathe up. Over halfway now. You're doing great.'

Laura means to be inspiring, but her words sink my hopes. If I feel this terrible now, I'm in for a world of hurt in the second act. I make an involuntary grunting sound. My lungs are stretched so thin they feel like burning paper. My legs are screaming with lactate and saliva pools in my mouth. It tastes metallic. I swallow it and close my eyes, counting out another five strokes.

When I look up, the room is spinning. It's so hot in here, the only air circulated by the wheels of the machines. My leg muscles shake and I'm desperate to stop. Even for a few seconds. My heart pounds in my forearms, neck and throat. The beat jumps around like a loose frog.

I look at the screen. It says 1250 metres. I have another 750 to go.

You're not going to make it, the voice says coldly. *It hurts too much. Stop. No one will mind. You can say you felt sick. Take the erg another time.*

'Water!' I croak.

I want to drop my handle and quit. It's all I can think about. That, and not vomiting. My lunch repeats in my mouth. *Don't vomit. Don't vomit. Don't vomit* I pray with each stroke. The resistance on the end of my handle is like pulling an anchor through wet sand.

Dad picks up my water bottle and dumps cool liquid on my neck and head.

'Nearly there, Leni,' he says, and I hate him for being able to stand there feeling no pain, just observing mine. 'Crank it up now. All legs, all heart. What you got left?'

The water helps and I can see The End. Taste the sweet Gatorade swishing in my pasty mouth, feel my heart rate thudding back to a slow, steady beat as I lie spreadeagled on a mat. Hear the conversation I'll have post ergo. 'Seven-twenty. Thanks I'm pleased. What did you get?' Everyone will want to know my score and I'll act modest, like it was no big deal.

Fifty more strokes. I start to count them.

One. Two. Ouch! Ouch! Ouch! Four. Or was that five? Oh my God. This hurts so bad. I can't do this. Seven. Ouch!

Dad starts yelling behind me. His voice irritates me so much I want to turn around in my seat and scream SHUT UP! GO AWAY! LEAVE ME ALONE!

'Go! Go! You break 7.30, Leni. Five hundred to go! Lift!'

Next to me Rachel is lifting too, and Laura is pushing her to the end. She'll beat me, I know it. My mind goes blank and black.

'I can't! I can't!' I shout. There's no more rev in me. My time starts to drop away. I'm fading.

'You can do this, Leni!' says Laura, seeing me fall apart. 'Bring back the power.'

I don't know why I stop rowing. One minute I'm about to break my PB and the next I've got my head between my

179

knees, my time slipping away. Rachel forging ahead with her slow, hard strokes.

'Come on, Leni!' Dad yells. 'Keep going! You nearly at end!'

Maybe if I pick up my handle I could scrape a respectable time. In the top four to five in the firsts. But not the best. Not 7.20. Everything is ruined. I've failed.

I tumble off the machine.

'This is your fault! Can't you just be my dad? I already have a coach!'

He couldn't look more shocked if I'd slapped him across the face. I burst into tears and Laura comes towards me, like she's going to try to hug me.

'No! Leave me alone.'

I use my last remaining modicum of energy to get the hell away from them and their sympathetic faces.

Cristian

It's thirty-five degrees in the shade and I'm wearing stupid red socks. As if having them on my feet makes me any better than the guys in the seconds. I roll them off my sweaty feet and dump them in the bottom of the boat. Sitting in the firsts again isn't nearly as satisfying as I'd thought it would. I've risked everything to get here. Put my body through hell and it feels like any other row.

'Where's Sam?' asks Damo behind me. 'Anyone heard from him?'

I shrug and there's a silence down the boat. Sam has disappeared into thin air. Nobody has seen or heard from him for weeks.

'Our captain's done a runner,' says Damo. 'That's bloody fantastic.'

'Just focus, guys,' says Charley into his headset.

That's the problem. There's nothing to distract us out here in the sticks. Flat brown water, overhanging trees and endless paddocks. The girls are off doing their ergs, so there's not even the hint of a bare leg or a pair of tits to help break the boredom. I chug back on some water, pull down my hat and anticipate a long, tedious outing.

'Forget about what Sam is doing. We've got our meat seat Cristian back,' says Charley. 'Although he has much less, er, meat these days.'

Westie zooms up on his tinny, ready to break us.

'Stop dicking about and row,' he shouts into his megaphone. I can't stop thinking about Westie having daughters and a grandkid. Which means someone actually loved him enough to have kids with him. Was it possible he did have a human heart and not a lump of stone?

We sit forward and it's like I never left. All the same bodies. All the same issues. When we break out of warm-up into full crew work, it's creaky and slow. Westie is back in my face, shouting out picky technique calls and generally making a pain of himself, when what we need is a bit of quiet to feel the stillness of this place. To find our rhythm again.

'Come on!' he shouts. 'This isn't the Portsea front beach! Sloppy technique! Let's go through those balance drills again.'

Just as I'm losing hope that I can survive the rest of the season, even if I am in the top boat, I feel a hand on my back.

'Nice to have you back man,' Julian says from the four seat. 'Wasn't the same without you.'

There's a click of realisation. I didn't miss the boat or the racing or the endless drills. I missed the guys.

Dad stops me as I go into erg trials later in the day. 'Your sister blew up her erg.'

'Leni blew up? What happened?'

'I don't know.' Dad looks worried, a frown creases his brow.

'No words of wisdom for me?' I say, expecting a full wind up. Dad's always full-on before trials.

'Row your own erg. I meddle too much already.'

'Really?'

'Yes. Do your best.'

Adam and I suck down a foul-tasting protein shake. The pact we made months ago is about to come to fruition. It occurs to me that maybe we should do well on our trials, but not too well. But it's too late for that conversation now.

'Boys. Time to jump on the machines,' says Westie.

As I pull my zootie over my leaner body I hear a hard, determined voice inside myself say, *bring it*. It's a voice I haven't heard in a long time.

I'm waiting for my turn, listening to eight machines whoosh, and the grunts and moans of the Year Eleven guys before us in complete, utter agony. As they finish up they stagger from the machines and roll on the floor, groaning, heaving for air and writhing in pain. One of them vomits into his hands, the rest crawl towards the showers and water.

Adam wipes down a machine dripping in the last guy's sweat, blood and tears. He means business today. There's a score to settle. I sit down next to him.

'The firsts,' I say to him and we bump fists.

He sits forward on the slide and grasps the handle, readying his body for the impact.

'Attention! Row!' shouts Westie.

Adam comes out of the blocks like a greyhound snapping for a rabbit. I steady myself, using relaxed powerful strokes to cruise along beside him. The other guys drop away from us in the second 500. We're so far ahead, I consider backing off, but my body doesn't want to. I'm so pumped, so primed, that I can't do anything *but* smash it. How far can I take it?

Westie stands behind us and it makes me find even more strength in my legs. I feel like I'm pushing down a block of flats.

'Easy you two. Leave something in the tank,' he warns.

Little does he know what's powering our tanks. We'd be thrown out of the team in a second if he could see what was in our bloodstreams.

The 2 ks fly by. I don't count strokes. Don't feel the searing pain of years past. I just eat up metre after metre until I'm staring at the finish line.

'Let's go!' shouts Westie. 'Final push lads!'

Everyone stands around for the finale and I can tell it's going to be a massive time for Adam and me. A PB by miles.

As we wind down the last twenty strokes, I'm pulling so hard I think I might pop a vein and Adam is super focused, closing his eyes and muttering to himself. My chest burns and sweat pours down my face, but I feel good. I'm breathing up big and I know I've got heaps left. This erg is mine.

The room counts us down and I reach the end of the 2000 first, dropping my handle dramatically, sucking up oxygen. Making everyone think this is a feat of muscle, bone and heart. I roll up and down on the slide, keeping my body moving so I don't cramp up.

Adam gets there next, thirty seconds behind me. He tips back his head and gasps for air. I thrust water at him, but he shakes his head. He dry heaves with his whole body, but nothing comes out. The other guys finish up – far enough away that it's a *fait accompli*. We are both back in the first boat. For the first time, I think that this idea of Adam's was the best he's ever had.

I grab Adam and lift him off the machine and even though his legs are jelly, I get him to walk around the room a few times with me and take a few sips from his water bottle. He looks awful. He isn't recovering as well as I am. We sit on the balcony for a while, looking out to the river and the girls getting ready to go out rowing.

'Feel better now?'

Adam nods, but he's still pale. 'Took it right to the edge.'

Westie comes over with his iPad.

'The rumours are true, then,' he says.

Guilt and shame force their way up to my cheeks and make them burn.

'What rumours?' I say defensively.

'That you two have been doing extra weights sessions. Training on the sly. I don't encourage it, but your results are dramatically improved.'

Adam manages to smile. We did it.

'Adam you rowed an impressive 6.22. Breaking your PB by ...' He consults his iPad. 'Forty seconds. Poppa, you broke the Australian thirteen to eighteen-year-old ergometer record in a time of 5.52. Congratulations boys, you are both officially back in the first eight.'

Leni

Rachel finds me in our room. I'm lying on my bed and turning over the erg trial in my head. The weather has turned and it's pelting down rain. Slabs of it are dripping from the window frame, turning everything to mud. Our break will be over soon and the afternoon session will begin. I have to leave this room somehow. There's a knock at the door and it opens slowly.

'Oh Captain, My Captain,' Rachel sing songs. I'm in no mood for her jokes.

She walks into the room and sits on my bed. I roll away from her.

'We're ready to get out on the water. You know the

rowing camp motto – monsoonal rain, hail or shine. Are you okay, after the erg test?'

'Of course I'm not okay. What time did you get?'

'Who cares?'

'I do. Laura does. The school does.'

'Put an erg on the water and it sinks. It's what we do *in* the boat that counts the most. Anyway, you weren't the only one to blow out. Meg hit the deck at the 1000-metre mark.'

'Meg? Are you comparing me to the worst rower in our boat?'

'If I was, would it matter?' she says. 'We're all in the same crew. We all win or lose together. If you didn't want to be in a team, you should've sculled this year.'

'What's everyone saying about my erg?'

Rachel puts her hand on my leg, gingerly.

'You know what people say about you, Leni? That you're amazing. Maybe the best rower we'll ever sit in a boat with. That one day, you'll go to the Olympics, like your parents.'

'You don't have to say that to make me feel better.'

'I'm not. I'll row this last season. Maybe a couple more at uni, socially. It's fun and it keeps me fit. But I'm not going to any Olympics. I'll watch you on telly and tell people I beat you on an erg test once.'

'But I'm the captain. I'm not supposed to die on an erg,' I say.

'There's a reason you were voted captain and it's nothing to do with your stupid erg score. We all look up to you. The younger girls want to *be* you. On the river, you're a rock star. So get out there. Talk to the other crews. Get your head out of your own arse and ask them how they're going. Give them someone to follow and be the best rower you can be. That's what a real captain does. Pull it together.'

'Are you always this blunt?' I say. 'I mean you could've sugar-coated it a little.'

'My mum never lets me get away with sulking. She says I've got it too good. I'm not going to let you either.'

Like in the boat I follow her lead. I change into clean training gear and pull a slicker over my head. Grab my water bottle and my hat.

'One more thing,' Rachel says. 'There's no point us being rivals. Whether I'm in the stroke seat or you are, when we line up for the Head of the River, we're going to need each other. Forget about erg scores and seat races. Let's be a crew. Row well, win some races, maybe even have a couple of laughs. Okay?'

She puts her arm around me, like she does with her besties. 'You gotta relax, Leni, you're far too uptight.'

We walk down to the boats together and even though Millie and Aiko are there too, Rachel keeps her arm slung over my shoulders, right through the crew chat. And I let her.

We row the rising, pockmarked river, Laura trailing us in a speedboat. Raindrops the size of peas roll off the peak of my hat and my hands slip on the wet handle. I shake my head, but the rain comes harder still. The rain soaks through my zootie, right through to my undies.

Usually wet outings bring a dark cloud over my mood.

187

But today, I see the funny side. When we stop to do roll up drills, water sloshes around our feet. The rain is attacking us sideways, above, below. I can't stop giggling. We can barely see a few metres in front of us. I'm blinded by the water running into my eyes.

'You find this weather funny, Leni?' Laura asks into her megaphone, huddling under a slicker.

'I don't know why I'm laughing,' I admit.

The unstoppable rain and my soggy undies seem hysterically funny. Then it starts hailing.

In front of me Rachel gets the giggles too and behind me Millie catches on, then Penny and Meg, all the way down to the bow. The whole boat cracks up. The harder it hails, the harder we laugh. Even Aiko gives up trying to get us into line.

'Bugger this,' says Laura, looking up at the grey, closed-in sky. 'Middle of summer and it's hailing. Let's ditch this session and get dry. At least you girls still have your sense of humour.'

As we pull the boat into the staging, we're still laughing and talking. The rain has broken up a dark stagnant pond, revealing clear water underneath. After we put the boat on racks, I spot a group of Year Nines in the rain. They've decided it's so wet they might as well have a swim in the river, and they're cavorting on the bank, sopping wet. Usually I'd ignore them but I have a job to do. Like it or not – I'm in charge of this rabble.

'Oi!' I shout at them. 'You lot!'

I gather up an armful of dry towels and beckon them inside. 'Let's go, girls. Get out of the rain!'

They run towards the shed and shiver around me as I hand out towels.

'Dry yourselves off. I'm going to make hot chocolates for everyone upstairs in the dining hall,' I say. Group hot chocolates. Could anything be less me?

They look at me in shock, drying off their hair and bodies, teeth chattering. I've never spoken to any of them. I don't know their names. That has to change. I remember how much I looked up to previous captains. How they never paid me the slightest bit of attention and I yearned for it. I have a chance to be a different type of captain this year.

'Wet gear off, hot showers, dry clothes and I'll see you in the hall in ten minutes,' I say, liking how my voice sounds. Strong, almost motherly.

'Training hard?' I say to one of them as she passes by. Tall and solid, she could be a future first-boat rower.

'Yeah.'

'Good. Having fun too?'

'Yeah.'

'Good. That's what camp is about. What's your name?'

'Amelia.'

'I'm Leni.'

'I know,' she says, and finally gives me a shy smile.

Dad pulls me into the empty training room before dinner. I flinch when I see the ergo machines. There should be crime scene tape draped across them.

'Come, sit,' says Dad, patting a seat. It seems so innocent now. Not the dreaded lump of steel that beat me to a bloody pulp.

I roll up and down on the slide, the wheels turning gently on metal. Dad sits on the machine next to me and does the same. Outside dinner has started. We can hear the muted roar of starving rowers clawing for plates of hot food. The smell of barbecued meat makes me hungry. I want this father–daughter chat to be brief.

'Why did I stop?' I say. 'You know everything about rowing. Everything about my rowing. So why did it happen?'

'I can't tell you that, Leni,' Dad says, switching to Romanian so I know this isn't going to be a short chat. 'Every trial is a mental game. You're fit enough to do 7.20. Your body was strong, but your head gave up today. You got spooked.'

'My brain was weak? Nothing to do with it being a furnace and going out too hard on your advice? I couldn't keep it up. I'm obviously not as good as you think. I couldn't even break 7.30.'

'Don't be the rower that makes excuses after a poor result,' Dad says. 'You're just starting out in this sport. In rowing years, you're a baby. If you progress to senior crews, you'll push yourself further than you can even imagine sitting here right now. You will scream for mercy. You'll summon every fibre of your being, every ounce of energy trying to claw your way to the line first. You'll be ten times fitter, stronger, faster and tougher than you are now. Today was a lesson. You'll face so many more in the future.'

'I learnt a lesson by falling apart during an erg?'

'Did you learn you can be beaten?' asks Dad.

'Yes.'

'You're human?'

'Yes.'

'You have weakness?'

'Maybe you're my weakness,' I say. I don't mean it, but I want it to be someone else's fault.

'Maybe,' Dad agrees. 'Maybe your lesson was not to listen to your silly old father.'

'Why *did* you tell me to go hard? It wasn't the right thing today.'

'It's tough for me not to guide you. I taught you and Cristian to row. I feel like I know you best. Better than these coaches. But I have to trust them. I have to let go. I've spoken to Laura. We've agreed I'll stay out of the way and not offer my opinion, unless I'm asked. I wish I'd been across the room during that trial, not in your ear.'

I feel torn. I've always loved having Dad by my side. He gives me strength.

'Sometimes I will ask you for advice. Would that be okay?'

'I'll always be there for you. You're my daughter.'

'Should we go and eat?' I ask. 'I'm starving.'

'Yes, go. Never get between a teenager and their food,' Dad says.

'You coming?'

Dad straps his feet into the ergo and picks up the handle.

'In a little bit,' he says.

His body may be ageing, but his rowing style is polished to perfection. Each stroke flows gracefully into the next, his tree-trunk legs revving the wheel slowly into a crescendo of power. He takes it up a notch, knowing I'm watching. Then he smiles and waves me away.

Cristian

Leni sits with me at dinner. Her plate is heaving and she shoves food into her mouth, stopping only to gulp down a glass of milk.

'Hungry?'

'Starving,' she says with a full mouth.

I'm picking at a flaccid salad and a gristly piece of steak. It's hard to choke it down, but I need the energy to get through camp. I suck back at a sports drink, trying to satisfy the awful thirst. Since I started on the pills, I can't get rid of the dryness in my mouth. I wish I could chuck the packets in the bin. I dream about Mum's cakes and stews. I'm starving, too, but in a different way to Leni.

'Okay after today?' I say. It's not right. I should have crashed out, not her.

'All good now. I heard you had a blinder.'

Nobody could have guessed this is how camp would turn out. Leni dying at the 1500-metre mark and me – former fatty – taking the whole thing out.

'Ergo gods smiled today.'

My record is all anyone wants to talk about, but it feels like a poisoned chalice. I didn't earn this time. I cheated.

'You'll get that 7.20,' I say to Leni. 'You're so strong, you just had a bad day.'

'Thanks, Cris.'

After our plates are cleared, everyone starts banging the sides of their glasses with their knives and Westie walks up to the front of the room.

'Someone in this room did something extraordinary today,' he says. He pauses for effect and the silence deepens. People turn to look at me.

'Cristian Popescu didn't just do an erg trial. He smashed the school, state and Australian record for under-nineteen-year-olds over 2000 metres. According to Google, our very own Cristian is now ranked the ninth fastest eighteen-year-old in the world. *In. The. World*,' he says, stressing each word.

Leni ruffles my hair as I look down at the table. I don't feel proud. I'm a cowardly, dirty con artist. Completely undeserving of all this attention and admiration. Everyone starts stomping their feet on the floor, like they're at a rock gig and they want an encore. I glance at Adam and he's leading the noise and clapping. I'm his science experiment gone right. He wolf-whistles between two fingers.

Thankfully Westie settles the room down and moves onto other news items.

'In other developments, we welcome Cristian and Adam Langley back into the first boat for the duration of the camp. Your co-captain Sam Camero has also recently arrived and is settling into his room. Sam has been absent due to a family matter and I expect you'll make him feel welcome. He's still a valued member of our first eight and will be making up his missed ergo tomorrow morning first thing.'

'He shouldn't have come,' I say, in solidarity with Leni. I still hate the guy for doing the dirty on my sister. I was right about him. He's shifty.

'Yeah,' she agrees.

Dad shakes my hand, then pulls me into a hug.

'Well done!' he says. 'Amazing, Cris. I knew you could do it.'

It feels good, even if I swindled my way back into the firsts, to bask in Dad's full, golden attention. To see pride, rather than disappointment on his face.

As we shuffle out of the room towards an early night, I catch the eye of Damien Yang. One of the guys dropped from the first eight to let Adam and I back in. He has tears in his eyes.

'Tough break, man,' I say to him. 'I'm sorry.'

He nods, but can't speak. There couldn't be a worse feeling than being dropped at rowing camp with three months to go until the Head of the River. I feel a surge of fresh guilt, but brush it aside. Rowing's tough. You have to be tougher to survive.

Adam claps me over the shoulders as we walk towards our room. 'Woo Hoo! Didn't I tell you we'd be back?'

I should feel like celebrating, but after the high of the ergo earlier, all I have the energy for is collapsing into my sleeping bag. I'm so exhausted. I'm usually up half the night, worrying about small stuff, blinking into the darkness, my pulse racing. I have to fire up my phone and watch podcasts until I can fall asleep again. It's hard to believe a few months ago I used to crash out all night in a warm, calm cocoon. I miss that.

'Long way to go yet,' I say. But we both know crew shuffles are unlikely now. 'I think we should play it down a little,' I add in a whisper. 'Don't you think maybe I did a little too well today?'

'Mate, you are Vasile Popescu's son, you could rip the handle off the ergo and no one would even raise an eyebrow. We are home free, Cris. Enjoy it.'

Leni

I don't hear him until he's right next to me in the dark, breathing loud enough to wake me, saying my name in a loud whisper.

'Leni ... Leni.'

I'm dragged out of a black sludge, 3 am sleep. The kind of sleep that whacks you over the head for ten hours. My body aches all over from training. When I move, it protests.

'Are you awake?'

I sit up, confused, and blink into the pitch black, reaching out with my arm. I'm frightened and I have no idea where I am or why someone is whispering my name. Is this a nightmare? It feels real.

Slowly, I see his silhouette. Make out his body shape. He catches my hand and I snatch it away.

'Sam? You scared me. What are you doing in here? Get out. If the coaches catch us, we'll be sent home.'

I'm still so angry with him. Anger mixed with desire. It's a confusing sensation.

I reach for the water bottle beside my bed, taking a long sip. I'm sweating inside my nylon sleeping bag and I unzip it and let my hot limbs free. Rain patters on the tin roof. My brain is in soft focus.

'I had to talk to you,' he says.

'Now? You could've called or texted. You've had all summer.'

'I wanted to say I'm sorry. For not telling you about Bee.'

Bee. Her name flattens my spirits. 'Did you think it was okay to muck around with me and not tell me you already had a girlfriend?'

'I stuffed up. Can I lie down?'

'No, you can't.'

'Please? I'll just stay a minute.'

'You hurt me. I've never done those things we did with anyone else. Didn't that Sunday at your place mean anything to you?'

Has he thought of me? I've thought of him every day of this unbearably long, slow summer.

'Of course it meant something. *You* mean something to me Leni.'

I want to believe him, but I won't be someone's bit on the side. Not even the heart-stoppingly gorgeous Sam Camero.

'Are you still with Bee?'

'Not right now.'

I feel a door open. Sam is single? I'm single. Is it finally okay for us to be together? It's what I want so desperately.

'You broke up?'

'We're not together. She's gone overseas on a study tour.'

'Oh. Okay.'

I let him lean into the space next to me. We lie in silence and his hand finds mine. I don't move it away, although I should. There are things I haven't yet forgotten or forgiven.

'What are you doing?' I whisper.

'Lying in the dark, holding hands with a beautiful girl,' says Sam. 'I've missed you Leni. I can't stop thinking about you.'

'Where have you been, Sam?'

We lie still and listen to Penny's heavy, measured breathing. Rachel moves in her sleeping bag and I wonder if she's awake, listening to this soapie.

Sam puts his fingers on my forehead and strokes along the hairline. I close my eyes. The feeling of his fingertips on my skin is so soothing I never want it to stop. I breathe in his smell and feel excited by his closeness.

'My parents split up,' Sam says.

'What happened?'

'Dad's moved into my apartment. His apartment. He told Mum it wasn't his dream to open a yoga retreat in the middle of hippyville. He doesn't even like yoga. He's gone back to his old job. Back to wearing suits and checking the stockmarket. He said they've lost more money than he can count with her silly pipe dreams. Now someone has to be a grown-up and accept it hasn't worked out.'

'You okay?'

'Yeah … nah. Better now that I'm here with you.'

'You should go back to your room,' I say, wanting him to stay with every molecule in my body.

'Do you want me to go, Leni?'

Sam turns to face me. We're so close, it's almost an accident. Like tripping. We start kissing. Really kissing. Kissing like we're going down on the *Titanic*.

'I want to make you feel good,' Sam says between head-spinning kisses.

Feeling good with Sam is all I can think about.

'We can't,' I say, trying to slow things down. Think this through. 'I don't have anything with me.'

'I do,' Sam says, knocking down my last hurdle of resistance. 'In my wallet. I can go get it. If you want.'

'Okay, but not here,' I say, letting go of the edge of the railing.

Dawn creeps under the curtains and throws a block of light onto the carpet. The girls are starting to stir in their bags. The night is over. Sam is gone. I'm an undone knot. Everything that was once tight is now unravelled. I lie on my back and look at the ceiling, smiling to myself, saying Sam's name like a prayer. I reach for my phone and text Audrey. Hoping she'll text back this early. Wanting to share what happened. I'm excited, my heart still drumming. I wait a few minutes and then hear her message ping back.

No way! RUOK?

I'm OK x

How did it feel? ☺

How did it feel?

I could only think how it *didn't* feel. It didn't feel wrong, bad or something to regret. It was quick, painless and as natural as breathing. And in the hazy aftermath, the build-up, the waiting, the importance seemed all at once, inconsequential. I wasn't a virgin anymore and that was that.

Good I think ☺

I want gory details.

Later.

PS: Who was it?

Sam.

:-o

All the details Audrey wants are fading. My strongest memory is how it felt when Sam held me afterwards. Closer than I have ever been held in my life. Skin to skin. Almost breathing for each other.

The day feels too bright and loud. I want to go back to Sam and I in the dark. Where I can say anything. Be the girl that lets go. I look for Sam at breakfast, before I remember he's making up his erg trial. I should be disappointed but I'm relieved. It gives me a few more hours to swim lazy laps in the memories of last night. To wonder how and when we will make our togetherness official.

I wander dreamily down to the water with an armful of oars. Take my place as usual at the seven seat. It's our last session today. This afternoon we will pack up and take the bus back to the city. I'll be leaving a part of myself here on this beautiful river. The part that holds on too tight.

'Leni, move up a seat,' Laura says as we put hands on the boat. 'I'm chucking you back in stroke for this last session. Don't get too excited. It's not necessarily permanent. I want to try you up front with Rachel behind. I think you two have some special chemistry going and I don't want to split you up.'

'Okay, thanks,' I say, stunned. She hadn't given me any hint she was going to try me back in stroke. She leans into my ear. 'Forget your erg. We all know how fit you are, but turn your head off, mate. Don't overthink it. Listen to the water, feel the other girls behind you. Don't go at it like a bull at a gate. What do I always tell you?'

'Have fun.'

'Exactly.'

The river is wearing a coat of mist, gum trees reflected silver on the glassy surface. I look over Aiko's hat at the boat slicing through the water, rudder leaving behind a straight ribbon of disturbance and tight, swirling eddies from the push of our blades. My arms swing loosely over my knees and the water seems to find the tip of my blade, with just a tiny lift of my knuckles. It's still cool out, and after all the rain, the river smells freshly washed.

The boat sits level, no one tipping it out of balance. Rachel gives me gentle encouragement to push up the rating. She's like a strong pair of hands, a boosting me up to a high window to see the view. There's no nitpicking, mindless chatter or laughing. We're all in the zone. One crew, not a gaggle of individual girls. I resist ripping my blade through the water. Thinking of Laura's words. *Feel the girls behind you. Turn your head off.*

I let my mind go clear and listen to the bubbles popping alongside and eight blades dropping gently into the catch together. Thoughts of last night rush past with the river

200

water – downstream and then gone. Instead of charging the slide, I roll up slowly, pulling my oar through the water with a slow rev of muscle and energy.

Nothing hurts, there's no strain. Even when we bring it up to a hard pace, I can't seem to find the aggression and anger that I usually feel in the boat. All I have to give today is quiet determination and purpose. When Laura calls for a light, easy piece to cool down I dial back the intensity and glide through the strokes calmly, thinking about my technique, and not worrying that we're missing out on hard pieces and wasting time.

As we pull into the staging, a sweat on my back, and a big hairy monkey off it, I can honestly say I've never had a row like it. For the first time ever, we feel like a winning crew.

'How good was that?' says Rachel as we wash and wrap our oars in bubble-wrap and load them onto the trailer.

'Pretty bloody fantastic,' I say, grinning. 'You're not upset about being taken out of stroke?'

'I'm better at follow-the-leader. Besides, you absolutely rocked it out there.' She pauses, narrows her eyes. Does she know? 'You seem different today, Leni. I can't put my finger on it.'

I dip my head and can't look her in the eye. Did she hear Sam and I last night?

'Different how?'

'You're happy or something. Like that stick up your butt has been removed.' She looks at me, cheekily, and we burst out laughing.

'Oh my goodness, you actually do have a sense of humour!'

I flick her with my water bottle and she sticks out her tongue.

Cristian

I drag myself through the final session of camp in a daze. I desperately wanted to stay in bed after another restless night. Along with my usual breakfast of egg whites and a protein shake, I've had a strong, black coffee. It hasn't helped wake me up. Everyone is getting on my nerves. Especially Sam.

He's late to our session, faffing about in the bathroom. When he finally does get ready and helps us get the boat on, he drops the oars on the ground with a clatter, totally distracted. He's just done his erg trial and come in second, behind me. He seems put out.

'Careful!' I say. 'Those cost five hundred dollars each.'

Sam picks up the oars and doesn't even look at me.

I'm still pissed at him for doing the dirty on Leni, but I'm trying to hold back my brotherly protectiveness. If we didn't have to row in a crew together I would've given him a full spray.

In the boat Sam can't find the rhythm. He's a fraction off at the catch each time.

'Quicker hands, Sam,' I hiss at him, although I'm not supposed to coach from the boat.

Westie gets on his case and it makes him more rattled. The balance goes and we spend most of the row trying to recover it.

Julian loses focus when we pass by the girls' eight, staring at Rachel.

'She's so hot,' he says, for the hundreth time this week.

'Shut up, Julian!' Nick says. 'We all know you have a stiffy for Rachel. Let's just try to have a halfway decent row.'

'Boys! Sit forward and stop pissing about!' says Westie.

'I hate this,' I mutter in the boat as Westie calls for another timed piece. Thirty minutes of heavy work. I miss the feeling of connection that we had in last year's boat. When every row got us closer to the victory podium. When we couldn't lose.

'Don't say that,' says Adam.

'I'll say whatever I like,' I snap. 'You know this crew is crap compared to last year.'

At the catch I smack my blade into the water in frustration, messing up the balance of the boat.

'Oooh, err, who's in a strop this morning?' says Mal.

'Back off, man,' I warn.

As we settle into a long row down the river, I can't even enjoy the incredible beauty of this place – its misty paddocks, fat, moony cows hanging over fences and staring at us. There's no time to be. No time to relax. The pressure is even bigger than it was in the seconds. We have to win. Now, I've broken all those records, everyone thinks I'm the guy that's going to win it for them.

★

Despite her best efforts to avoid me, Penny and I end up standing on the trailer together at final loading, feeding the boats carefully onto their steel racks. Our job is to throw straps over the curved hulls to secure them in place. My knots look like a dog's breakfast, hers are neat and precise. Seeing her calms the anxiety beating like a bird in my chest. Being near her makes me feel okay.

'Nice. Girl Guides?' I ask, as she winds the rope nimbly around her fingers.

'Sailing. Dad has a catamaran at Port Melbourne.'

I find it easier to talk when my hands are busy, so I keep chattering nervously. Sensing the ice starting to thaw with her.

'How was your summer?'

'My family travelled overseas. Sri Lanka and India. It was amazing.'

'I'd love to go to India,' I say. 'And Europe. Africa. Eygpt. South America. America. Everywhere actually.'

'Romania?' Penny asks.

'Especially Romania. I was born here, in Melbourne. But we went back when I was five to visit my grandparents. I can't remember it. Not properly. Where did you go?'

'Unawatuna in Sri Lanka, for the beaches, mainly. Mum said she wanted to do the whole lie on the sand and do nothing thing. Which personally I can't stand. Then we went to India which was Dad's pick.' She sighs, looking wistful. 'We did a tour to Delhi, Agra, Jaipur. Temples, amazing people. Crazy, delicious food. I want to go back as soon as I can.'

'Hey, Pen, sorry about that night at the party.'

She stops knotting and looks up. 'Sure. I'm over it,' she says lightly.

It feels so easy. How come I made it such a big drama in my head?

Another boat cuts between us in the trailer. I imagine Penny and I backpacking across India. We're at a bustling train station waiting for our ride to the next town and she's leaning on her battered backpack, writing in her journal. I'm behind her, taking her photo. We have the whole trip ahead of us and she looks back at me and smiles.

Leni

After training Laura gives me the news I've been waiting for. Longing for.

'Good news, Leni, you're back in stroke.'

'Permanently?'

'Nothing is permanent in rowing, but I don't have plans to make more crew changes.'

'Thank you so much,' I say. 'I won't let you down this time.'

'Don't thank me. You were a different rower out there today. Usually you try to bully the water but today you let it run. There was light and shade. Controlled power. It was beautiful to watch. Keep rowing like this and you've got a huge future in this sport.'

I smile and feel a burst of happiness in my chest.

Yesterday I thought I was a failure, today I have a huge future and a new boyfriend.

Rachel and I make a run for the bus. There's a double seat in the middle, which means I have to walk past Sam to get there. He's been out with his crew most of the day and we haven't had a chance to talk. He must be exhausted. I try to make eye contact, but he's got a window seat, head rested on the glass, eyes closed.

'Take me home Mr Bus Driver,' says Rachel. 'Rachel needs hot shower. Mum's cooking. TV. Sleep.'

The back of Sam's head is three seats away. I wish we were sitting together. That he was running his thumb along my hairline, lulling me to sleep. I can't wait until we're officially a couple.

Ten minutes into the ride home, Rachel is slumped over, snoring. Half the bus is out cold. Even some of the coaches. My body aches and my eyes are heavy, but I can't drop off. Sam has his headphones in the entire way home, sleeping and then texting on his phone. We can talk once we're back in the city. There's so much to work out between us, but I know how he feels now. How I feel. That's all that matters.

The bus stops outside the boatsheds. We don't get to go right home, even though we're tired, hungry and stinky. We have to unload the boats and get them back on the racks in the shed. Everyone complains about having to do more work. I can't – it's my job to be positive and captainly. Luckily, so does Sam. We'll be here working side by side for another few hours.

'Come on, get off you lot!' shouts Laura. 'Go help Mr Poppa get the boats ready for next week's first session.'

Rachel uses the edge of her T-shirt to wipe drool from her bottom lip.

'When will this torture end?' she asks.

Rachel shuffles in front of me down the aisle. Sam tries to cut in front of her, but she pushes past sleepily, leaving him no choice but to step out in front of me.

I smile at him and we make eye contact. I'm expecting him to give me a wink or even surreptitiously touch my hand. But the moment I look at his guilty face, hunched shoulders and sad eyes, I know. Sam regrets last night. Deeply.

'I'm sorry,' Sam says. 'But I can't do this.'

I'm lying on the floor of my room, in the dark, curled up in the foetal position. I'm listening to break-up music, crying so hard my throat is raw and there's salt on my tongue. There's a knock at the door. I made it through dinner, but only just. The second I closed the door to my room I fell apart.

'Go away!' I shout.

'No!' Cristian says, letting himself in and turning on the lamp next to my bed. My room is too neat, orderly and clean for this level of heartbreak. It needs to be trashed, like my heart.

'Adele's greatest hits. That bad?'

I can't even lift my head off the floor. I stare at his feet, tears running down my face. I'm not sure I can survive this. Cristian sits down on the floor and puts his hand on my head. It's warm and familiar.

'Broken heart?'

'Smashed.'

'Sam?'

'How'd you know?'

'I hoped you'd get over it. He's *such* a douche bag. What did he do to you this time? Give me a reason to deck him and I'll do it.'

'Lied. Cheated. Stole something from me that he didn't deserve. I thought he was single and he wasn't, so I let my guard down, let him in.'

'Leni Popescu, you let someone past the armed guards?'

'I regret it.'

'Don't. You could afford to off-load a few pieces of chain mail. Okay, put your hand on your heart,' says Cristian.

I roll on my back and place my palm over my chest. We have always done this. Since we were little kids.

'Repeat after me: I am braver than I believe, stronger than I seem, and smarter than I think.'

'I'm not.'

'You are. Say the words.'

'I am braver than I believe, stronger than I seem, and smarter than I think,' I say. 'Where's that from?'

'Winnie the Pooh,' says Cristian. 'It's on *your* inspiration board.'

I look over at the board. Vaguely remember writing it down on a piece of pink paper in silver pen when I didn't know anything about anything.

'There's only one thing for a smashed aorta and that's to get your head off the ground and go and look at something beautiful.'

'No, thanks.'

Cristian pulls my arms off the floor and the rest of my body follows.

'Yes, you'll thank me later.'

Cristian takes me to the *Birrarung Marr* parkland, on the North Bank of the Yarra. Far enough away from our boat-shed to allow me to feel peaceful.

'*Birrarung* means river of mists,' says Cristian, as we wander the park, the sun dimming in a cloudy sky.

'And *Marr*?'

'Means side. *Riverside*.'

'How do you know that?' I ask.

'I know lots of things. Come on. I want to show you something.'

He makes me stand in the middle of the Federation Bells. A small forest of golden cups, held up to the city skyscrapers on steel poles. The tops of the bells glow orange, like fire pokers.

'Listen. They're about to play.'

We wait with a handful of tourists getting their phones ready to capture the moment. The bells begin to clang and chime like church bells, making my skin crackle and my lips hum. It's wonky, out of tune, pure and beautiful all at the same time. It matches what I feel inside so perfectly. How did Cristian know this was the right place to take me? Of the two of us, he got all the sensitivity. When it's finished, Cris buys me a hot chocolate from a cart and we sit and drink together, looking out to the water.

'Feel a bit better?'

I shrug my shoulders. They feel heavy.

'A bit. Thanks for getting me off the floor.'

I'm far from okay, but at least I can see myself getting out of bed in the morning. Maybe I'll survive this.

February

Two months to Head of the River

Cristian

Mum drags me out for coffee on my rest morning at local institution, *Aquilana Pasticceria*. We've been coming here with her forever. She won't be lured into the hip organic-coffee, free-range-egg and biodynamic-tomato places that have grown up around it like weeds. She says it's because the coffee here saved her life. When we were little she would bundle us into the double pram and come here to escape the house.

'Someone would always talk to me,' she told me. 'Even though I had mashed banana on my T-shirt and I was going out of my mind from lack of sleep. This place would plug me back into the world, and give me a strong dose of caffeine to get me through the day.'

We walk in past the glass cabinet of old-school pastries, shell-shaped and heavy on the marzipan, and take our regular seats at the window. The tables are plastic and wobbly and have been here as long as I've been a customer.

'Jodie! Cristian!' says the owner, Angelo, beaming. He always wears a pristine white apron and treats me like I'm his long-lost grandson. 'The usual?'

The usual is an espresso for mum and a chocolate milk-shake, extra ice-cream for me.

'Yes, thank you,' says Mum.

'No thanks, Angelo, I'll get a skinny cap,' I say.

I'm grumpy this morning and can't seem to wake up. I need caffeine. I'm also off ice-cream, full-cream milk and sugar. Looking around the café I couldn't eat anything on display. Mum turns to me with an intense look as Angelo busies himself behind the counter.

'I won't muck around. Darling, I'm worried about you.'

My heart sinks. She's taken me to a public place so I won't be able to throw a fit, walk away and close the door to my room. I'm trapped.

'Why Jodie?' I say, using her first name to remind her I'm an adult now.

'What are your plans for next year? You seem a bit … lost.'

My plans didn't extend much further than the Head of the River. After that I'd try not to fail my Year Twelve. I couldn't see myself at a desk studying next year. Or the year after. I didn't want to go to uni but I couldn't say the words out loud.

Like most migrants my dad had big dreams of Leni and I becoming mega-rich doctors or lawyers. Mum was a bit more realistic but she didn't want us to potter around on a minimum wage like Dad or work shifts at midnight like she did. She also imagined us in clean offices, driving nice cars and buying big houses. I didn't know how to tell them they weren't my dreams. I wanted to walk the earth and see as much of it as possible.

'I'm not lost,' I say, cringing at the snap in my voice. The muggy café closing in like an unwanted hug.

'I'd like you to think beyond the Head of the River. Your dad was so focused on the Olympics. Afterwards, he was like a rudderless boat, going in circles. He hadn't planned for life after that event. Think about the big picture is all I'm saying. University choices, your exams. These things are far more important than one race.'

'I'm stressed, Mum. I'm doing eight training sessions a week plus regattas. Trying to get my marks back up. I don't need you putting any more pressure on me.'

'Okay, okay. Don't get angry. That's the other thing, Cris, you don't seem yourself these days,' she says, carefully. As if I might detonate.

'What does that mean?'

'You've lost a lot of weight, very quickly. I'm worried it might have taken a toll.'

'What do you mean?'

'You seem withdrawn, sweetheart. Tired. You haven't been sleeping well either, have you? I've seen your light on at night.'

Angelo produces our coffees with a flourish and puts a heavy almond biscuit on the side of my cup. I ignore it and stay quiet, stirring the fluff on my tasteless coffee.

'I see this sort of thing at the hospital. Kids struggling with eating and weight loss. It can be easy for it to get out of control. To become a problem.'

'I'm not struggling with anything. Are you insinuating I have an eating disorder or something? That's a girl thing. I lost the weight. Made the crew. You should be happy.'

'The question is, are you happy?' Mum says.

'Of course I am,' I lie. 'Why wouldn't I be?'

We sit in silence until our coffees are finished. Under the table I tap my foot on the floor impatiently.

'I'll be late for school, can I go now?' I ask, leaping out of my seat.

Mum stops me as I try to leave, putting her hands on my shoulders.

'I love you, Cris.'

'Mum, this is a public place.'

She hugs me. 'I don't care. Remember I'm here for you if you need to talk.'

'I don't need to talk,' I say, 'I'm fine. Stop worrying so much.'

Leni

I'm lying in a sweaty puddle on the floor of my room, listening to sad music. It's a billion degrees and the overhead fan is doing nothing but moving hot air around.

I'm pining for Sam. He told me he'd had second thoughts after our night on rowing camp. That he wasn't properly broken up with Bee. That he really couldn't start something with me because he wasn't technically single. Blah-blah-de-blah. I should be consumed with bitter rage, but I feel ripped off. Stupid. Used. This wasn't how it was supposed to be. I thought the first guy I slept with would love me back. Or at least be unattached. Why did I believe him, so easily? When he'd deceived me once before.

Thankfully, my phone rings. 'Yeah?' I answer listlessly.

'I'm sweating like a whore in church,' Audrey says. 'Meet me at the pool in ten.'

I haven't had much time to catch up with Audrey since her trip. I've been so bunkered down with rowing and my misery over Sam.

'But I ... '

'No buts, get your bathers and come.'

The pool is the Fitzroy Pool. We're lolling in the toddlers wading section dipped in a few inches of heavily chlorinated water. It's past seven at night, but the air's still toasty. There's no other place to be than in a body of water. The rest of the suburb is here as well, and it's hard to find a spot to put your bag, let alone your body. Audrey is eating a red icy pole and I'm eating a banana and biting back my feelings. My heart is badly bruised. Lately I'd been crying for no reason, sitting in my room or watching TV. Big, fat silent tears.

'Are you okay?' Audrey asks. 'You seem so sad.'

'I just don't get it. Sam and I had this amazing night together. I really thought it was the start of us. But then ... nothing. He won't even look at me at rowing.'

Audrey lowers her sunglasses.

'Can I give you some tough love, sugar?'

'Not too tough.'

'I've only been with Kezza, so it's not like I'm the expert in matters of the heart. But I think real love is supposed to go in both directions. Sam isn't the one for you. He only seems to love himself. Plus, he's probably a psychopath. He certainly appears to be emotionally void.'

I start to cry, knowing that Audrey is right and wishing she wasn't.

'He two-timed you. Beautiful, perfect you. He needs his head read.'

'I know, but the *jtzooum* was fierce,' I say, through tears.

'Let this Bee character deal with his broody, damaged, lying, cheater shtick. There are plenty of other dudes lurking. Kieren has this friend, if you can get around body odour, he's hot.'

I laugh, feeling cheered up. 'Not Gavin?' I picture Gavin. He's nerdy cool, but not my type.

'Yes, Gav! Don't you think he's sort of gorgeous in a *Big Bang Theory* way?'

'No!'

A group of guys in speedos walks past us on their way to night-time squad training, carrying bags of flippers and kickboards.

We both stop talking and check them out. Audrey licks her icy pole suggestively.

'Maybe we just need to ogle these swimming boys for a while. Get some eye candy on our plate. I missed you when I was on the road. Six weeks was too long to be away from my girl.'

'Did you? I thought you'd have been too busy going to music festivals.'

'Yeah, we did that 5 per cent of the time. The rest of the trip I had to live in a van that smelt like Kieren's feet and truck-stop food. The reality of driving off into the sunset, my dear.'

I smile. That's what I love about Audrey, she didn't try to airbrush her life.

'Hey, Auds.'

I pause, wondering if she might tell me to get lost. Knowing that I can't survive Year Twelve without her. A lot rests on her answer to my next question.

'Yeah, doll.'

'Would you mind if I sit with you and the knit bitches again at school?'

Audrey sits up, her face serious. 'I dunno. Things got weird there for a bit. You basically dumped us for Adam and his fancy mates. You really hurt my feelings.'

'I made a mistake. You, Maz, Luc, Yvette. I want to hang out with you in my last year of school. Not just after hours. You're my tribe. I don't know what crazy juice I was drinking when we agreed to be friends outside school. I want more. I want recess and lunch access.'

'You won't dump us for some hottie with a new car and good abs?'

I put my hand on my chest.

'Brownie's honour.'

'Well, okay then. I'll tell the girls. You'll be expected to craft with us, of course. Maybe you can crochet some rowing shorts.'

We smile at each other goofily and then Audrey grabs my head and dunks me under the cool water.

The Green Cup is a predictor for the Head of the River. Kind of like the Golden Globes, before the Oscars. It's been run by Parkview School since the 1960s and is a chance for everyone to show pony after rowing camp. Unfortunately for us, Melbourne's latest brutal heatwave won't break. At 9 am it's already thirty degrees and shaping up to hit forty by lunchtime. Everyone's trying to sniff out the cool change. When will it arrive? Where the hell is it?

'So hot,' moans Cristian out the car window. 'Why don't we have air conditioning?'

'You want car with air con, you pay for it,' says Dad. Mum's working, so it's just the three of us today.

'Let's get this over with,' Cristian says, looking like he's going to the gallows. Meanwhile, I'm itching to race. Since camp our crew feels united.

We pull up at the gates of Parkview and follow the ushers' direction to a space between a gleaming Range Rover and a BMW. Dad pulls gingerly into the grassy square.

'Careful!' Dad barks as Cristian flings his door open and nearly takes a chip out of the BMW's immaculate paintwork.

'I didn't even touch it,' Cristian says, glowering. Cris has been so on edge lately, everyone's been walking on eggshells around him.

'What time's your heat, Leni?' Cristian asks as we wander towards our boat trailer in a throng of kids.

'Ten thirty-two.'

'Good luck out there,' he says, heading for the trailer. 'Stay cool.'

'Always.'

Dad and I keep walking towards the water. A shaved-ice stand is doing swift business, next to a table selling T-shirts and rowing gear. I peruse the goods and decide to spend some of my Target cash buying Rachel, Penny and I a pair of lucky undies. I know they're lucky undies because it's printed on the front of them, with a four-leaf clover embossed on the back.

'Leni! Good luck!' says Amelia, the Year Nine girl I told off at rowing camp. She's wearing a green wig and fluoro zinc.

'You too, Meils!' I shout back. 'Stay out of the sun!'

'I will!' she calls back.

We walk past a roped-off VIP area with the best view of the river. A sign states: INVITED GUESTS ONLY and inside waiters are serving chilled orange juice and croissants to a select few.

'VIP?' my dad mutters. 'What this VIP? This is rowing. Not nightclub. Ridiculous.'

I leave Dad and find Rachel and Penny in a physio tent set up by our school. Rach is getting her calves warmed up on the table. Penny is stretching on a mat.

'Hey Captain!' Rachel says.

Her hair is in plaits, tied with green ribbons, even her toenails are school colours. If I'm the heart of the boat, Rachel is the spirit and Penny is the balance.

219

'I got you girls something,' I say, taking out the undies and throwing the pairs at them. 'You have to wear them for this race.'

Rachel finishes up her massage, grabs Penny's hand then runs to the loos to change. They return and flash me the waistband.

'I won't wash them until the Head of the River,' says Rachel.

'Eewww,' laughs Penny.

'Laura wants us at the trailer in ten minutes for a race briefing,' I say. 'Let's go.'

Cristian

I feel average today, but it's probably the heat. I strip off to my swimmers before the race and lower myself into the inflatable plunge pool our school has set up down by the sheds. I bob in the chilled water, looking up to the blue sky. There's not a single cloud to block out the pounding heat.

'Ready to race, Poppa?' Adam says, getting into the pool beside me.

'Sure, let's race,' I say, feeling my body temperature drop, my heart slow. I could almost fall asleep here. I'm missing at least four hours sleep and my body wants it back. I woke up at two and slept fitfully the rest of the night.

'You might want to show a little more enthusiasm,' says Adam.

'Yeah? Judging by how crap we've been training, I think getting too enthusiastic might be counterproductive.'

'Come on, we're about to turn a corner. Today's the day, I can feel it. Let's rub Stotts's faces in a dominating win.'

'Is your dad here?' I ask. Adam always gets more antsy when Mitch watches him race.

'Took his private helicopter down from Portsea. Landed on the rugby fields. It's time to put our energy supplements to good use. Show the old man we're worth the dollars he pours into this rowing program.'

I stand up and let the water gush off my body. There's virtually no fat left on it. I'm skin, muscle and bone. 'Time to zoot up for the race,' I say.

A group of Year Ten girls wolf-whistle at the sight of my transformed body, but even that doesn't make me happy. It's only Penny's opinion that matters, and it seems like a hot body isn't the way to her heart after all.

We're heading back from our heat when the ambush happens. Two guys in white polo shirts, wearing plastic lanyards around their necks are talking to Westie. At first I think they're US scouts, but they're too official for that. They're flashing Westie their badge IDs. He seems confused. We lower our boat onto stretchers and hang around to see what Westie thought of our race. We didn't do too badly. Second to Stotts and a ticket to the final. We got there mostly on grunt and not much finesse. He should be pleased.

'Doping control? VADA?' says Westie. 'I've got kids here. Some of these boys are not even eighteen. Who gave you the authority to test here?'

The guys take out official-looking papers and start waving them around. It's nearly forty degrees but I feel a chill run right through my body. Anti-doping? Why are they here? And what do they want with our crew?

'These students compete at national level, in a sport that's governed by anti-doping laws. We have every right to test them unannounced. Just as we do all high-level athletes,' says one of the guys.

I glance at Adam and we share a look of mutual panic and terror. Our blood is tainted and these two polite guys have the equipment to prove us both liars and cheats. This can't be happening. I was told there was no testing for drugs at school sport.

'Why would my kids bother doping?' says Westie. 'You're wasting your time and ours. Why aren't you at a cycling race? Rowers don't dope.'

'Mr West, with all due respect. No sport is clean,' says the official. He's completely calm and I get the feeling testing will go ahead today whether Westie likes it or not.

I wonder if it would be possible to run. To go to the toilet and make a break for it out a window. It couldn't be more than a kilometre to the nearest bus stop. There's money in my bag.

A crowd of parents, coaches and onlookers has formed quickly. Discussions buzz around me. I try to hold it together, but I'm now sweating like a racehorse, my pulse flying. It's too late to get a clean sample of wee and I don't have the first clue how to pull off a complicated switch during a test.

'What's going on here?' Mitch elbows his way next to Westie. 'Where are you blokes from and what right do you have to test our kids without our say so. They're minors.'

'Sir, we're from VADA – the Victorian Anti-doping Authority. You have the right to be present at their testing as a representative.'

'You're damn right I do. No one gets a drop of piss or blood out of my son without my permission.'

Dad arrives on his bike and stands there with his helmet on, trying to catch up. It's difficult for him when people speak quickly.

Adam comes up behind me and hisses in my ear. 'Fuck, Poppa,' he says, sounding close to tears. 'Drug testing? We're screwed.'

'Shut up,' I whisper. 'Don't freak out.'

But we have every reason to freak out. Big time. This could spell the end of our time at Harley as well as a swift exit from the firsts.

Julian's mum gets in on the debate.

'My son takes steroids, for his asthma, are you going to ban him from rowing if that shows up?'

'We routinely test minors for performance-enhancing drugs,' says the official. 'They will each have a chance to notify us of any other substances they are currently taking, which we can exclude. If everyone calms down we will explain the procedure and get the testing underway so you can go back to the competition.'

'And if we refuse?' says Mitch. 'I should get my lawyer on the phone. This is outrageous.'

Mitch is beetroot red and about to blow a fuse.

'Let them do job,' Dad says. 'Our boys have nothing to hide. Sooner done, sooner back on water.'

Dad's been drug tested dozens of times, it's no big deal to him. He has no idea his son could be unveiled as a drug cheat if he continues arguing for the tests to go ahead. If I did run, where would I go? I've got a few thousand bucks in my account and nowhere to live. I'd last a few weeks on the streets. Should I confess instead? Come clean before I test dirty?

'These standard tests,' says Dad. 'We do and then go race.'

Bloody Dad. I want to run over and gag his big mouth.

'Look this kind of blatant breach of human rights might be all right where you come from. But here, it's unacceptable,' says Mitch.

For once, I'm willing Mitch to win this fight.

Dad looks furious. 'Where come from? I live here twenty years, *mate*. Let them test. What does it tell boys if we stop this? If we don't follow rules? These rules stop people cheating. We need them.'

'Vasile is right,' says Westie. 'Not taking the test is as bad as taking the test.'

He sighs and runs his palm down his face, as if to wipe away the stress. The pit of my stomach drops away as I realise in shock that I'm about to get caught. My deceit will come to a messy end. Our plan has failed. My brain skips to the near future. My parents' humiliation. My shame and expulsion from Harley. Penny wouldn't want anything to do with me.

'Boys! Gather round!' shouts Westie. 'Oh, you're already around. Look, this is a pain in the backside, but these guys are here to do a random drug test for VADA. God knows why they want to test you lot, but let's get it done as quickly as possible. I'll pass it over to them to tell you the rules and regs.'

He gives the VADA officials a stern look. 'Don't make my boys miss their final. Otherwise I'll start being a lot less cooperative.'

Dad's my official representative. He's on my right side and the VADA official is on my left as I report to the testing station with an impending sense of doom. I might as well be in a line-up at a police station. Dad and I sit in chairs with the other guys and their parents or coaches. I'm pretending to sip from my water bottle until my bladder is full enough to test. I'm actually completely busting. My bladder aches from holding it. I'm trying to distract myself from pissing my pants. Singing songs in my head, saying the alphabet backwards. Basically packing death.

Adam sits a few seats down from me, his face pale and serious. He picks at a scab on his knee and whispers something to Mitch. I'm humming the chorus of the catchiest stupid pop song I can think of. Over and over. It won't work forever. I will have to piss eventually.

'Do you think anyone's actually juicing?' Charley asks Nick behind me.

'I dunno. Maybe. Why else would VADA be here? Why would they pick out our school?'

'Boys, this is no time for gossip,' says Westie.

The gossip had already started. Since rowing camp I'd been under more scrutiny than Adam. He was thicker and stronger, but his appearance wasn't vastly different. Meanwhile I stuck out like a sore thumb. The more weight I dropped, the more my muscles popped. I'd heard a few guys from other schools comment on how quickly I'd stripped off the chub and how big my ergo score was. How I'd gone from pie-eater to pin-up in a few months.

My bladder can't take the pressure any longer. I put my hand up and the VADA official ushers me into a toilet. He watches, and so does Dad, as I piss like a racehorse into the cup, trying not to overfill it. I'm completely naked from the knees up and I feel totally exposed.

'Don't worry,' Dad says as I dress and take my sample cup over to be put in a proper kit, filed and sent to a lab. 'When you row internationals, you get used to weeing with other people watching.'

He laughs, but I feel sick with guilt. What will he say when this sample finds its way to a scientist in a lab coat? I'm a fraud, a liar and a terrible son. He'll never forgive me for this.

I'm numb as I sign the paperwork.

'Have you ingested any unusual foods, drugs or alcohol today, Cristian?' the VADA official asks.

'No,' I say, remembering how I'd casually swigged back two pills this morning with a bottle of water. 'Not that I can think of.'

'Good boy,' says Dad, patting my back. 'Now go and warm up for your final. Put this all behind you.'

Leni

We're driving to an emergency meeting of the Harley Grammar Rowing Committee to discuss the drug bust at the Green Cup. The story moved quickly from the river, to online, talkback radio, even television. As rowing captains, only Sam and I are allowed to go to the meeting. Cris is at home, studying. Or at least that's what he says he's doing.

Sam is the last person I want to spend time with. But this is official duty.

I'm looking at the latest story on my phone while Mum drives.

'VADA OFFICIALS DEFEND SCHOOLBOY BUST!' the headline screams. Usually Harley's rowers would be in the sports section doing a puff piece about our excellent chances at the Head of the River and whether our boys could back up two years in a row. This year it's a different story.

'Would you be okay being tested for drugs?' Mum asks me.

'Yeah, of course.'

'Do you know anyone who takes performance-enhancing drugs?'

'No.'

I can't imagine a single person on the rowing team using any kind of drug to get an edge.

'We looked for steroids on the internet,' says Dad. 'It took us ten seconds to find them for sale. Girls can take too you know.'

'I would never, ever cheat.'

'We know you and Cris wouldn't do something like this, but school sport can sometimes seem like life and death,' says Mum. 'Don't forget the world will keep turning and we will still love you, even if you come last at the Head of the River. We said the same to Cris earlier.'

Sam meets me at the lecture theatre, which is packed with parents, teachers and coaches. I'm exhausted and want to be in bed with my laptop, catching up on homework. I didn't bounce back well after the race on the weekend. After racing in the heat I still feel drained. When the season ends I will slow down and get my system back to normal. Recover.

'Hey,' says Sam, still looking guilty.

'Hi,' I say.

Sam and I have been successfully avoiding each other for weeks. Ducking out of each other's way during training, not making eye contact. Not speaking unless we absolutely have to. He'd made his position clear. He didn't want me. Bee was his choice. Now that I'd had a chance to grow some backbone, I didn't want him either. I was keeping myself busy, focusing on the Head of the River and trying to move on and forget him. That wasn't possible tonight. We were here to represent the whole squad as captains. To work together.

'Are we okay to do this?' Sam says as we go in the side door and head for the stage where we will sit with the coaches and our principal, Mr Kentwell. Sam's gone to an effort to iron his school uniform and brush out his curls. We are both wearing our official captains' blazers. He looks gorgeous but I have to steel myself against it.

'Let's get it over and done with,' I say. 'What's the latest?'

'Mitch Langley has hired a fancy lawyer. He wants to block the results on the grounds that kids shouldn't be forced to provide urine samples without their parents' permission. Not all the parents were at the regatta. Including mine. Mr Langley reckons it's violating our rights.'

'What do you think?'

'I think cheaters should get caught,' Sam says.

'Do you?' I say sarcastically, raising my eyebrow. I can't help having a dig at his double standards.

He goes red and stares at his feet. I silently high-five myself.

Drugs have never been on the agenda at a HGRC meeting. It's usually fundraising drives, new equipment, coaching appointments and crew disputes. There's an excited buzz in the air, which dies down as Mr Kentwell approaches the lectern. Everyone sits up tall, ears pricked.

'Judging by attendance tonight, there is justifiably some concern over Saturday's visit by VADA to the Green Cup regatta at Parkview,' he says. 'From my perspective, I was alarmed to hear that the students in our boys' first eight were required to urinate in front of strangers and that due to the surprise nature of this testing, some students did not have parents present. The question facing us is do we allow this testing to take place at our school regattas? I person-ally don't believe there is a performance-enhancing drug problem at school sporting levels, but I'm prepared to be disappointed. Before we decide what action to take, I'll open up a group discussion. Questions may be directed at any party on the stage, but please raise your hand.'

Of course, my parents' hands go up immediately.

'Yes, Mrs Popescu,' says Mr Kentwell. 'Your views are very welcome here tonight.'

'We'd all like to see school sport as innocent,' says Mum. 'And we should grieve that loss, but as an Olympic-level athlete, how can we refuse to cooperate with an authority which stands to make our sport clean? By refusing random tests, are we not telling our kids they're exempt from anti-doping rules that all athletes live by? Are we giving them a safe place to cheat?'

Mitch stands up in the crowd, flanked by a man in a suit I assume is his fancy lawyer.

'A safe place to cheat? How about just giving them a safe place? Shouldn't our regattas be free from this sort of violation?'

'Drug testing isn't a violation, it's a standard process. And it's highly regulated,' says Mum.

'I won't agree to this VADA mob traumatising our kids to tick an official box,' says Mitch. 'Call me idealistic, but I believe in the purity of school sport. Doping is for footy players and crooked cyclists, not our kids. I think what we should be discussing here tonight is potential legal action and blocking the results that have already been obtained.'

Dad stands up to speak. I worry he'll get nervous and lose his words again. But he doesn't seem rattled tonight.

'You are competitor in a sport,' says Dad, choosing his words carefully. 'And that sport has anti-doping policy then you must abide by rules of competition. One way we tell our kids doping is wrong is to make sure they know consequences. VADA not want catch kids, they want stop them starting in first place.'

Dad sits down and several parents clap him.

'Why was VADA there in the first place?' says Nick's dad.

Westie takes the microphone on stage.

'A tip-off was made by an anonymous parent, concerned that specific members of the first squad have had a rapid increase in size and performance on the ergometer machine. Doubts were raised.'

Someone shouts something inaudible from the back row and there's a rumble of laughter.

'Something you would like to share down the back?' asks Mr Kentwell.

Damien Yang's father stands up to speak. Damien was chucked out of the first boat for Cristian and has been dark ever since.

'If we're talking about specific cheating in the first eight, then there are some obvious suspects. Look at Cristian Popescu. The kid looks thirty years old, not seventeen. His erg score went through the roof in a matter of months. He's rapidly changed body shape. We've all thought maybe he's on the gear, don't tell me you haven't,' he says, looking around the room. 'We should allow the test results to go ahead. I'd like to see if our boys are clean.'

'My son not drug cheat!' Dad shouts, so loudly that I jump in fright.

Before Mum can talk him out of it, he runs to the back of the room and throws a punch at Damien's father.

He misses and they tumble out of the room with half the committee trying to pull them apart.

Mr Kentwell adjourns the meeting until the parents can stop acting like 'absolute animals'.

'Did that really just happen?' Sam says to me.

I'm already running in the direction of the fight to see if I can talk Dad out of punching Damien Yang's dad into next week.

Cristian

With Leni and my parents at the rowing committee meeting I'm left to drift around the house on my own. I take out my drug stash, lay it out on my bed and consider flushing it all down the toilet. I call Adam first.

'Your dad at that meeting?' I say.

'Yeah. Yours?'

'Yep.'

'What are we going to do, Ads? I was thinking of getting rid of the evidence.'

'Why would you do that? So you can go through steroid withdrawals right before Head of the River?'

'Withdrawals? You didn't tell me anything about that.'

'Every high has a comedown, Cris. My advice is do nothing, mate. I'm not changing my plan.'

'What if they catch us? As soon as the school finds out our results, we're gone.'

'Dad's spending heaps of cash on a lawyer who's going

to get those test results burned up. We won't get caught. I promise you.'

'You promised there was no testing at school level, look how that turned out. My parents will disown me if I test positive, won't your dad flip too?'

Adam pauses on the line. 'You don't know?'

'What?'

'Cristian, you are so naive, I love that about you.'

'What do you mean?' I'm getting frustrated and edgy with this weird conversation.

'My dad already knows because he helped me get the 'roids. He's got connections at the gym. He didn't want to see me rowing from the seconds in my final year. He bankrolled the whole thing. He knows about you, too.'

I feel totally let down.

'What kind of parent buys a kid drugs?' I ask. This makes no sense.

'Listen, mate, I gotta go. Promise me you won't do anything stupid. Dad will get us out of this. Money talks. It does, Cris.'

'There are some problems that even money can't fix,' I say.

'Wait and see.'

I hang up, reeling from the phone call and Adam's deception. I was a fool to follow him blindly into this mess. I spend a few more minutes looking at the drugs I still have left to take. If I can hang on, I might get away with all of this.

Instead of dropping the pills down the toilet while the house is empty, I pack everything away in its hiding spot, turn off the light and pretend to be asleep when my parents come home.

I don't move when Leni knocks on the door wanting to talk. I've deceived her, too, and she's always been the one I tell my truth to. There's nothing left to do now, but wait it out and hope for a miracle.

Six agonising days after the rowing club meeting, Westie gathers the entire squad to deliver the verdict on the drug testing. He reads out an email after training to the entire squad. It's short and to the point.

> Dear coaches, parents and friends of the Harley Grammar Rowing Club,
>
> The results of the VADA test taken on the 19/2 will be released today the 25/2. You and your children will be notified of any irregularities in individual tests by phone today and you will be asked to come into school to meet with myself and coaching staff.
>
> Regarding the matter of further drug testing, I have met and had numerous discussions with the heads of APS schools over the past week. Collectively we have signed an agreement stating we will not cooperate with drug testing at APS regattas and informed VADA of our decision.
>
> VADA has defended its right to test young athletes, but provisionally has agreed not to do any further testing this season or in the future.

We consider this matter now closed.

Regards,
Robert Kentwell
Principal

Everyone starts chatting amongst themselves but I'm silent, staring blankly ahead. My entire world imploding.

The results of the VADA test taken on the 19/2 will be going ahead. Results will be released today.

We're caught. It's over.

I try to find Adam in the crowd, but he's already gone. He must have slipped out the back. I bolt down the stairs, pushing past other rowers, out onto Boathouse Drive. I watch, helpless, as his Mini speeds off.

'Adam!' I shout, knowing he can't hear me.

I kick at the ground and run my hands through my hair.

'Fuck!' I shout.

I run around trying to find Adam before class, but he's disappeared in a cloud of magician's smoke. I'm jittery and my chest feels tight and hot. Any moment I'm going to be collared and hauled off to Mr Kentwell's office. Turns out, I'm not being paranoid. I go back to my locker to grab my books for English and find a note slipped inside. At the same time I get an SMS telling me to go directly to Kentwell's office before school starts.

I try to call Adam, but I go through to his message bank.

'Adam, I've just been called to Kentwell's office. They know, man. It's over. What should I say?'

I hang up and wait for him to call back, but the phone stays silent. I'm on my own.

When I open Mr Kentwell's door, I'm not surprised to see my parents are there, as well as Westie. There are no words for the shame I feel. It's so big it fills the room.

Dad doesn't look at me, but there's a seat next to Mum and she pats it solemnly. I want to confess everything, but it's so quiet and I don't know where to start.

'Good morning, Cristian,' says Mr Kentwell.

'Morning, sir.'

'Do you know why you're here?'

'I think so, sir.'

'Let's not delay the inevitable. The results from VADA came back positive for you.'

He holds up a piece of paper and reads from it.

'More specifically it showed a banned steroid. As your parents have confirmed you don't have any problems with asthma, we can only assume you were taking it to improve your rowing performance, is that correct?'

'Yes, sir.'

'There was also a positive result for a prescription-only weight-loss drug. You don't have permission to take this?'

'No, sir. I needed to drop weight fast. I was desperate.'

Mr Kentwell leans forward on his elbows and frowns.

'This is most disappointing, Cristian.'

'I know, I'm sorry, sir.'

'Don't apologise to me. Apologise to your parents and your coach. Your crew. Those who trusted you and had faith in you. You've let them down, son. But not as much as you've let yourself down.'

I turn to Mum, whose face is stony.

'Sorry Mum.'

'I'm sorry Dad.'

Dad grunts and looks away, at the wall. My eyes sting with tears.

Mr West waits for his apology.

'I'm sorry Mr West,' I mutter.

'Cris, I'm gutted you made this choice,' says Westie. 'Is there any way we could keep Cris in the boat? It's only weeks until Head of the River. Is there any point upsetting the applecart? Potentially this crew could turn around. They could win it again.'

'I think we have every reason to remove a cheat from the crew,' says Mr Kentwell. 'If we compete at the Head of the River, we have an obligation to send a clean team.'

Mr West nods, but looks upset. 'I'm sorry, mate. Just don't let this be the end of a promising rowing career. You can come back from this. You're young, you made a silly mistake.'

'I'd like a full review of Cristian's coaching and management,' Mr Kentwell says to Westie. 'I've been talking to VADA's president about bridging the gap. We desperately need anti-doping education in the curriculum and for our students to be taught the dangers of performance-enhancing drugs. On a more grassroots level, I'd like to gather our senior coaching staff to workshop ways to provide our senior rowers, and all our young athletes with more emotional support. I understand how caught up we can get in the Head of the River, but it's just a race. To start, we need to ask you some tough questions, Cristian. Are you ready?'

I wipe my snotty nose with my hand. 'Okay.'

'To your knowledge did anyone else in the squad take performance-enhancing drugs?'

Is this a trick question? Did Adam squirm his way out of getting caught and leave me to hang.

'Not that I know of.' I'm a cheat and a liar, but I'm no dobber.

'Who supplied these drugs?'

'A guy at a gym. I don't know his name.'

'What gym?'

'I don't know. We didn't meet there.'

'You might have to think harder, if we refer this matter to the police,' says Mr Kentwell.

The air con seems like it's up too high and I'm shivering. The police?

'Why did you do it?' asks Mum. Her voice cracks and she starts crying. Dad puts an arm around her and glares at me. In my entire life, I've never felt worse. My entire body is twisted and wrung out with shame. My head throbs with pain.

'I don't know,' I say, tears dripping onto my knees.

'That's not good enough, Cristian,' says Westie. 'These are your actions. Be accountable. It's the least you can do now.'

'I panicked when I was dropped from the firsts. All anyone cares about at this school is winning. So I had to win, didn't I? I had to be in the firsts. Keep my scholarship. I couldn't see any way of doing that without taking these drugs.'

'They were the easy way out?' asks Mr Kentwell.

'Yes, sir. But there's nothing easy about today is there?'

'Do you have any idea how dangerous these drugs can be? Especially when you mix them?' says Mum. 'You were playing a very foolish game, Cristian. You're lucky you were caught.'

'You need to see your family GP,' says Mr Kentwell. 'I'll also make you an appointment with the school counsellor. As this is a significant breach of disciplinary expectations, we should also discuss an appropriate punishment.'

I'm suspended from school until the Monday after the Head of the River. I won't compete in the race. My team-mates will be told I hurt my back lifting weights and I'm out of action due to injury. Even though I've dreamed of being free from the numb early mornings, the pain, testing, endless training rows, runs, all of it ... I'm sad. Being kicked out of the firsts a few weeks before Head of the River is like being dishonourably discharged from the army. I'll never row for Harley Grammar again.

I'm allowed to play rugby for the firsts, but there'll be at least two random urine tests carried out by a school doctor. I'll be watched like a hawk all year. I have zero credibility and I've proved I can't be trusted.

My marks have to reach at least a B average if I'm to hold onto my scholarship. I'll have to work like a dog. The only good news is that the police won't be called in. God knows the school doesn't want that kind of media attention.

VADA has agreed not to file my records so I won't forever be marked as a drug cheat. On the proviso that Mr Kentwell gets the ban on random drug testing at APS events overturned.

He said he would do his best to make it happen.

When I get home, my room has been ransacked – everything I own is tipped out on the floor. My bed sheets have been stripped and every drawer and cupboard cleaned out.

'Did we get robbed?'

'Your dad wanted evidence,' says Mum. 'He found it. You'd better clean up here and start studying. Lie low. I need to talk Dad down from the ledge. He is absolutely furious, Cristian. I've never seen him like this. Given our background in rowing and the natural gifts you've been given as an athlete, he feels so betrayed by you.'

'I'm so sorry, Mum. It was a stupid mistake.'

Mum puts her hand to my cheek.

'I know. Let's get you to a check-up later today. It's not my area but I understand the detox from steroids can be rocky. You might feel low, a little sad, lethargic. That's normal, okay? Make sure you tell me if you're feeling down. We'll get through this, Cris.'

She leaves and I pick up my clothes and re-fold them into the cupboards, listening to my parents fighting in their room. It's more intense than any argument they've ever had. I hate that it's because of my actions. The bedroom door slams and footsteps thunder towards my room. I put my back up against the wall and brace for something terrible. My father has never hit me, but today could be the day.

Dad stands at the door, his eyes hollow and red. He looks at me like I'm a stranger.

'I'm sorry, Dad. Please don't take it out on Mum. I'm the one you should be shouting at. Punish me. Whatever you say, I'll do. Anything.'

'You study, work, sleep. No phone. No TV. No go out. I don't want talk to you. You shame our family today.'

As soon as Dad leaves for coaching and Mum for work, I sneak out. I want to do the right thing and abide by his punishment, but there's something I have to do before lockdown begins. I'm on the number 8 tram, scuttling away from the graffiti and housing commission flats into a world of high fences and hedges. After pacing up and down Adam's street a few times, I pluck up the courage to press the intercom at the ornate iron gates. I jab the button more times than I should, desperate. I need to find out how Adam didn't get caught and why he won't answer any of my texts or calls. How did I end up in this mess all by myself, when I had an accomplice?

'Hello?'

'Adam?'

'No, it's Mitch. Come in, Cristian.'

The gates open automatically and I walk down the driveway, the eye of a security camera following me.

Mitch is drinking a tumbler of something icy and golden as he ushers me into the marble foyer, with cowskin rugs and a black grand piano in one corner. A chandelier hangs above us, sharp crystal pendants aimed at my head.

'Adam isn't home,' says Mitch. 'He's at the river, of course.'

I'd forgotten this afternoon was a group ergo. I feel almost guilty for missing it.

Mitch makes no move to invite me in. In fact he seems to be blocking me from going past the foyer.

'You got caught, didn't you?'

'Yeah. You know everything, don't you?' I say, bold with a new anger. 'I never asked to take the fall for this.'

'I don't like your tone,' says Mitch.

'Adam told me you got him on the gear.'

Mitch puts his drink down on a nearby stand, knocking it heavily onto the glass.

'If I started it, you finished it, son. Take the blame. Be a man. Have some backbone.'

'And you? Do you have any backbone?'

'I'm in real estate; a lack of moral standing is good for my business interests.'

He looks me over and his smile fades.

'People are talking about you, Cristian. They'll be talking even louder when you mysteriously resign the firsts with, what was it Adam said, a back injury? I'd try to play the part, by the way. You're supposed to be bedridden. My son, in the eyes of VADA, is clean. I don't want you two mixing together anymore.'

'How did Adam get away with it?' I ask.

'There are ways of masking any kind of drug, if you know the right people and you have the right colour of coin.'

I back away. Trying to talk to Mitch is a waste of time.

'You might have gotten Adam through the net, but if he feels anything like I did before I was found out, he's not in a good place. Mentally or physically. I'm glad I got caught. At least I don't have to lie anymore.'

'Some of us have less trouble lying than others,' says Mitch, closing the door in my face.

I'm in a park when my phone rings.

'Hi Mum.'

'Where are you?' she asks.

I look around the little park, with its kids' play set and yummy nannies sharing coffees and gossip.

'Some park in Toorak.'

'Come home. I've got dinner on. We'll work this out, I promise you.'

March

One week to Head of the River

Leni

Cris and I have a coffee after my rowing training, at a café in Southgate. His face has already filled out. He looks healthier. We sit on the outside balcony, overlooking the late crews starting their sessions.

'Are you okay?' I ask.

The house is too quiet. Dad barely speaks to Cris and Mum's furious with Dad for not resolving things. The whole house hums with resentment.

'Are you going back to school, after your suspension?'

'Yeah. Why not? Got my last rugby season to play.'

'And after that?'

'Travel maybe? Go back to Romania. Visit Bunica and Bunela. Backpack in Europe. I'm saving. I think I can make enough to buy a round-the-world ticket. Maybe I'll pick up some work over there. Who knows?'

Maybe it's because he's out of uniform, but Cristian seems years older.

'You can meet me overseas, if you like? We could travel together.'

'That would be cool. It was too much pressure for you, wasn't it?'

Cristian nods. He seems loose and relaxed in a pair of shorts and thongs. The stress has gone from his face and body.

'I was never cut out for rowing. Not the way you are. I didn't have the hunger. In the end I don't care who wins and who loses.'

He gestures at the chocolate cake between us.

'And I like the sweet stuff too much.'

'Don't ever mess with your body like that again.'

'I won't. Promise.'

'Think you and Dad can patch things up? Bit tense around the homestead.'

'Maybe.'

We share the cake, silently, until there's one more bite left. Just like when we were kids, we cut it in half and share it. Cristian looks at his phone.

'I gotta go. I've got a shift tonight. See you at home?'

'Yeah. Maybe I'll run back to Fitzroy. Fit in a bit more training.'

'You're nearly there. You deserve to win the Head.'

Friday, 1 April

Day before Head of the River

Our first official Head of the River business is to appear at a send-off at our boatshed on the Friday night. We get into minibuses to drive to the Yarra to stage a formal 'row past' for old boys and girls. I sit down next to Penny, who is white with fear. It's her first Head of the River as a senior rower.

I put my arm around her. Neither of us will sleep well tonight. There's no escaping the raging nerves. 'Don't worry, Pen, we've done the work. It's up to us now.'

We drive down the long road towards the school gates and hear a roaring, drumming sound in the distance. As we get closer, it gets louder.

Adam rolls down the window and the sound is deafening.

'No way,' he says. 'Guys. You've got to see this.'

Outside the school band's drum section is thumping and the entire senior school has lined the road as we slowly drive past. Kids are screaming and jumping. This is our goodbye and good luck from the school. It happens every year. We just never know where it's going to happen. Sometimes the basketball courts, sometimes at assembly. This year, they've taken over the driveway.

'Win! Win! Win! Win!' shout the students, fists in the air.

I hang my arm out the window at some Year Sevens who high-five me, feeling like a rock star.

Penny grins at me and we grab hands, excited.

'This is it,' Penny says. 'I can't believe it's tomorrow.'

At the river we dress in our zooties and head out for a demo row. No hard strokes, just a show-off for invited guests.

'This is weird,' says Rachel behind me. 'I feel like we're on stage.'

'We are,' I say.

Our rowing is better than ever. Strong, balanced and together. Everyone's been talking about our chances at the regatta. We are equal favourites with St Ann's. Anything could happen. The boys' first eight do their row past after us. With Cristian out of the boat, they're struggling to connect and catch up to the other lead crews. They're fit but look a little scratchy. Is it too late for them?

On the staging we get out of the boats and meet a few of the old Harley oarsmen and women. Members of the winning crews from 1953, 1966, 1971, 1984, 1995, 2003 and last year wear medals, sip on free drinks and reminisce about the big race.

It may have been a while since they saw a podium finish, but they all have a winning quality.

'Leni Popescu,' says a very short, round man wearing a tarnished medal around his flabby neck. 'I rowed with your old man. When I say rowed, I mean I steered him straight. He was quite an athlete. As are you, young lady. It comes as no surprise to see you stroking such a fine crew.'

'What was it like, winning the Head of the River?' I ask, eyeing off his medal. We are so close now, I can taste victory.

'It was the happiest moment of my entire school career. Even when they threw me in the wretched Barwon River. Good luck out there, Elena. Do your school proud.'

He shakes my hand and I smile. 'Thank you. I will.'

Afterwards we have a boat-club barbecue and everyone hangs out on the balcony.

Amelia and her Year Nine mates come up to me with a wrapped present.

'Leni, the Year Nines wanted to give you this,' she says. 'To say thanks for being our captain this season.'

I take the present and feel a surge of emotion. This is all really coming to an end. In a few days I won't be their captain anymore.

I unwrap the gift. It's a photo of the first eight, in a silver frame. It obviously has some parental involvement. They also give me a massage voucher for a spa in the city and a bar of my favourite chocolate.

'Aw, thanks, girls,' I say, giving Amelia a hug. She's sweet and funny. I'll be keeping an eye out for her in the future. Maybe one day I'll even get to coach her.

'Win it for us?' says Amelia. 'For Harley?'

'I'm going to try,' I say.

After a restless night's sleep in Geelong, Rachel, Penny and I are on a secret mission. Before breakfast, we sneak out to the McIntyre Bridge on the racecourse. We have a message for our crews.

'Did you get any sleep?' I ask Rachel.

'Not a wink,' she says, looking as tired as I feel.

We've taken over a motel near the course. An eighties throwback with peach-coloured bathrooms and a TV bolted to the wall. When the lights went out, I lay in the dark, coursing with adrenalin and nerves. I was desperate for the morning to come so we could get our races over and done with. I didn't need a wake-up call. I was already up, dressed and sitting in the toilet with the light on, reading, when Rachel knocked lightly on the door.

We walk onto the footbridge together. The other schools have been here too and space for our banner is limited.

We check out the other banners.

Row like there's no tomorROW, Ren!
The body achieves what the mind believes. Row hard!
It's in Y-OAR hands St Ann's!
This is it Stotts. Make it count!

I can't believe we are really here. No more training rows. No more preparation.

'Are you ready?' Penny asks.

'Let's do it,' I say.

Together we unfurl our white banner over the edge and tie it in place with ropes. It's a serious moment. Our moment.

'Let's go down and see how it looks from the bank,' says Rachel.

We stand on the grassy bank, looking up as the sign flaps gently from the bridge. It's simple, but it's the first thing every crew will see as they come down the home stretch in three hours' time.

IT DOESN'T HURT WHEN YOU WIN. GO HARLEY!

As we walk back to the motel, Rachel holds my hand and Penny's too.

'This is it,' she says. 'Game day.'

'No turning back now,' I say, nervous goose bumps rising on my arms.

Today I will remember every ergo, every freezing cold morning, every weight lifted, every blister, every seat race, every lost race, every painful stroke, every time I said no to a drink, a movie, a party. I'll remember it all and row my heart out. Not just for me, but for my crew and my coach.

'Wait. I want to tell you guys something,' says Penny, looking serious.

'What?' says Rachel. We both stop and stare at her.

'We are Harley, couldn't be prouder!' shouts Penny into the wind.

'If you can't hear us, I'll shout a little louder!' we join in.

We run along the bank, singing our hearts out. Letting go of some of the awful tension.

Back at the motel, Rachel heads towards the dining room for breakfast and I notice Sam hanging around in the courtyard. We've been forced to work together and get everything ready for this weekend, but I've been careful to keep my distance. With Sam Cam, if you get too close, he can pull you into his tractor beam.

'Can we talk?' he asks coming into the empty room.

'Of course. Everything okay?'

'I just wanted to tell you how amazing you've been, as a captain. We all appreciate it. I appreciate it.'

There's wistfulness to the way he says it and a lingering silence.

'I broke up with Bee,' he says. 'Like, for real. It's totally finished.'

'And that's supposed to make everything between us okay?'

'I still think about that night. About us,' says Sam. 'Do you?'

Before I can answer Sam leans in and kisses me, gently, on the mouth. This time, I'm ready for it. I don't let his Sam-ness blur my clean lines. My focus for what lies ahead. I steel myself and gently push him away.

'You don't want to try again?' Sam, asks. 'Now that things are less ... complicated?'

I feel a rush of bittersweet pain at what could have been. That lost fragile thing that neither of us could label or take ownership of. It would be so easy to go back to obsessing about Sam. Pining and waiting.

I take a step back from him. What we had is over. I'm different now. I've moved on.

'No, I don't want to try again, Sam,' I say firmly.

'What do you want, Leni?'

'An apology would be nice.'

'I'm sorry.'

'Good,' I say, smiling.

As I walk away, I put my headphones on and play 'Roar' by Katy Perry – the kick-ass song that helped me recover from Hurricane Sam.

Saturday, 2 April

Head of the River

Leni

My stomach gurgles as it tries to digest the toast and eggs I forced down at breakfast. Laura gathers us in a school minivan before our heat, air con up. It's going to be a scorcher. We've drawn tough competition in the heat – we'll go head-to-head with our arch rivals St Ann's. Our confidence has dimmed a little, knowing we have to race them first up. We'll have to win to go through to the final. Everyone else will fight out a repechage. We don't want to race the rep. Laura has already gone through the technical aspects of the race, now all that's left to do is inspire us. She leans forward and everyone in the van falls silent.

'In no other sport does the word *team* mean so much than in rowing,' she says. 'You guys know that already. If one of you is having a bad day, then the whole boat will feel it too. If someone is rowing a perfect race on their own, who cares? This morning, don't go out there as nine separate schoolgirls. Go out as one amazing crew. It'll hurt. But I've made sure you're ready for that. Embrace the pain. Stand up to it. Don't let it win. If it wasn't hard, everyone would row. It's the hard that makes it worth doing.'

She glances at me. 'Leni will take you there, guys. But you have to back her up. Be there for her every stroke. You can win this heat. You *will* win this heat. Okay, huddle up.'

Everyone gathers in a circle in the middle of the van and puts their clammy, nervous hands in on top of each other.

As usual I feel tired, washed out and nauseous. My head throbs.

'Cheer! Cheer! Win the race! Pull your oars to win first place! Let's go Harley, let's go! Show our school how good we row!' Everyone shouts as we clap our hands.

For extra motivation Laura fires up the stereo with our crew song, The Script's 'Hall of Fame'.

As we listen, every one of us feels like we could be a hero and get the gold.

We pile out of the van and Rachel leans into me.

'Let's be champions.'

On my way down to the boats, I bump into my parents. Mum has the weekend off to watch the racing, and they're both decked out in school colours. Mum hugs me and Dad gives me a firm handshake, which I push aside and hug him.

'What happened to no PDAs ever?'

'I've grown up.'

'You sure have,' says Dad.

'Any last-minute words of wisdom?' I ask them.

'This is your race. You have your coach's instructions. Go out there and do your best. Whatever happens, Leni, we are so proud of you,' says Mum.

The announcer calls marshalling for the girls' first eights and a jolt of nerves runs through me.

'I gotta go!'

'Good luck!' calls Dad.

I run my hand over the bow of the boat as we do our last-minute checks. Today, as Harley's best shot at Head of the River glory, we've been allocated the newest boat in the fleet, the *Vasile Popescu*. It makes today even more special rowing in a boat named after my father. I go to my seat and triple check everything. Gate tight? Check. Slide oiled? Check. Foot chocks secure? Check. Oar handle smooth? Check. I'm grateful Dad's sturdy hands have been here first. Mine are shaking.

I'm visualising the race as I walk down to the water's edge, so focused I nearly miss what the younger crews have done. They've set up a guard of honour with their oars and are throwing confetti at us. I walk through the archway of blades first, trying to act serious and focused, holding my side of the boat firmly on my shoulder, standing up tall. I end up cracking a massive smile.

'Go Leni!' Amelia shouts as she tosses confetti.

'Thanks, Meils,' I say. 'I ate your chocolate, so I've got extra energy.'

A few months ago I wouldn't have known her name, or cared. Thanks to Rachel, I now know every Harley crew member.

At the end of the group Cristian stands in his plain clothes, next to Audrey and Kieren. I wave to them and Audrey holds up a homemade sign that says GOOD LUCK LENI! It's the first time she's ever been to a regatta.

She runs up to me.

'Leni, take this,' she says, slipping something over my head.

I look down. It's a necklace with a silver oar and four-leaf clover charms threaded on.

'It's for good luck, but you won't need it,' she says. 'Just be the rowing legend we all know and love,' she says. 'I'm so proud.'

Cristian doesn't say anything to me as I pass by. He doesn't need to, I know what he's thinking. He knows how I'm feeling. He lifts up a single index finger. Meaning: Number One. It's a big deal for Cristian to come down when he's not in a crew. I'm racing for both of us today.

We lift the boat up over our heads and swing it down to our knees, placing it gently on the water's surface. Our blades screwed in tightly, we push of and sit forward to row to the start line, the cheers of our supporters making it hard to hear.

'Are you ready Harley?' shouts Aiko. 'Let's go kick some butt.'

We roll out our best practice starts behind the start line. So do St Ann's. We eye each other off, comparing technique. They look good. But so do we.

'Half! Half! Three-quarter-full!' Aiko says calmly into her headset as we smash out a warm-up start and check the

256

run off the boat. 'Eyes in the boat, girls. If there's anything worth looking at, I'll tell you about it.'

We drift around waiting for our race. My throat hurts and I feel washed out. I splash water on my face and slap my cheeks lightly. Rachel puts her hand on my shoulder. I turn my head and look down the line of my crew. Each one has a hand on the shoulder of the girl in front. I reach forward to Aiko and take her palm.

'This is your race, Harley,' Aiko says. 'Steady your nerves and believe in yourselves.'

We are so quiet I can hear the splash of water against the bow and Rachel's breath behind me. I release Aiko's hand and we look at each other.

'Are you ready, Leni?' she says.

'More ready than I have ever been in my life.'

'Crews! Attention! Row!' says the starter, breaking the unbearable, still silence. I spring out of the blocks, winding up too quickly and missing a stroke. Behind me, Rachel reminds me to relax.

'Find your rhythm, Leni. Lengthen out.'

I bring down the intensity and focus on feeling my crew behind me. Our boat edges into the lead. Pushing our legs down together, each of us works to find the thread that binds us down the boat. St Ann's settles in beside us at the 500-metre mark, pushing us along. Their stroke girl is beside me. I can hear her ragged breath. They want it badly, too. Their cox is screaming at them to push away from us.

'Okay Harley, you know what to do. Give me ten with the legs!' says Aiko. I remember every squat I did in the last six months and slam down my thighs. St Ann's lifts as well. Laura yells from the bank, but I have no idea what she's saying. Dad's voice is there somewhere too, but I don't dare to look out of the boat to find his funny old bike in the scrum.

My legs hurt, arms hurt, lungs hurt. We hit the 1000-metre mark. Normally I'd feel okay at this point, but I've dug deep and gone out hard. I blow air out of my mouth and get ready for another effort. We're sticking closely to our race plan. So far it's working.

'Come on Harley, this is it!' shouts Aiko as we go past the McIntyre Bridge, our sign hanging down in front of me.

'It doesn't hurt when you win!' pants Rachel at my back. I go for another twenty hard strokes and she's with me. St Ann's drops away by a quarter of a boat length. Out of the corner of my eye I can see they're getting sloppy and tired. I keep the rating high and we're at 250 metres to go. We row past the first of the caravan of school tents that line each side of the river. Now we can hear the crowd shouting, see the balloons and flags flying.

'Let's go now!' shouts Laura from the bank. 'We want this Harley. Nice and strong, Leni. Wind it up Harley. Thirty strokes left. I can see the finish line!'

We put everything into it but St Ann's crawls back into the race, sharpening up their act and managing a final push, working together beautifully. We're matching each other, stroke for stroke. It's so close our coxens are level. The horn goes off twice as we cross the line together.

It's impossible to tell who won. There's a confused silence as we drift away from the finish line and wait for someone to tell us who gets the golden ticket to the final.

'Wow, that was a close heat,' says the announcer. 'In a photo finish, St Ann's got it by a bow ball from Harley Grammar. Look out for these crews later in the program, folks. It's going to be a red-hot race for the Senior Division One Schoolgirl Eights. A bit of trivia, Harley Grammar is stroked by Leni Popescu, daughter of Olympic rowers Jodie and Vasile, so she'll be looking for more gold for the family trophy cabinet today.'

I put my head between my knees, dizzy from giving it everything. Wishing that for once, the announcer wouldn't mention who my parents are.

'How did we lose that race?' I ask.

Aiko looks like she's about to cry. She's sitting in the most frustrating seat in the boat, not being able to help us actually row the boat faster. She has no words of wisdom. Nobody has much to say.

'Looks like we'll be rowing the repechage,' says Rachel, behind me. 'These lucky undies better start doing their job, Leni.'

Cristian

I wasn't going to go to the Head of the River. I'd planned on going to a movie by myself and pretending it was just another Saturday. But then I thought of all the times Leni had stood on a chilly rugby field, cheering as I scrambled in the mud. How she'd been excited, not jealous, when I won The Head last year. I owed it to her to turn up.

I feel left out. Everyone huddles in their crew meetings, all polished and shiny in their uniforms. Their parents ridiculously proud. I have nowhere to be. No one to talk to. Everyone is busy and has a job to do. Without a crew and stupid red socks and a seat in the firsts, I'm no big deal. Another face in the tens of thousands of spectators.

I walk up and down the banks, lost in the crowd. Looking over the program for the millionth time. Eating a Mr Whippy soft serve for something to do. My appetite has returned and my weight is climbing steadily upwards. I'll never be as skinny or hungry as I've been these last months. It's messed with my head, too. That's why I'm seeing a counsellor who specialises in eating disorders. She's helping me change the bad ways I think about myself and food. It might take some time.

My crew will race in twenty-six minutes. A tough semi-final. If they finish in the top two crews, they'll go through to the A final. The bottom two and they'll be relegated to the B final. Nobody wants to race the banana final. Westie rides down to the start line. My crew rows past, pumped up and ready to have a crack. If Adam sees me, he doesn't show it.

I see Leni wandering back from the food trucks and she smiles and runs up to me.

'Cris! You came!'

'Of course I bloody did. What sort of a brother would

260

I be if I didn't watch my twin sister win the Head of the River?'

'You saw our heat?' Leni asks, looking worried. 'We have to row the repechage.'

'We rowed the rep last year,' I remind her.

'Did you?'

'Yeah, but you don't remember, do you? You just remember that we won. Don't worry, Leni, this rep is yours. Settle into your work and don't waste energy. You'll win it by a mile.'

Leni nods. 'Thanks, Cris.'

'Go on, get out of the sun and stretch. Get your crew together. Don't get sucked into the crowd. Stick together. Keep your heads on. You only have two more races to row. Enjoy it.'

Mum and I take a pair of folding chairs to a grassy hill to watch Leni's next race. She usually likes to take a bike and ride along, but today she says her legs are shaking too much to pedal. We're all nervous for Leni.

'Here comes Leni,' she says, peering through her old binoculars. 'They're in front.'

We stand up and peer at the spidery dots in the distance, which gradually focus into five crews.

We cheer as Leni and her crew smash through the repechage, winning by four lengths.

A peloton of bikes screams past. Laura out in front looking relieved.

'A final!' I say and we hug each other. This is what Leni has wanted for so long.

'She could go all the way,' Mum muses. 'She reminds me so much of Dad at the same age. He was all grit and no finesse. So single-minded. She's the same.'

Mum turns to me.

'You could go all the way too, Cris. I heard on the grapevine that the US scouts are interested in you for their college program?'

Going to the US is appealing, but not on a sport scholarship.

'They called. I told the scout I'd talk to you about it. I'm not sure.' I take out my phone and look at the scout's number. It's a big college. Somewhere lots of people would want to study. I suppose it makes sense. My erg score put me into the top handful of guys in the world. They don't know I've been cheating.

'They have some concerns about my … back. But they said I'd be a good fit for their program.'

'Cristian, this might be your second chance. They don't come around that often.'

I tap the number on the screen. Does it have a hidden message for me? *Cristian, take this scholarship. You will end up meeting hot cheerleaders and spend all your time at keg parties.*

I sigh and delete the contact before I can make another huge mistake. If he calls again I'll say I'm not interested.

'I don't want to row anymore. Besides, I don't feel like I earned this. I cheated. Why don't they take Leni? She deserves an opportunity like this.'

'They say she's not ready.'

'Why?'

I'm stunned anyone wouldn't want my smart, hard-working sister. The white to my dark side.

'She needs refining. But she wants it with all her heart. She'll get there. What do you want with all your heart?' Mum asks.

'Mum, don't be cheesy.'

'I'm serious.'

I look out to the river. My former crew is finishing up their race. Damien Yang sits in my five seat. It could've been me out there. All I feel is relief that I'm on the bank instead.

'They can't make up that ground,' says Mum as we watch Sam, Adam and the boys battle over the line in third place. *Third*. The A final has slipped away. There's no second chances for them. No more time. No more training. It's over. They'll row the B final. The best they can hope for is overall seventh. I look out to the guys' faces. They are utterly devastated. Adam bends over into the boat. Is he crying? Possibly. Westie and Mitch Langley cycle past in a cloud of anger.

'Not this,' I say, gesturing to my crew.

'Good enough,' says Mum, and she picks up my hand. Squeezes it.

'Sometimes you have to figure out what you don't want, before you can figure out what you do.'

Leni

We win our repechage easily. Smashing the rest of the boats by four lengths. The A final is next. The big one.

The only race that counts. We've drawn lane three. Once again St Ann's will be next to us.

We have our last crew meeting away from the crowds. We sit so close we're touching shoulders. We've all had our last trip to the loo, filled up our water bottles, stretched, done our warm-up run and said goodbye to our parents. It's just us now. Us and our boat. Laura has done a visualisation of the race with our eyes closed. The start, the middle, the finish. In her version, we win. In mine we do, too.

'Okay girls, you rowed the best time of the heats in your repechage. I don't see any reason why you shouldn't win this final. I have complete faith in you. All I really have to say is good luck. Leni, anything you'd like to add?'

I look around at the girls I'm putting my trust in. That I can't win this race without. That have become my friends. Somewhere a few hundred metres from us, St Ann's is having their pep talk too.

'We want to win this race,' I say. 'But so does St Ann's. We all want the same thing. To cross the line first. To take home those medals. To be the best in the state. The question is, who wants it the most?'

I look at Rachel and she's more serious than I've ever seen her. Not even the trace of a smile on her face. Next to me Penny fiddles with the top of her water bottle and jiggles her foot up and down, nervously. On her legs and arms is our race plan, written in black texta on her skin: *10 hard, 30 settle. Long and strong. Push. Sit back. Quick catches. Quick hands.* She won't even look at it when the race starts.

'Who's prepared to suffer the most to get it?' I continue, my voice confident. I don't want to let my crew know my heart has already broken out of the blocks and is racing hard under my ribcage.

'I am,' says Penny.

'Me too,' says Rachel.

'I'll suffer the most,' says Millie.

'I'll hurt more than St Ann's,' says Meg.

The rest of the crew joins in.

'Good. Because winning means we are prepared to pull harder and row better than anyone else out there. Let's win this race. No second chances, right guys? There's just this moment.'

The girls clap and hug each other, and everyone draws in a big breath. There's nothing left to say.

'Everyone, I want you to take five minutes alone,' says Laura. 'Pick a spot somewhere quiet. I have something for each of you.' She hands out a letter to each of us.

'When you finish reading, come back to the shed and we'll get our boat out for the last time.'

I take my letter and walk down the river to my favourite willow tree. It's bent over with age, limp branches dragging in the water. Nearby is a fine arts college with grafitti across its brick wall: *Motion & Emotion*. It seems to be a sign written for me today.

Under the willow tree's shade I open the sealed envelope and read the carefully written note.

Leni, I've seen you grow so much this season. You've earned your place in the stroke seat and as the leader of your crew and the entire Harley rowing squad as Captain of Boats. You've blossomed in confidence and rowing ability. I'm very lucky to have coached you this season and I fully expect you to join me in the senior ranks after you finish school. Maybe one day we will even row together. Be proud of yourself and your achievements today. Enjoy this race. Don't forget that after all the hours of training and all the blood, sweat, tears and drama – you're here today because you love the sport. Go out there and have fun. Whatever happens you are all my champions.

Love,
Laura x

I find myself crying, not because I'm sad, but because after this race, I won't see Laura and my crew every day. I'll miss them. I'll miss the magic we have together. I stay under my tree for a minute, looking out to the wide brown river, wondering what the future will hold. Win, lose or draw. I wipe away my tears, tuck the letter under the leg of my zootie and go to meet whatever this race throws at me.

We row up to the start carefully, but with confidence. Along the bank it seems like the entire school is there to cheer us on. Harley has hired buses to get a load of spectators here. People I don't even know, who couldn't care less about rowing, are shouting my name. Kids are dressed in their school uniforms (mandatory), ties wrapped around their heads, war paint on their cheeks. Someone plays a bugle like a call to arms. There are whistles and drums beating.

Parents fly the school flags overhead and the younger kids run beside the boats, screaming. Teachers ask for decorum. Police stand at the banks, arms crossed, in case anyone should decide to dive into the water and swim out to the boats gliding by.

'WE ARE THE HARLEY TEAM, THE MIGHTY HARLEY GRAMMAR TEAM!' shouts a kid down the front as hundreds of students shout it back at him. 'AND IF YOU CAN'T HEAR US WE'LL SAY IT IN LATIN.'

This is it. There's no room for mistakes. No dodgy strokes or missed catches.

'I'm scared,' Rachel whispers at my back.

'Me too,' I say. 'Now shutup and row.'

Dad rides along with the pack, his own coaching medal swinging around his neck. His third crew just won their A final. He went bananas after the race, but now he's quiet. Now is not the time to scream or yell. Now is the time to put our heads down, concentrate and get it right. In the transit lane we brush past St Ann's during our hard strokes, our oars clashing on the bow side. Clack, clack, clack. They look over at us, pull their oars in and try to stare us down.

'Calling the finalists for the Schoolgirls Senior Eight, Division One,' calls out the starter.

It's funny, I've been desperate for this moment to arrive, but now I'm actually here, it seems to be moving too fast.

'I'm looking for Kilcare Grammar in Lane one, St Ann's in two, Harley Grammar in three, Roberts Ladies College in four and Jubilee High in five. Coxens, I'll have you move your crews into position please,' says the starter.

My mouth is dry and I'm terrified. Aiko gets the bow four to touch it up to the start line and finally we are in position.

'Good luck,' the St Ann's stroke calls out to us.

'You too,' I echo weakly.

I look along their boat and realise they are made of flesh and bone and ponytails, like us. We can beat them.

'Sit forward Harley,' says Aiko, and I snap my eyes in front. 'Be ready, Leni. Good luck, girls.'

We sit in position, perfectly still, perfectly balanced. There's a light wind across the course, the sun directly overhead in a cloudless sky. I grip my oar tightly and think only of the first ten strokes. There is nothing more we can polish or perfect. All we have is us nine girls and the next six minutes.

I take one last, deep breath and let it trickle slowly from between my lips.

'Crews!'

We sit up and dip the tips of our blades into the water

'Attention!'

I tense up and lightly press back on my toes, ready for the start.

'Row!'

We pull back on the water and take our quick strokes. Half-half-three-quarter-full. It's all rush and splash and I try to grip the water as it gushes past. I listen hard for Aiko's directions over the yelling from the bank and the other coxes.

'Sit up! Push away! Legs Harley!'

The first 250 metres are a blur as each boat tries to snatch the early lead. We fall a few metres behind and I fight the urge to hurry our strokes. Instead, I hold the pace steady and strong. We can row through in the second half.

Let the others get tired and we'll come home like a train. We're still a quarter of a boat length behind the lead by the 500-metre mark, but we pull up on St Ann's and Jubilee falls away with Kilcare and RLC fighting for third. I feel good in second position. Like a jungle cat ready to pounce.

At the 1000, Aiko asks us for an effort and I feel the boat lift up and surge backwards. Everyone has shown up today. Nobody is slacking off and taking a free ride. We move further up on St Ann's, until we are a canvas short of them. It's another two-boat battle for the line and we row through the McIntyre Bridge to the snap of dozens of cameras hanging above us.

'I have the seven seat, give me the stroke!' yells Aiko and we creep up another notch to level the boats.

This time, I vow to myself. We are not going to lose. I lift the rating again and the crew comes with me. I'm pushing them harder than I ever have. I'm at thirty-six strokes per minute. Pulling each stroke through the water violently. I keep digging deeper for gold, ignoring the burning in my chest and throat.

We go under the final James Harrison Bridge level with St Ann's. Two hundred and fifty metres left to race. I can hear the announcer excitedly calling the race and the screaming of kids on the bank as they run along beside us, waving our school colours. From the corner of my eye I can see Laura going mental as she pedals fiercely on her bike.

'Thirty strokes to go! Give it everything, girls! This is it! No guts no glory! Come on!' shouts Aiko. She's red in the face and spit flies out of her mouth. She's leaning so far forward I worry I might hit her in the face with my handle. 'What have you got left? Give me everything you have!'

I grind my teeth, make a grunting sound and focus on one painful stroke at a time. I remember back to the pain of every run, every erg. *Dig deeper* I tell myself. *This is it. You'll never be back here again.*

The crowd is going crazy, but all I can hear is Rachel in my ear.

'Come on, Leni! Go mate! Go! I'm here, let's do this!'

I go, with Rachel right behind – ten perfect, hard strokes. Harder than I've ever rowed in my life. St Ann's slips a few centimetres away from us.

'We're moving through them!' screams Aiko. 'We've got this race!'

There's a metre in it. If that. I can't tell if we've got them or they've got us. It's so close.

We cross the line with absolutely nothing left. I fall back in the boat, the taste of metal in my mouth, breathing so hard I can't speak. My head pounds with a blinding headache. I'm dizzy and disorientated but I know this time we won it.

'Harley Grammer, stroked by Leni Popescu, takes out the Senior Eight, Division One in the narrowest of margins,' says the announcer. 'What an exciting race and a wonderful way to finish up a competitive season.'

Rachel grabs my shoulders and shakes them

'We won, Leni! Get up and take a bow!'

She punches the water, splashing me. I sit up and raise my fist above my head.

'Yeah!' I shout.

I reach back and grab Rachel's hand, squeezing tight and laughing.

As we row our way back to the staging to collect our trophy and medals, I smile so wide I'm not sure it fits on my face and feel a happy so big I don't know where to put it.

We stand up on the podium. Arms around each other. All nine of us and Laura. I duck my head as an Olympic gold medallist – my mum – hangs the champion's medal around my neck and gives me a huge trophy. She stands up on the podium and kisses me. Behind her, Dad takes photos and beams. What with his crew and my crew winning, he's floating a few metres off the ground with pride.

'I'm so very proud of you, darling.'

'Thanks, Mum. Now get down and give out the other medals.'

We pose for a photo with the local paper, our school photographer and the *Age* sports section. Me hugging the precious trophy and everyone else holding up their index fingers. Crossed oars and the river behind us.

'I was sweating bullets down that home straight,' says Laura, who hasn't fully recovered from the race. 'You guys kept me guessing right until the line.'

All the tension of the past year has disappeared. I feel like I don't have a single thing to worry about. Penny and I keep grabbing each other and jumping up and down, squealing.

Rachel seems stunned. 'We actually won. We did, didn't we? This isn't some fantasy dream sequence?'

'We won. We really, really did,' I confirm.

'You know what happens now?' Rachel says, looking at Aiko.

'No, what?' says Aiko.

'Tradition says we have to chuck the cox in the river,' says Penny.

'Yes, it is tradition,' I agree.

Aiko starts to back away but we drag her towards the river and push her in. She dog paddles around in the weeds. Then Rachel links hands with me and Penny.

'1-2-3 …' she says and we run towards the water and take a flying leap off the staging.

'We did it!'

Cristian

I'd decided I wasn't speaking to Adam ever again, but when I see him looking like the saddest, sorry sight on the riverbank, I can't help it. He's tucked behind a trailer of Harley boats, his head in his hands. He looks up and grimaces. It's hot and he's sweating and crying, his face streaked with dirt. I hand him my bottle of water and he takes his hat off and pours it down the back of his neck. He's short of breath and panting.

I sit beside him on the grass, my anger dissipating.

'You okay, Adam?' I ask.

'Did you see our heat?'

'Yeah. I'm sorry, I know how much you wanted to get through to the A final.'

'Maybe the B final is what I deserve. I bailed on a mate.'

'What happened?'

'Dad talked me into letting you take the blame after my results came back clear. He got me into the masking drugs, just in case. If I'd known we were going to get tested I never would have left you hanging. Who the hell cares now? All that gear and I'm still a loser.'

'You're not a loser.'

'I can't wait until this is all over. I rowed like a hack in the heat. Every stroke was an effort. I'm done. I don't think I have it in me to row the stupid B final.'

'Then don't.' I put my hands on his shoulder. 'You've got to stop living your life for other people, Adam. Fuck what your dad wants. What Westie wants. What people expect of you because of your last name. Do what you want for a change.'

Adam nods, rubs his jaw tiredly and pulls his hat back on.

'Just one more race. I've got to see this through to the end. I'm sorry, Poppa, for all of it. You're a good mate. I don't deserve a mate like you.'

'Yeah, yeah, I know. See you for a cheeseburger later?'

'Absolutely.'

I stop lurking in the shadows, find our school's cheer section and stand amongst the rabble. A few of the guys give me sideways looks.

'Why aren't you out there?' asks a Year Ten boy in full face paint and a jester's hat.

'I don't deserve to be,' I say truthfully.

'Oi, your sister's coming down the course,' says his mate.

They start up a chant and I join in. I feel a swell of brotherly pride as I sight Leni's boat in the distance. I'm caught up in the banging of drums and whistle blowing.

Come on, Leni, I say to myself, as if I am whispering in her ear. *You can do it, girl.*

'Leni! Leni! Leni!' shouts the crowd.

I see her go for the last push. It's so close I couldn't call it. The lead changes back and forth. But as they cross the line, Harley edges out St Ann's – the crew that's beaten them all season. I knew she had the heart to get there.

'Yeah!' yells the Year Ten kid, slapping me on the back. 'Your sister rocks!'

I slap him back and smile. 'She sure does.'

After Leni's race, there's a ten-minute medal break and then the boys' first eight B and A finals. The last races of the day. I can't get down to the podium in the crowds to see Leni get her reward, so I decide to stay put and watch Adam and my crew finish off our strange season. For some schools it's no disgrace to race in the B final, but for Harley Grammar it's considered a whipping.

'Coming down the course now we have the second last race of the day and more quality eight racing with the Schoolboy Division One B final,' says the announcer. 'Leading at this stage by a long margin is Harley Grammar. You'll all know Harley won the Head of the River last year, so this is rather an upset. Still, they're rowing very well and look to have this sewn up.'

The cheering on the bank doesn't dim for the consolation B final. Harley's cheer master peps up his disciples as Adam and my old crew smashes through the final 250 metres. The sad thing is they finally look like a crew that deserved to row in the A final. *Too little, too late,* I think. As they cross the line, a hush falls over the part of the crowd that's closest to the boat. I strain over the tops of heads to see.

'What's going on?' I shout to a guy next to me.

'Someone's passed out!' he shouts back. *Who is it? Which seat?*

I push my way to the front of our school's barricade and look out to the crews. In the six seat Adam's slumped over his oar handle, blade trailing limply in the water. I consider jumping the fence and swimming out to him. I have no idea what I'd do if I got past the cops and the water safety boats. I can't remember any of my first-aid training. *Is it two breaths, one compression?* I think wildly.

'What's wrong?' I yell at a teacher near the barricade.

'I don't know,' she says.

Adam falls back in the boat, letting go of his oar, his arms limp, head lolling on Damien's feet behind him. The cheer section is now completely silent. I run down the side of the bank towards the staging in total panic. Damien is splashing water on Adam's face and shaking his shoulders. I should be in that seat right now. Would I be doing any better job than Damo? Adam looks unconscious. Sam calls out for help to the bank, waving his arms over his head. It seems to be taking so long to get help out to him. *Come on!* I think. *Rescue him!*

Seconds tick past. The crowd of over fifteen thousand is hushed and worried. Me, most of all. Unaware there's been a collapse, the main race keeps coming down the course. Officials on the bank and the course boats try to stop it and fail. The coxens, rowers and bike packs are completely in their own world. A rescue boat speeds out to Adam, the eights reach the final bridge. Who wins seems pointless now. Why did we spend so much time and effort on it?

'Eights! We have a medical emergency on the finish line. Rescue! Rescue! If you can hear me please stop racing!' shouts the announcer. 'St John's Ambulance will assess the situation immediately and we have paramedics on their way to the course. Please stay calm in the spectator areas. We will update you as soon as we know more.'

The A final comes across the line. The big race. The race that matters. The Head of the River. The crews look around, puzzled by the silent crowd. This is supposed to be their moment of glory. It's been snatched away from them.

'Who won?' a boy says behind me.

'Who cares?' his friend answers, before I have the chance.

The rescue boat speeds Adam back to a landing area on dry land. St John's Ambulance workers lift him out of the boat but his body is still limp. They start doing chest compressions right away. Mitch is by his side, his brother, too. They look devastated.

I try to get closer, to see if Adam's eyes are open, but the crowds are huge.

'Can you move?' I say, pushing at a group of guys who are rubbernecking in front of me. 'That's my best friend! I have to get to him!'

'Mate, he wouldn't know if you're there or not,' says one and it takes all my self-restraint not to deck him.

By the time I get close enough to see Adam, the ambulance has arrived and paramedics have taken over CPR. I hear his rib crack and flinch. They get out a defibrillator and attach the pads to his bare chest, delivering a shock of electricity that doesn't seem to do anything.

'Still no pulse. Let's get him out of here,' says one.

Before I can tell Adam to hang on, the ambulance doors have closed and he's left the area, lights flashing and sirens blaring.

After Adam's collapse, nobody is in the mood for celebrating. We file soberly out of the regatta and try to find our car in the chaos. I check my phone obsessively, hoping for a text from Adam. Something that tells me he is fine – just dehydrated or heat affected. There's no word.

'That time the Harley crew got would've won them the A final,' a St David's rower says to his mate in front of us.

'Someone should tell Adam Langley that,' says the mate.

'If he's still alive,' says the rower.

A ripple of uncertainty crosses my mind. Leni must feel it, too.

'He's fine, Cristian. Don't listen to them,' she says. 'Let's just go home and wait to hear something other than gossip.'

Leni

After the regatta I don't feel well. My throat hurts and I'm dragging myself around the house trying to get ready for the official Head of the River dinner.

'Are you sure you're up to this? You look pale,' says Mum, putting a palm to my forehead. 'You're hot.'

'I'll take a couple of Panadol. I think I overdid it in the race,' I say, backing away from her before she sees my puffy glands and the bags under my eyes. Make-up has only gone so far.

'You could skip it, you know. Have an early night? It's been a big day. You must be worried about Adam, too.'

I look at the couch where Cris is lying, his feet up, playing with his phone, Banjo curled over his size twelve feet. I wish I could pull on my ugg boots and join him. Order some pizza for dinner. But duty calls. Dad and I are expected to be there tonight. We are both in the winners' circle. It's our moment.

'I have to be there. I'm the captain. I'm giving a speech.'

'Okay, well let Dad know if it's too much. He'll bring you straight home to bed.'

I'm sitting with my crew at the front of the room. We all look different. Gone are the sweaty zooties and crusty caps, replaced by skirts, dresses and blow-dried hair. The Head of the River cup is placed in the middle of the table and every now and again someone will come by and want to touch it. I can't take my eyes off it. I can't believe it's really mine. Ours.

I pick up the fancy place setting outlining the night ahead.

Harley Grammar School
Boat Club Dinner – Proceedings
7 pm – Doors open
7.30 pm – Guests seated
Captains of Boats speech – Elena Popescu and Samuel Camero
8 pm – Main course served
8.30 pm – Presentation of year books
9.30 pm – HGS boat song
Close

Laura stops by our table and puts her hand on my shoulder. 'Ready?' she asks. I nod and take out my carefully written speech, feeling the first shot of nerves since our race. The painkillers have done their job and I don't feel too bad. Sam and I walk together to the front of the room and he's introduced first. He takes the microphone and the room erupts in wolf-whistles and cheers and then falls silent.

'I want to thank every rower for giving it their all on the Barwon River today. The racing was fast and fierce and every one of our crews put in a good showing. None more so than the girls' first eight who we can now call Heads of the River. Well done to Leni and her amazing crew.'

The entire room stands up and stomps their feet, including Dad. It's a zoo. I smile, so happy and relieved.

'Our boys had a tougher day out there,' says Sam, a note of sadness in his voice. 'In rowing, you don't always get to go fast at the right time. We tried our best, but couldn't produce what we needed when it counted. That doesn't take away from the hard work my guys put in.

I want to thank each of them for their dedication, but most of all Adam Langley, our six seat, who collapsed on the course today and is currently in hospital recovering. You're a legend, mate, and we hope you get better soon. I'd like to thank our coach, Mr West, and express our gratitude for the chance to be part of the great tradition of rowing at our school. We will go our separate ways, but the club will continue and we wish it the best of luck and fast racing in the future. Finally, to the Year Nines, Tens and Elevens here tonight – good luck for next year and keep the flag flying high. We'll be the ones cheering you on the bank.'

I take the microphone from Sam. Down the back Dad whistles and starts up a chant.

'Leni! Leni! Leni!'

I was going to give a formal speech, but I fold up my bits of paper and decide to do something different. Something really not me.

'I couldn't have won the Head of the River on my own today,' I say. 'So I don't want to give this speech on my own. I'd like to ask the winning girls' eight to join me up here, as well as our coach Laura.'

Everyone claps as my crew steps up from the table and crowds around me. It feels right to have them by my side. This is not just my victory.

'This is how we won today,' I say. 'We stuck together through everything and found a way to work as one.'

I hand the microphone to Penny next to me. 'You first.'

When we all finally finish talking and thanking everyone Rachel puts her arm around me and squeezes. 'You're a bloody legend, Leni.'

Stuffed with pumpkin soup, some fancy meat dish called chateaubriand and chocolate baskets with berries, I look over the year book given to me and the rest of my crew. I've seen it before. Every page has my fingerprints on it. As part of my captain duties, I organised for the books to be put together and printed weeks ago and given out as a keepsake tonight. The hardbound leather book is full of club rowing photos, quotes, regatta results and official crew photos. Along with the school crest, the names of my crew are stamped in gold lettering on the cover.

Harley Grammar School
Girls 1st VIII
Bow: M. Aitkin
2. A. Bishara
3. G. Johnstone
4. J. Sweeny
5. S. Hao
6. P. Mission
7. R. Wilson
Stroke: L. Popescu
Cox: A. Tanaka
Coach: L. Muston

I run my hand over the raised lettering and the names of the girls. *My girls.* I flip through the photos of the entire boat club. All of us training, rowing, winning, losing. It's been an incredible season. I'll never forget how much these past six months have made me grow up and become a leader.

I read over the inscriptions from my crew. One stands out.

Leni, You were amazing. We did amazing things.
Love, Rach x

I lean over and hug her spontaneously.

'*You're* amazing,' I say.

Sam gets up and announces we will sing the Boat Club Song and then wrap up the night.

'This song has been sung at every Harley Head of the River dinner for over a hundred years,' he says. 'Tonight I'd like to dedicate it to Adam Langley, who should have been here with us tonight.'

My crew links arms as everyone stands up to sing. The entire room filling up with voices low and high. Old and young. I catch Dad's eye across the room and he smiles at me. This is what he meant when he said rowing brings people together. Makes them loyal and bonded for years after their races end.

Long live Harley Grammar and our lasting pride
The love of the river, that nothing divides
May the good old dark greens never weaken or break,
Till the coxswain calls out 'easy oar, easy mates'.

Down the Yarra we glide,
True friends at our side.

This fellowship nothing on earth can divide.

Fair play and hard rowing, by these do we steer,
To triumph unbeaten, our victory clear.

From our heroes of old,
To the novices bold,
Our courage in racing is untarnished gold.

Here's to the eight and here's to the four,
And here's to the boys and girls strong to the core,
And here's to our school, dear to our hearts,
And the Head of the River, where we made our mark.

Cristian

On Sunday I get up early and know I can't drift around the house like a lost sock all day. I have to do something. In the kitchen Mum has tea on and Dad is listening to a Romanian radio station. They look up when I shuffle in and sit at the table.

'Would it be okay if I went out?' I ask them. 'I want to visit Adam in hospital.'

They share a look like it's not the best idea. I get it. There's no love lost between Mitch and either of my parents.

'You'll have to get permission from Adam's family,' says Mum. 'I think I still have Belinda Langley's number. I'll dig it out for you.'

She gets the number from her phone and scribbles it down for me.

'Thanks. I'll call her now.'

'He's at the Alfred, isn't he? Want some company?'

'Nah, I'd rather go by myself.'

I leave Leni a note and let her sleep. She's completely wrung out from racing and had a late night at the boat club dinner. She'll be annoyed she missed out, but it's too much for both of us to go and I don't want to drag her out of bed.

At the hospital I walk into the main entrance and ask for Adam.

'Adam Langley. He's in ICU. Level four. Are you immediate family?'

'No.'

'Do you have permission from his immediate family to visit?'

'Yes.'

'Okay, pop up and speak with his Unit Nurse Manager first. It should be okay.'

In the waiting room, I see Adam's brother Oliver. I know him from the river. Two years ago he rowed in the crew above me. He was Captain of Boats in his final year.

'Cris,' he says, standing up. He's fatter and taller than Adam, but they have the same freckled face and intense blue eyes. I don't know what to do so I shake his hand. He smells like stale coffee and body odour. Like he hasn't showered in days.

'Mum told me you were coming in this morning. It's what Adam would want.'

'Can I see him now?' I ask.

I'm impatient to see him. To talk to him about the fright he gave us. To tell him to hurry up and get better.

'The nurses are doing some checks. Mum will come out in a minute.'

'Where's your dad?' I ask. I'm steeling myself for an encounter with Mitch. He may not want me here.

'He's gone for food. The grub here is terrible.'

A nurse in scrubs approaches me. 'You're visiting Adam today?' she asks.

'Yes. I'm his best mate, Cristian.'

'Have you ever been to an ICU unit, Cristian?'

'No.'

'Okay, then there's a few things you need to know. Be prepared to see lots of lines, tubes, wires and monitoring equipment. Some of it will beep and make loud noises. That's okay. It doesn't mean it's an emergency. We're just keeping a close eye on your friend. Adam isn't conscious, but feel free to touch and talk to him. He may be able to hear you. Wash your hands with gel before you go in.'

I scrub my hands with antibacterial gel from a dispenser and sit down with Oliver in a plastic chair, listening to the sound of beeps and alarms going off. The quiet bustle of nursing staff attending to the sickest of the sick. The smell of disinfectant is overpowering.

'How is he?' I ask.

Oliver shakes his head. 'Not good, Cris, not good at all.'

Adam's mum comes out of the room. I haven't seen her in over a year. She's lost weight and changed her hair colour. She hugs me, tightly. I spent a lot of time around her kitchen bench when I was younger. She was funny and warm. I never could understand why she was with Mitch and it didn't surprise me when she left him.

'Cris, you made it. It's so good to see you. You ready to come in?'

She takes me into the room and I nearly sink to my knees when I see Adam. He's hooked up to a machine that's breathing for him. Every space on his skin seems to be attached to a tube or wire. I have no idea what to do.

'Do I sit on the bed?' I whisper.

Adam's mum smiles and pulls a chair over to the side of Adam's bed. She takes Adam's hand and places it in mine. His skin is warm.

'Talk to him,' she says. 'Tell him how great he raced on Saturday. What mischief you boys are going to get up to this year. Big Year Twelve boys. I can hardly believe it.' She backs away, closes the door behind her.

I look at Adam's face. It's peaceful and still. Then I start to talk.

April

One week after Head of the River

Leni

It takes a few days for the blood tests to come through. By then, I'm already in bed. My neck swollen, my throat so raw it hurts to swallow. Even taking a shower requires extreme effort.

'Infectious mononucleosis,' says Dr Chang on the phone.

'What's that?'

'Glandular fever, otherwise known as the kissing disease, though you can get it from sharing water bottles or eating utensils. It's spread by infected saliva.'

I think of kissing Adam and Sam. All the saliva we swapped in our little love triangle. Of the water bottles I casually shared with my crew.

'I'd like you to take a fortnight off school and six weeks off your training.'

'*Six weeks?*' I'd miss nationals, state selection. The AIS trials. In terms of my rowing, this was a disaster.

'I can't. Not now.'

'Yes. If you don't rest, you're in danger of getting even more ill. By rest I mean no rowing, running or heavy socialising. Stay at home, keep your fluids up, eat healthy food, sleep. Come back and see me in two weeks and we'll see how you're doing. Put your mum on, I'd like to talk to her too.'

I hand the phone to Mum and go to my room to lie down, again. I turn my laptop on to check Facebook and see that Adam has posted a status update. I smile and sit up, excited. Cristian went to see him a few days ago and said he was still unconscious. His condition had obviously improved.

Hi everyone,

I'm Adam's brother, Oliver. Early this morning my brother died, peacefully, in his sleep. We are so incredibly sad and heartbroken by this terrible loss and feel like a piece of us is missing. I can hardly breathe. My family can hardly breathe.

I'm sure you all know that Adam was an amazing bloke with a bright future ahead of him. Thanks for all your messages, they are helping us come to terms with this tragedy. I wanted to say – I love you, Adam. You were an amazing little brother and we will miss you forever.

0 Likes 117 Comments

I bury my head in my pillow and scream. I only stop when Mum comes into my room and holds me in her arms.

Cristian comes home early from school. He drops his bag heavily in the hallway and runs into the kitchen, crying. Mum grabs him and hugs him and so do I. We stay like that, a little triangle of grief, until Cris pushes us away. He paces up and down the kitchen.

'No, no, no,' he says. 'This wasn't supposed to happen.'

'Sit down, Cris,' Mum says. But he doesn't.

She puts the kettle on and goes through the motions. Spooning out the dry tea-leaves, filling the pot, leaving it to steep. She has been through this before. Countless times. The death of a child is part of her world.

I look at Adam's Facebook page, now an online memorial to him and the best place for any updates from his family on the funeral plans. Funeral plans. I can't believe he's gone. Completely gone.

'Cris, come here,' I say. He's making me jumpy with his pacing.

We sit together at my laptop as Mum puts tea in front of us. She stands behind Cris, her hands on his shoulders. He's shaken to the core. We both are. I feel scooped out and hollow. Shocked.

'A fit seventeen-year-old dropping dead of heart failure?' Mum muses. 'This is a tragedy.'

'Why did it happen, Mum?' I ask. I should be in bed, but I can't sleep. I'm confused. Adam was so strong. So young. It didn't make sense.

'I don't know,' says Mum. 'Adam may have had a pre-existing heart condition. It's hard to say.'

Cristian and I scroll through Adam's Facebook page, hoping to add our own comments. There's nothing else for us to do.

In total shock. Miss you Ads
Rachel xxx

Devastating news. So so sorry and sad
Aiko x

Oh no. no. Not my beautiful nephew.
Susan

Big hugs and love to all your family, you are in our prayers
DX

Very sorry. Very sad. Too Soon.
Nick

Hundreds of comments have been sent from all over the world, all of them dripping with loss.

I type out one of my own.
Adam,
I love you. I'm sorry I never told you that.
Leni x

Cris tries to type one out, but he can't. Instead he drops his head to his knees and howls. Punches the table with his fist.

I close the computer screen. We put our arms around each other and cry.

Cristian

In my room I take out my phone and go to my contacts page. Adam is the first name on my list. I'd often call him by mistake when my phone was in my back pocket or I dropped it. There's a thumbnail photo of his face next to the number. I press it and hold the phone to my ear.

'Hi, It's Adam. Leave a message or send me a text. Bye.'

I hang up and dial the number again, and again, and again. On the sixth call I leave a message.

'Adam. It's Cris. I don't know why I'm calling, I know you're not there but I needed to hear your voice again. Guys aren't supposed to say shit like this, but I love you, mate. I'll miss you.'

I hang up, undress and put on my zootie.

There's only one way I can stop this hurt.

Dad pulls me off the ergo machine in the garage. I'm sweating, crying. A wreck. He wrenches the handle from my hands and forces me off the seat. The floor below me is puddled with sweat. I've been here for two hours, revving the handle like a robot. Pull, recover. Pull, recover. Pull, recover. Counting strokes, watching the kilometres tick upwards. I was almost at 20 ks. I wasn't intending to stop.

I crouch on the floor, totally exhausted, still not feeling any better.

'Dad, I need to tell you something,' I say. 'Adam took steroids too and other stuff. We did it together.'

Dad doesn't look surprised.

'Of course together. Your mother and I, we already knew in our hearts.'

'That's why he died? The drugs? Wasn't it? *Wasn't it?*'

Dad throws a towel over my shoulders, rubs my arms dry.

'Cristian. We make this right. I promise you.'

Adam's funeral is held at St Paul's Cathedral in the city. It's the only church big enough to hold everyone. There are hundreds of people here. Maybe even a thousand. This is what happens when someone dies too young. The community comes out in droves to protest the unfairness of it. The cruel snatching away of promise and a future. Leni insists on coming to say goodbye, even though she's sick as a dog. I don't think Adam was the love of her life, but she's cried for three days, because she lost a friend, too.

'We'll take Leni inside to sit down,' says Mum, squeezing my arm. 'Are you okay to do the guard of honour?'

'I'll be fine. Take Leni inside before she passes out,' I say.

Dad and I stand in a guard of honour as the coffin arrives. All the oars from the boatshed are here. Sweep oars and sculling blades, fibreglass and waterlogged wood. Some painted, some plain. They cross over each other, forming a long, sad hallway. The coffin is pulled out of a black hearse. Adam's brothers – Oliver and Matty – and four of their cousins steady the weight of it on their shoulders.

As they make the slow walk down the guard, I feel like I should step aside. Could I have stopped us going to that dodgy gym? What if I'd said no to Adam's plan to get us back in the firsts? Would Adam have had the guts to go through with it alone? Right now, it's pretty hard not to wonder why I didn't die, and Adam kicked on to eighty. Who decides these things?

But I hold up my oar as the coffin passes because it's the right way to honour him, standing there straight and tall in my school blazer and polished shoes. The coffin is draped in the school's rowing flag. I'm not sure that's what Adam would have wanted, in the end, but it does the job of stopping us from looking too hard at the wooden box, and thinking of Adam lying inside it.

'We go inside,' Dad says, taking my oar and putting it back in the trailer.

Inside the church it's stuffy and everyone fans themselves with the picture of Adam's smiling face. There's a few prayers and hymns and his brothers speak at the pulpit, their voices cracking.

'Easy oar, Adam,' says Oliver, a traditional call to stop rowing. 'Rest.'

Adam's mum sits bent over and shaking through the service. Mitch changes seats in the middle of the funeral and goes to sit beside her. Sharing their unbearable loss.

A final song is played over the loudspeakers, filling up the cavernous, gothic cathedral, right up to the vaulted ceilings and down the long aisle. On a big screen are scrolling pictures of Adam. Adam as a cheeky little boy on a bike, Adam jumping on a trampoline with his brothers, Adam rowing in last year's winning first eight, me behind him. Adam in black tie going to our Year Eleven formal with Leni. All our memories of him in one stupid montage.

There isn't a single person in the room who isn't bawling. Leni cries from the moment the funeral begins, to the moment it ends. When it's over, Mum takes her back to the car to fold her – crumpled and exhausted – in the back seat.

I walk slowly down the aisle behind Dad, who is dressed in a dark suit and tie, his hands and fingernails clean, hair brushed. Outside, the light is so bright it hurts my eyes. Trams ching their horns, cars drive, people walk to their jobs, sipping takeaway coffees. The world keeps moving, even if I feel like it should be still and silent.

I stop behind Dad as he claps Mitch on the shoulder and says loud enough for me to overhear.

'If my son died, they must bury my heart with his body.'

He hugs Mitch. Longer than I have ever seen two grown men hug, and Mitch lets out a high-pitched sob. Dad releases Mitch, grabs my hand and walks towards the car in a very straight line. The last time he held my hand, I was in kindergarten.

I go to the wake at the Toorak mansion I was thrown out of last year. There's no security guard at the door. No caterers or bar staff. Everyone's brought a plate of food and Adam's brothers and other relatives are fetching drinks. There's no laughing. No smiling. No short skirts or flirting. The dress code is black. This isn't a celebration of a life well lived. It's a mourning of a life cut short. I drink a beer and sit with my former crew by the pool, peeling the label from the slippery bottle. I stare into the water and the shimmering blue tiles, feeling numb. An early autumn leaf the colour of a red delicious apple flutters down on its surface and there's a chill in the air. Summer is winding down.

Penny has been standing with the girls' eight, but she opens the child-gate to the pool, walks over and sits down next to me.

'Hey,' she says.

'Hey.'

We sit in silence for a few minutes, and for once, I don't try to fill it.

'I've been meaning to say thanks, for the flowers,' Penny says.

I stare at her.

'How did you know?'

'You're a giant,' she reminds me. 'You can't hide behind a tree.'

'I was trying to say sorry.'

She puts her arms around my waist and leans in, so I can smell the shampoo on her hair. That coconut scent I've longed for. I close my eyes, breathe it in. A tear drips from my nose. I feel released.

'Why are you hugging me?'

'Because you need it.'

'And what about you?' I ask.

'I need it too. Don't worry. It's all going to be okay,' she whispers.

For some reason, I believe her.

I gather my old crew outside the Langley mansion. We stand in a cold wind by the hedges I once tried to pull down in a rage.

Nobody knows what I have to say and how hard it is for me to say it.

'What's up, Poppa?' asks Julian. Everyone is tired. Emotional. We all want to go home to our families.

'I didn't hurt my back,' I say to the group. 'I was caught taking steroids and diet pills. I was kicked off the team.'

'I knew it!' says Damo. He's angry. I don't blame him.

'I don't want to get into a fight, not today, but I do want to apologise to all of you. I was told I didn't have to admit my guilt, but I want to. It's the right thing to do.'

Nick looks at me, shaking his head. 'We could've won with you in the boat.'

'I doubt it.'

'How are we ever going to know that now?'

Mum picks me up from the wake. Dad's in the car with her.

'Still want to do this?' she asks.

'Yep. But drive quickly before I change my mind.'

We park outside the police station and my parents come in with me for support. Their standing by me makes it easier to do this.

We walk past the parked white cars and the blue-and-white checked sign outside. I push on the door and into the sterile reception area and straight up to the desk.

'Can I help you?' asks a receptionist.

I can't seem to find my voice and Mum leans into the counter.

'My son would like to report the supply of anabolic steroids and performance-enhancing drugs to minors at the Fitness Now gym in Toorak.'

She squeezes my arm and I feel no regrets. It's too late to get Adam back, but I can tell the truth, all of it, even the bits that make me look bad.

Leni

I'm feeling pretty low in the days and weeks after Adam's funeral. Stuck at home, only my books and study for company. The walls of my bedroom are starting to close in. I'm supposed to be resting but a knock on the front door is a welcome surprise. I put on my ugg boots and get out of bed. Through the glass I see Sam Cam standing on my doorstep. I open the door, even though I'm not sure I want to see him.

'Hi Leni,' he says, smiling.

'How are you feeling?'

'Blah. What you got there?' I ask.

It's hard to miss. He's carrying an oar in bubble-wrap.

'Shall I bring it in?' he asks.

I hold open the door and he brings the long oar into the house, puts it down on the living room floor.

'Am I allowed to open it?'

'Yes, of course. It's yours.'

I rip off the bubble-wrap. The blade is painted with the names of our crew. Head of the River champions. It's my very own trophy oar.

Sam looks at the oars already hung up on our walls.

He holds mine up underneath. 'Should go nicely, right about here,' he says.

'Did you do this?' I ask.

'No. Everyone in your crew got one.'

'Oh,' I say, feeling silly that I thought Sam had gone to any special trouble.

'They had a ceremony at assembly. I volunteered to bring it over to you. Thought it might cheer you up. I'm also saying goodbye.'

'Where are you going?'

I knew Sam wouldn't stick around, but I thought he'd stay until the end of the year at least.

'Dad's relocating to California. I'm going to finish my last year of high school over there and then transfer to Berkley.'

'Berkley college? Ivy league?'

'Yeah. They offered me a sporting scholarship. I'll be rowing crew for them for a few years.'

'Oh. That's really far away.'

I feel deflated. Sam's heading off on a big adventure, and I'm stuck spinning my wheels here. Hoping to be able to get enough strength to walk around the block. I'm jealous.

'I thought maybe you'd get an offer, too,' says Sam.

I'm still smarting from being snubbed by the US scouts.

From not being able to trial for the AIS or win the gold medal at nationals with the rest of my crew. Not doing anything is more frustrating than anything I've ever done.

'Not this year. They said I needed more time in the boat. Doesn't matter. I didn't want to go to the US anyway.'

'Will you keep rowing?' Sam asks.

That's a question even I can't answer. 'I dunno. Maybe.'

Sam hugs me and I know I probably won't see him again for a long time. Maybe not ever. He's gone, like he said he would be. 'I'll miss you, Leni Popescu.'

'Me too, Samuel Camero.'

I watch him leave from the doorstep and realise, finally, who it was that Sam loved the most. Not me. Not Bee. Not some random American girl he was sure to fall into bed with. Sam's one true love is rowing. It had been all along.

When I'm finally able to take a shower without having to rest afterwards and my throat doesn't hurt to swallow and my face stops looking like a glob of marshmallow, I decide to go for a walk.

'Where are you off to?' asks Mum, thrilled I'm leaving the house. My bum has left a permanent imprint on the couch and I've watched more TV than I have in my whole life. She's been fussing, too, worrying how I'm coping.

'When Dad gets home I thought I'd put a barbie on. Maybe some steaks? Get some iron into you. You look so pale.'

Dad's at land training at the Victorian Institute of Sport with his new crew. After the school season he was asked to coach the state under-22 crew for a trans-Tasman regatta in

New Zealand. Westie says he'll move him up to coach the second boat next season. I'm proud of him. He's worked hard on his English and there's no one on the river who knows more about the technical side of rowing.

'Just a walk, I'll be back for dinner,' I say. 'Thanks for looking after me, Mum.'

'Take it easy,' Mum says. 'You're still getting your strength back remember.'

'It's a walk, Mum.'

I leave the house and look right, then left. It's one of those walks where you set off, not sure where you're going. As well as getting out of the house I need to get out of my head. It's been a few weeks since the funeral, but I think about Adam every day. I miss him.

'How ya going, luv?' a homeless man says, sitting in a pile of his belongings outside the TAB.

'You look happy,' he says.

'I am happy. I'm walking. I'm out of the house,' I say.

'God bless you, gorgeous. You keep on walking.'

'I will.'

I take a tram to the city and wander around the uneven pink stones of Federation Square, past Cristian's bells that mended my broken heart, past the tram stop that once took me to Sam's lonely apartment; down to the boatsheds that welcomed my dad to Australia; past the river that made me stronger; the ergos that broke my spirit and the photos and plaques that tell the history of who I am.

There's been so much going on since Adam's funeral. The news that he died as a result of performance-enhancing drug abuse shocked everyone, but not our family. The huge training and steroids use combined caused his heart muscle to overgrow and shut down.

The school swung into action, putting into place random drug testing across all senior sports. A new anti-doping education program funded by the Langley family trust will be rolled out next year. Charges were laid on the trainer at Fitness Now gym, thanks to Cristian's testimony. I was proud of him standing up to the label of being a cheat. It helped that he had Penny to back him up. They turned out to be the perfect couple after all. At least one of us got a Disney ending.

I end up facing a crammed noticeboard at the Mercantile Club.

SIGN UP!

VICTORIAN YOUTH 8 SQUAD

I run my hand over the paper and look at all the names that have already signed up. There are forty at least. Girls from all over the river. All schools. All abilities. All sizes and shapes. All of them throwing their hat in the ring. Wanting to be part of it, still.

I step out to the balcony, looking at a crew of masters women getting ready for a late row. They're wrinkled and weathered, bellies stretched from babies and living. They gossip and laugh as they set up oars on the bank, fill up their water bottles and lightly carry the boat out to the staging. One of them looks up at me, smiles and waves.

'Leni!'

I look closer. It's a friend of Mum's. A former crewmate she sometimes had round for coffee. I don't remember her name. My parents have so many rowing friends it's hard to keep track. For some reason, they all know my name.

'See you out there?' she calls.

'Maybe!'

She laughs. 'You can't fight it. It's in your genes.'

I laugh, too. Because she's right. This sport runs through my veins like river water.

The four women roll up together and take off with a set of beautiful, precise strokes. The light is fading and all that's left are the dark outlines of their bodies. For a moment, they look like a schoolgirl crew.

I turn to head down the stairs, back home for dinner before my parents begin to worry. But I can't shake the feeling I've forgotten something. I backtrack to the notice-board and the sign-up sheet. I stare at it for a few minutes, listening to the sound of my heart beating in my wrist and neck. I take the pen and write my name down in capital letters.

LENI POPESCU.

I add my mobile number, knowing that when my phone rings for the first training session, I'll be ready.

Acknowledgements

This book would still be half-finished without the generosity of the Australia Council Arts Literature board.

Thank you to my family, Dale and Sophie, I'm so lucky to have you. To Mary Harry, world's best Mum and my inspiring sisters, Sarah and Nicola. To my sensitive and wise 'first readers' Michael Harry and Sarah Minns – you were the perfect choice to entrust with a book that was still taking shape.

The subject matter of this book is very close to my heart. Many thanks to my father, John Harry, for introducing me to the sport of rowing and sharing a love of competition. Melbourne's Yarra River will always be 'Dad's River' to me. Thanks to Donna Harry for babysitting Soph so I could sneak away to the Surry Hills Library to write.

A section of this novel was written in the cottage at Ten Ten farm. Thanks to my hosts, Ann and Michael Keaney, for the beautiful setting and sustenance.

Thanks to those who took a special interest: Ian and Heather Saynor, Margaret McKenzie, Ken McKenzie, Mike and Penny Clarey, Rachel Smith, April and Maz Huxley, Eddie and Monica Buck and Susan Kelly. To my mother's group for being there (with coffee) and Sharlene Miller-Brown for steadying my nerves on the tricky business of writing a second book.

To all the rowers I sat in a boat with, but especially Kate Barnett, Ingrid Just, Lucinda Johnson and Yvette Keating.

To my agent Sophie Hamley and the lovely UQP team – Kristina Schulz, Michele Perry and Meredene Hill.

And to my editor Jody Lee who was there for long chats about the intentions of heart-stoppingly gorgeous boys.

To Olympic oarsman Ion Popa, for talking to me about Romania and adjusting to life in Australia, and Simone Bird for giving me an insight into school rowing. To Annabelle Eaton and the MGGS rowers who let me ride along with my notepad while they were training. And to my cousin, Dr Jamie Clarey, who provided medical advice. Any mistake is the fault of the arts graduate.

To the book bloggers – you know who you are. Thank you for loving Australian YA.

I'LL TELL YOU MINE

Pip Harry

Kate Elliot isn't trying to fit in.

Everything about her – especially her goth make-up and clothes – screams different and the girls at her school keep their distance. Besides, how can Kate be herself, *really herself*, when she's hiding her big secret? The one that landed her in boarding school in the first place. She's buried it down deep but it always seems to surface.

But then sometimes new friends, and even love, can find you when you least expect it.

So how do you take that first step and reveal yourself when you're not sure that people want to know the real you?

'I loved it. It has three of my favourite ingredients: boarding school, great characters, and a lot of heart.' Melina Marchetta

'What an angst-ridden, passionate and funny story!' *Good Reading*

'A beautiful debut told in a crisp, clear voice by an author who has expertly captured the struggle to find your identity, fall in love, and survive high school.' *Viewpoint*

ISBN 978 0 7022 3938 0